Knives, Forks, Scissors, Flames

PANHANDLER
BOOKS

UNIVERSITY OF WEST FLORIDA | PANHANDLERMAGAZINE.COM

KNIVES, FORKS, SCISSORS, FLAMES

STEFAN KIESBYE

Panhandler Books
Pensacola, Florida

21   20   19   18   17   16   6   5   4   3   2   1

Library of Congress Control Number: 2016907060
ISBN 978-0-9916404-2-3

Panhandler Books
Department of English and World Languages
Building 50
University of West Florida
11000 University Parkway
Pensacola, FL 32514
http://www.panhandlermagazine.com

University of
West Florida

For Michael, Jo, and Sanaz

"Knives, Forks, Scissors, Flames,
have no place in children's games."

—German Nursery Rhyme

PROLOGUE

When the children found her, the oldest boy broke a branch off the tree under which she lay and pressed the tip to the dark nipple. Then he shook the chest, and even the girls laughed, it just looked too silly. But the countless cuts and bruises made them quickly fall silent. They knew the signs, even if they were too young to have ever seen them before. Everyone in the village knew them.

The smell coming from the dead woman was very strong; something was sticking out of her belly. A boy muttered, "They have to find a new king." The others nodded in agreement.

They couldn't see the village behind them, not even the church tower. Probably no one would have found the corpse in the next few hours or even days, had Sybille Antler not encountered the pastor in his red jogging suit and given in to her guilty conscience. She broke her promise never to tell anyone about what she had found.

1

Benno was in the garden, trying to repair the rickety swing set. He had been finding ways to avoid Carolin's tight-lipped zeal since morning. It was quiet around him, so quiet that he could hear her cleaning the cupboards in the kitchen. He looked at the old thatched schoolhouse, half of which now belonged to them, and wiped the sweat from his brow. Parsonage and school stood together on a small hill, encircled by several old houses, and when Benno looked through the trees, he could see the road to Grevenhorst and the car dealership glittering in the sun. The next moment he heard the hasty and irregular steps of the pastor running toward the church. The stout man suddenly stopped, walked up to Benno, and with some difficulty said, "Something very bad happened. The children . . . Sybille . . . they've found . . . do you have a car?"

Benno looked at Mr. Cornelius and nodded. "Sure. Right now?"

When the pastor returned from his house, Benno was already waiting by the curb. Cornelius' wife had taken the kids to a soccer practice or a track and field event, the pastor couldn't remember. "We have to get there as fast as we can," he said. His forehead and thinning hair glistened with sweat. "Before anyone else does. How in the world did she get out? Wait, I must call the police."

Benno didn't understand what the pastor meant; Cornelius hadn't told him yet why and where they were taking the car. But he remained silent and followed Cornelius' instructions. He had decided to embrace whatever kind of life this new place had to offer. Carolin had insisted.

Strathleven meant a new beginning, a life without smog, subways, bums and gangs. No trash in the streets and no sidewalks full of dog shit. No Wall. Her son Tim was seven years old, and would soon have to enroll in school. It was time, Carolin had decided, to move away from Berlin. She had said it over and over again. Benno had been forced to choose between city and family. And with Strathleven they appeared to have made a good choice: the place was just twenty minutes away from the beach, and he could drive to Lübeck in a little more than half an hour.

And so it came to pass that Benno was one of the first to learn of the dead woman. He parked the car at the edge of the sandy path and then hurried after the pastor over grassy lots and meadows until they stood in front of the corpse, Cornelius' red windbreaker partly covering her chest and face. Benno was out of breath, the air was humid, and mosquitoes buzzed around his face. During the drive, the pastor had only given Benno confused hints and spoken of a disaster. The sight that greeted him now was strangely disappointing. He felt neither fear nor disgust while he spread the cheap plaid polyester blankets that Cornelius had brought over the naked body. Out here in the pasture murder made no sense. It was a sunny afternoon, a perfect day for swimming; he thought he could smell the sea. The body simply did not fit the scene.

Cornelius picked up his jacket with two fingers and stared at the woman with his head bowed. His lips moved, perhaps speaking to her or his God. She hardly looked human anymore.

The woman lay twisted; she could not have been very tall. The eyes were half closed, as if she were still squinting into the sun. She was maybe 35 or 40, the hair stuck to her head, thick and sandy-colored, her features harsh and clear. The pale skin was covered with cuts and bruises that looked almost black and had bluish edges. The stench was pronounced, and her toes were swollen.

Cornelius took Benno aside and made him promise to say nothing of Sybille Antler and the other children, who had initially found the body, because they should not get dragged into a police investigation. He alone had found the corpse.

Benno nodded, though he didn't understand what Cornelius was asking of him. Sybille Antler? What about the other children? What had they done? How long had they lingered here and examined the body? Silently, he stood with the pastor at the edge of the cow pasture and waited until the blue lights of the police and ambulance appeared out on the county road. The sirens had not been turned on, hurry was no longer needed. Crows or ravens—Benno could not tell them apart—hopped around nearby. Perhaps they felt cheated when the body was placed in a plastic bag and carried off.

A young, bear-like policeman asked him questions and took a report. No, Benno had never seen the woman before. No, he had no doubt about that, he was new here, he didn't know anyone in the village. The next day, his name appeared next to the pastor's in the regional paper and not just in the local section that probably no one outside of Strathleven ever read. This time the village had made it onto the front page.

―――――

At night Carolin asked him about the woman. Her voice was breathy because they had to leave the door open. Tim was suffering from laryngeal spasms, and she had to be able to hear him at all times. What the boy overheard of their talks, Benno couldn't tell. He often felt as though the boy lay awake at night to snap up their every word, their every sigh. Sometimes Benno could hear Tim snoring softly—he could never get quite enough air through his nose—but maybe the boy was a lot smarter and more cautious than his mother and stepfather. Maybe his ears were better than those of Benno and Carolin, and maybe he shared in their secrets.

"What did she look like?" asked Carolin. Her breath tickled his ear, one of her small, powerful hands stroked his arm. In her youth she had been a gymnast and won prizes and medals. The pregnancy hadn't touched her lines.

Benno gave her an approximate description and tried to sound sad and concerned. But he kept quiet about the blackened wounds. "And we only just arrived," he added, "in this small, clean, decent dump." He couldn't help himself.

"This has nothing to do with Strathleven," Carolin hissed in his ear. "Somebody just dropped the body in the field."

"How do you know that?" he asked.

"Otherwise, you would have found her clothes."

"The murderer could have taken them," Benno said. "In Berlin, I never found a corpse. And I lived there for eighteen years."

In response Carolin punched him in the kidney, and he stifled a groan. "You've got me and Tim," she said. "Isn't that enough?" Her chest pressed against his shoulder. "Did that hurt?"

"No," he said.

"Next time I'll hit you harder," she whispered. Not a sound could be heard from Tim's room.

Tim cut out the article that mentioned Benno's name, pasted it into a new composition book, and stared at the columns through a magnifying glass, as though somewhere in the small print he could find the solution to the murder case. He insisted on being driven to the spot where the body had been found, and Benno finally gave in, after making him promise not to tell his mother.

It was hard to find the exact location again. Benno got lost on the country roads, and when he finally found the spot where he had parked that afternoon, he was not sure which direction the pastor had taken. Yet Tim didn't mind and followed him patiently. Finally Benno stopped at the edge of a grassy pasture, and said, "This is it." Grazing cows watched the two of them quietly.

Tim crawled through the bushes and tall grass trying to discover evidence. Benno reminded him not to scratch his skin on branches or fence posts or some rusty barbed wire. Every little gash would scar and disfigure him. The boy nodded, but hardly seemed to have heard Benno's admonitions. He wasn't even disappointed when he didn't find a thing.

If you glanced at Tim in passing, the boy didn't look unusual—a seven-year-old with the flaxen hair of his mother, the same bad eyes, the same thick glasses. But maybe because of his biological dad, or maybe because of some random incident, he had this illness nobody could explain, and for which there was no entry in the medical textbooks. Not even a name. Carolin had consulted every specialist in Berlin, and doctors at the University Hospital had analyzed blood and skin samples and shaken their heads. They hadn't been able to do or explain anything. Whenever Tim cut his skin, it healed all too quickly, and a second layer of skin seemed to spread over the wound. With every scratch his skin grew visibly thicker. Six months ago, he had fallen from his bike, broken his glasses and received a cut just below his right eye. A scar had formed almost immediately, and made his right eye appear slightly narrower than the left. They had sold the bike before leaving Berlin.

Carolin blamed herself for Tim's illness. She hadn't wanted to get pregnant, "especially not by that guy." She'd never told Benno the father's name. "I really believed Tim was eating me from the inside, I wanted to stab him with a screwdriver." Benno had tried to convince her that her feelings had nothing to do with Tim's condition, but to no avail. "He must have felt the hatred. Just look at him!"

———————

The old school where they lived belonged to the widow Schmied who lived with her son Manfred on the second floor. She had to be in her sixties, always wore gray skirts and gray jackets, together with white, starched blouses. Her hair was tied back in a bun. Even Manfred only wore gray suits, and they always seemed two sizes too small, making him appear like a giant. His skin and face were always flushed, his voice loud, as though he were nearly deaf, and he didn't seem to be aware of his size and strength.

A few days after the publication of the newspaper article, the widow came to Benno and Carolin's door to tell them of the scheduled heating oil delivery, when Manfred suddenly appeared behind her. With child-like curiosity he pushed his mother aside to gawk at the unknown family. "Good morning," he said in his booming voice. Then he stared at Tim, extending his hand.

Mrs. Schmied lost her balance, and before Benno could catch her, she yelped and fell to the ground. Manfred didn't move from his spot, seemingly unaware of his mother's fall.

Mr. Heintz, who lived next door on the first floor, must have heard the cry, or maybe he'd been in the garden and had seen the accident, because a moment later he appeared at the door in a blue coat and shouted at Manfred as though he were a little boy. "Go, you silly boy," he exclaimed. "Come on. Get out of here."

Manfred stared at him with a blank face, then finally hung his head and left.

"He means well, he really does," said Mr. Heintz as he helped Mrs.

Schmied to her feet. He was a short, stocky man, shorter than the widow, with a broad face and rough hands. Benno and Carolin had never talked to him before and had only seen him once or twice on their way to the car. He didn't seem to leave the house very often. "He's just a little slow. He still thinks that he is your son's size."

Benno nodded in agreement.

"I haven't even introduced myself yet," Mr. Heintz said. "How do you like it in Strathleven?"

"We like it," Benno replied. "It's very nice here."

"What do you do for a living?"

"I'm the new sports editor at the *Strandkurier*," Benno said, taking Mrs. Schmied's other arm. Her hair was a mess, she'd lost several of her pins, but she didn't seem to have injured herself. "I'm not that good on my feet anymore," she said apologetically.

Mr. Heintz turned to Tim and asked, "Would you like to have a look at my workshop? Of course, you are all welcome to come along," he added.

The boy hesitated, looked questioningly at his mother, then at Benno.

"What kind of workshop do you have?" he asked.

The wood workshop took up almost the entire apartment, leaving only a small room in back furnished with a table, a bed, and two chairs. It smelled of cigars, fresh wood, and fresh paint. The wallpaper was old and had a gold pattern. "I used to make furniture, when there was still a small factory in town, but I've since retired." He scratched his bald head. "Now I'm only doing these here." 'These here' were neatly sawed and sanded wooden figurines, and Heintz painted each and every one by hand. They covered most of the walls, there seemed hardly any space left for new ones. There were fairy-tale characters—Hans in Luck with his lump of gold, Cinderella, who had lost a shoe, Mother Holle shaking out the beds—and sailing ships, moons with friendly faces and nightcaps, churches, and legendary deities with four faces.

Tim ran from room to room and marveled at the curious collection.

"Do you sell them?" asked Benno.

"Every now and then," Mr. Heintz said.

"He is too modest," said Mrs. Schmied, who sat down on a chair and tied up her hair again. "He supplies all the souvenir shops in the area."

"What's that?" Tim asked, pointing to a tree on the wall that seemed to have a hole in the middle.

"Please," Carolin corrected him.

"Please," Tim repeated.

"Superstition," Mrs. Schmied replied in a firm voice. "He shouldn't make those. It's sinful."

"Oh," said Mr. Heintz. "It's quite harmless." Then he bent down to Tim and said, "That is the Miracle Oak. The ones who manage to crawl through its opening will be cured of any disease. Whether you're blind or crippled, the Miracle Oak can heal you."

"Does it really exist?" asked Tim.

"It really does. Here in Strathleven."

"Where?"

Mr. Heintz stood up with a groan. "Just keep your eyes open. Here," he took the Miracle Oak off the wall, "take one with you."

———

Carolin was preparing dinner in the kitchen, and the smell of her beef stir-fry wafted like a childhood memory through the rest of the house. Benno looked around—the light that came from a single lamp in the dining area illuminated Tim's face as he sat at the table and kept humming to himself, the sound mixing with that of the rain pounding the windows—and he realized that he knew this picture only from the movies. He wanted to hold on to this image, hang it on the wall or lock it away in a safe. Benno's childhood had not been idyllic, and he had spent it in constant fear of an unpredictable mother.

This was still a sore point between him and Carolin. He no longer spoke to his parents, had not called them in years and discarded their letters unread. She respected his decision, but she didn't understand it. Her own parents had died early. Both had been diagnosed with cancer at almost the same time, as though they had eaten it from a shared plate. Her mother had survived her husband by two months.

"No family is perfect. You must be able to forgive," Carolin had said more than once. But he couldn't. His parents had always treated him like a talented and entertaining dog. When at age fifteen he had met his first girlfriend, his mother had called and visited the families of two ex-boyfriends to inquire about the girl's character. His father had initially seemed more sensible—and then flirted with the girlfriend, jokingly, as he claimed. But Benno knew better.

"Can you help me with the meat?" Carolin's voice sounded annoyed. As soon as he entered the kitchen, he was in the way. The stubborn chunks of meat cheered him on, he was glad that the little moment of perfection was over.

Later in the evening, when Benno came out of the upstairs shower, he saw Tim in his room, standing by the window. The boy had a pair of binoculars lying on the windowsill to watch birds and squirrels. In the garden stood the repaired swing, an old slide, and a large sandbox, and Tim looked silently down at his little kingdom and did not seem to be happy with it.

The floor of his room was strewn with school supplies, sports gear and newspapers, but the desk was perfectly clean. A dictionary stood on the right, along with a book about the local birdlife. A huge monthly planner took up almost the entire surface of the desk, and an old-fashioned pencil sharpener stood on the left side. Homework assignments were neatly entered into the boxes for each day, along with birthdays and afternoon activities. Paper clips, pencils, pens, and erasers were arranged in separate containers.

The walls, however, were just as chaotic as the floor: posters and newspaper clippings of bands and actresses fought for space. A huge image of a submarine hung above Tim's own drawings, and plastic figurines—cowboys, superheroes, and dinosaurs—were taped to the wall in-between.

Perhaps he hadn't noticed Benno. His shoulders drooped, and in his right hand he held the Miracle Oak that Mr. Heintz had given him. Benno came up to the boy and his eyes followed his gaze outside, where Manfred sat on the edge of the sandbox and was writing in the wet sand with a stick.

"What's going on?" Benno asked.

Tim shrugged.

"He doesn't know any better. His body is huge, but he hasn't really grown up."

Tim nodded impatiently. "I'm not stupid," he said, and fell silent again. Together they watched Manfred as he diligently recorded things that they could not decipher. Finally Tim asked, "Is that contagious?"

"What," asked Benno.

"Meningitis," said Tim.

"No."

"How do you get meningitis?"

Benno only remembered the admonitions of his mother. "When you ride your bike in the winter and your hair is all wet, or if someone else has it and you get infected." Maybe that was complete nonsense, but every answer was better than silence at this moment.

"So it *is* contagious," Tim replied in a low, firm voice.

"Not with Manfred, not anymore. The illness is no longer contagious. Manfred is harmless."

"What are the symptoms?"

"High fever and headaches. But I'll keep an eye on you."

Tim seemed to think about it while he turned the tree in his hand. "Promise?"

"Promise."

"Do you swear?"

Benno raised three fingers. "I swear."

"Tell me," muttered Tim. "Miracle Oaks don't really exist, do they?"

"No," Benno said. "Not really."

2

Strathleven was a collection of crooked streets and leaning houses and home to not even a thousand souls. It might have looked quite picturesque once, but modest wealth and new developments had eroded its charm.

The hilly streets were named Village Street, Church Street, School Street and Mill Pond, but there was neither a mill nor a pond anymore. The mill had been demolished after the war and the pond had been filled in to make room for the new county road. The village had a Spar supermarket; the restaurant Zum Storch, which attracted the occasional visitor from Lübeck; and a car dealership, whose owner, Otto Friedrich, had promised Benno a good trade-in offer for his old VW Bug, should he ever need a new car. Then there was a John Deere dealer, which also sold lawnmowers and tools, a gas station, two pubs, two doctors, and a consignment store. Cakes and pastries people bought at the Spar market, and they were supplied by a large, commercial bakery in Lübeck. For everything else, the townspeople went to the nearby town of Grevenhorst. The only true eye-sore was a concrete-pipe plant outside of Strathleven, on the road toward Wegsten, but the factory stood surrounded by trees, and only the trucks and construction vehicles hinted at its existence.

Even before he had set foot in the Spar market, all the villagers already knew Benno's name. "What a disaster," they said. "Not even here for a week, and already witnessed something so terrible."

After a few days he was no longer sure what the locals meant by those words. When a neighbor came to the door to ask if he could mow their lawn for a small fee—he already cut the widow Schmied's grass twice a month—and Benno considered whether buying a lawnmower would be cheaper in the end, the neighbor shook his head in disgust. "Such a mess," he said. "You've hardly arrived, and now this. You have to pay me in advance."

"Why?" asked Benno.

Christensen didn't answer, counted the money he was given and went to work. Benno watched him as he lifted the mower from a small trailer and pulled the starter. What had Christensen meant? Did these people believe that Benno had something to do with the murder?

The mower sprang to life with a clatter and startled Benno. It couldn't be. He hadn't even known the woman. In fact, no one in the village had known her.

After ten days, the summer holidays were over. A few crates and boxes remained unopened in the living room, but Benno's study, which was located behind the kitchen and looked out on an overgrown garden, was ready. The electric typewriter sat like a small altar on his desk.

Carolin had not been able to get a position as a physical education teacher. Tim's school in Grevenhorst—Strathleven was too small even for a primary school—had no need for one, and no school in Lübeck had responded to her inquiries. At least she would be home when Tim came back from school in the afternoon.

Tim started school on a Thursday, and Carolin bought him a large blue bag, shaped like a magician's hat, and packed it to the brim with pens, sweets and colorful erasers. Tim walked very erect and with eyes wide open from the car to his new school, and Benno and Carolin stared after him. Would he settle in? Would the other boys tease him because he didn't know their games and hiding places and said 'bread roll' instead of 'bun'?

After two hours, he came running back to the car, beaming. He had exchanged pencils and erasers with Daniel and Jens, who also lived in Strathleven. They had asked him if he wanted to ride his bicycle with them. Tim looked at his parents expectantly. "Please," he said. "Can I get one?" Carolin and Benno exchanged glances and promised to think about it.

The next morning they accompanied Tim down the road to the bus stop, where a group of children was already waiting. Benno and Carolin were the only adults. After Tim had stared intently at his shoelaces for a while, Carolin gave him a kiss on his hair and left with Benno.

"Too late," he said on the way home.

"For what?"

"We have destroyed his reputation. Daniel and Jens will laugh at him. Which ones were Daniel and Jens?"

Carolin laughed coarsely. "And I even kissed him."

"This calls for punishment."

"Empty threats." She smirked.

That was the reason why Benno was late for work on his first day in Lübeck. Fortunately, the editor in chief had gone to visit a customer and arrived half an hour after him. Benno was in charge of the sports section and would also help out with the ads. It was not the job he had dreamed of, but he didn't plan to grow old at the *Strandkurier*.

The publisher, Jochen Hecht, introduced Benno to his new colleagues, who occupied three floors in an old building on Hüxstraße. He got his own cubicle, his own desk, his own electric typewriter. During the first hours of work, with a cup of coffee next to his phone, he felt very grown up. It almost seemed as though he had been born for this life and had always wanted to wear a tweed jacket. He was now responsible for a large apartment, a wife and child, a car, a job. He was 37 years old. He just had to keep from screwing up.

Benno flipped through the pages of the *Strandkurier*, which was published three times a week and consisted mainly of ads. Yet he noticed that the dead woman had made headlines even in Lübeck. The article by Holger Wienast—which, as he told Benno with a broad grin, he had copied with only minor changes from another local paper—reported on the results of the autopsy. The woman had been raped, though some time before her death. The cuts and bruises, on the other hand, had been inflicted shortly before she died. She had bled to death, that much was certain, but the nature of the wounds was peculiar, as though the killer had stabbed her in his kitchen, using whatever he could find. Knives, forks, scissors. The tools had been dull, her death had come slowly.

So far, no one had recognized the photo of the dead woman, and no one seemed to miss her. Her picture had been published in the regional press, but none of the calls to the police had revealed anything. At the end of Wienast's article, it said that the coroner had determined that the woman was pregnant at the time of her death. "But where is the child?" asked Benno.

"Not even the *Gazette* has an answer to that," Holger, a small, dark-haired student who wore a tweed jacket with leather elbow patches, replied. Comparative Literature. He was working on his dissertation and had been at the *Strandkurier* for four years. "It was cut out in the most brutal way. You can only hope she was dead by then."

On Saturday, Benno went to three soccer games in the area and became acquainted with coaches and colleagues.

"Strathleven?" said the coach of SV Grevenhorst. "The only village that can't get together a team." His turquoise tracksuit gleamed in the sun. Few places, he told Benno, had either too few people or too little money to not at least join a regional beer-league. Yet money and people didn't seem to be the problem in Strathleven. He laughed and said, "They are holier than thou. Their church is very peculiar. A little bit crazy. Are you one of them?"

Benno shook his head. "We're only here because of the fresh air."

"Baptist air," he laughed. "Family?"

Benno nodded.

"Have you ever looked at the Miracle Beech? Is it still there?"

"Oak. Miracle Oak. I haven't found it yet. But I've heard of it."

"You should go see it," said the coach, a man in his fifties with a remarkable belly. "My parents showed it to me once when I was a little boy. But perhaps the Christians have cut down the tree by now."

On Sunday morning they had breakfast at the restaurant at the inn, Zum Storch. The parking lot of the restaurant was already nearly full, and even a police car stood in front of the entrance. But Tim had eyes only for an old Jaguar. It was an E-type with the long hood, and the special feature of the car was that it hadn't been painted, but was covered with a black material that looked like velvet. Before Carolin could admonish him, Tim ran his hands over the fenders. "Cool," he said.

Families sat in the crowded taproom. Young women in floral dresses, old women in beige dresses, all of them wearing perms. The men were talking shop. Grain prices were discussed, someone predicted that this year's crop would be even worse than last year's.

"The March frost killed everything," said a white-haired man in a plaid shirt at the next table.

"Next year everything will be different," said another. He also wore a plaid summer shirt, and looked like a younger version of the old man. "This is a new beginning, dad."

"Really?" asked his father scornfully. "Do you want to take the reins next year and make rain?"

When Benno excused himself after drinking a second pot of coffee, he noticed that there was a third room between the taproom and the actual restaurant. Guests were seated at a large, round table, the air was full of smoke, and instead of coffee the men were drinking beer and liquor. Curious, Benno paused for a moment. He thought he had recognized the green uniform of a police officer. The next moment one of the men turned to look at him and waved. It was Friedrich, the car dealer. Benno waved back. He felt caught and hastily turned away. The group of men seemed too serious to be disturbed. As he paid at the counter, the waitress asked, "Aren't you the new guy? The one who found the woman?"

Benno nodded. He waited for a reaction, but after the waitress had given him his change, she left without another word.

The rest of the day they spent together at the beach. It was sunny, the sky clear and blue. Tim built a sand castle and Benno thought he almost looked like an ordinary boy. He squinted through his straw hat into the sun, feeling the sand on his belly and legs. He and Carolin had made it;

in the eyes of the other beach visitors, they had to look like a normal family.

Around six o'clock they packed up their mats and towels and walked back to the car. Two kilometers before Strathleven, Tim suddenly yelled, "A wolf, a wolf!" Benno slowed. And really, not far from the road he saw something move in the tall grass. The animal seemed to have heard the approaching car and lifted its head. It did look like a wolf or a coyote. Benno's heart still beat wildly after the animal had turned and disappeared into a cornfield.

When he climbed into bed—he could still feel sand between his teeth, and his nose and neck were sunburned—he felt completely at peace. Carolin had a dreamy smile on her face, and the boy had had a wonderful day and was now snoring in the next room. Not a sound came through the open window. "I didn't think you would enjoy the country life," Carolin said. Her hand lay on his chest.

During their first night together, she had told him that at age eighteen she had stopped going to the gym to train every day and started to drink and go out with men who beat her. Most of them had been alcoholics or drug addicts. For several years she hadn't even had an apartment. Only after her pregnancy did she start seeing a psychiatrist.

Benno had been lying in the darkness of her room, her mouth pressed against his ear, her body wrapped around his. He hadn't wanted to start anything serious with her. Earlier that day, he had slept with another woman and arranged to meet her again. But Carolin's whispered confession had a peculiar effect on him. Since that night he hadn't cheated on her.

Yet as he listened to the silence outside, he suddenly missed the rattles and squeaks of the S-Bahn, the rumble and roar of passing trains. His sense of peace was gone; instead he missed his studio in Wedding district, missed even the smoke that wafted up from the pub on the ground floor to the windows of his third-floor apartment. The Baltic coast was so disgustingly healthy.

3

"Come home immediately. Please, Benno. Please!"

He apologized to the advertising customers, who sat across from him at his desk, and didn't even think to grab his bag. He ran down to the lobby, cursed loudly, returned to the office to get his keys, and then ran to his car. Benno needed just 20 minutes to get to Strathleven. Carolin's hoarse voice in his mind urged him on, and he suddenly felt cold. He had notified Holger that he would miss a District League volleyball game. Maybe he would lose his job in only his second week. But that didn't matter now.

As soon as he got out of the car in front of the old school, he heard several voices coming from inside the house. Carolin's excited voice mingled with a very high one he hadn't heard before, and with that of Pastor Cornelius. Someone was crying.

As he stepped into the hallway, Carolin threw herself into his arms and the small group fell silent. A woman was standing at the table with a big cake in her hands. "They are still children," she said in a pleading voice to Benno. "They just wanted to see. They didn't want to harm him. They are just stupid."

Carolin turned around and screamed at the woman, "Just wanted to see? You call that 'just wanted to see'?"

"But Mrs. Stroth . . ." Mr. Cornelius bit his lip and swallowed whatever he had wanted to say.

Carolin took Benno by the hand and led him to the sofa where Tim sat in silence, his face very white. He was wearing long pants since Carolin wouldn't allow shorts anymore. His left shirtsleeve was pushed up, and when Carolin pulled away his right hand, Benno could see the cuts. There were two, forming a 'T.' They were red, deep, and clean.

"Jens and Daniel! Her son did that," shouted Carolin, pointing at Mrs. Stroth. "And now this woman comes into my house and offers me a cake. A cake!"

"I just took it from the oven," said the woman, setting the cake down on the table and wringing her bony hands. She looked haggard. She was wearing a flowered dress and a dark red cardigan. Her varicose veins were encased in brown pantyhose, her feet stuck in beige sandals.

"What happened?" asked Benno.

"The kids . . . they cut him," said Cornelius and told him what had happened. After the school bus had dropped off the children, Daniel, Jens and Tim had made plans for the afternoon. Jens had received a kite for his birthday and wanted to try it out. But Tim didn't own a bike and the boys had teased him and called him a mama's boy. They couldn't understand why Carolin was afraid of Tim getting hurt. Tim had tried to explain it to his friends, but then had become angry. Finally, Daniel had taken out a pocketknife and cut Tim's arm. "I have no idea what got into them," said the pastor.

Benno turned to Tim. "Is that true?"

Tim nodded. "Yes. But . . . it wasn't bad."

"Not bad?" Carolin's voice was shrill. "With your skin? Not bad?"

"Did you tell Daniel and Jens about it?" asked Benno. "What would happen?" Tim was too quiet, his face without expression, or maybe defiant. Something was wrong. He avoided his mother's gaze and nodded wordlessly.

"Told them what?" asked the pastor, but Benno ignored him.

"Did you hold still?"

Tim lowered his head and began to cry.

"What?" asked Mrs. Stroth. "You allowed them to cut you?" She stepped slowly toward the boy. Tim's open wound offered a strange sight. The cuts had narrowed and were no longer red, and the edges looked raised and were turning a light brown. Tomorrow there would be only two lines, as though two worms were crawling underneath Tim's skin.

"What is this?" She bent down and grabbed Tim's arm. Carolin wanted to pull her away, but Benno stopped her. The boy let Daniel's mother inspect the wound.

"Is it always like this?" Her conciliatory tone had given way to a certain sharpness. She stared at the red 'T.' "That fast?"

"It's a rare disease," Benno said.

"Disease?" asked Mrs. Stroth and stood straight. Her back was no longer bent, her eyes sparkled. "A miracle is what it is! The boy was born with a caul!" She turned back toward Tim, took his arm and quickly pressed her lips to the cuts. Then she let go of his arm and ran out of the living room toward the entrance. At the door she turned her head one last time. "I guess we are done here," she cried in a piercing voice. "Your son made them do it. And you yelled at me. Called my Daniel a criminal." Then she opened the door and nodded at the pastor. "You enjoy the cake."

The next morning, Benno still had his job; Jochen Hecht had neither called nor fired him. Only Holger had called to ask if everything was okay. When Benno entered Tim's room to remind the boy that they would have to leave in five minutes, it was empty. The sound of running water was coming from the bathroom.

Tim had always called Benno by his first name. Carolin had never encouraged him to say "Dad," although his real father had never even visited. The boy had been almost four years old when Benno and Carolin had met on the subway, both on their way to a seminar, and by then he had already been used to the sight of unknown men. After the first night that Benno had spent at Carolin's place, the boy had hopped into their bed, sat down on Benno's hairy chest and asked, "Did you bring me a present?"

Benno was about to go downstairs again when he noticed a collection of carefully clipped images on Tim's desk. Normally, these would have been photos of stars or race cars that one could find in every seven-year-old boy's room. But these clippings showed victims of car accidents, fires, and fights, and next to each of them lay a second image of the surgically repaired face. The features still looked mangled. A man who had been attacked by his own dog was still missing lips and a nose, another man's eye had been torn and the lid sewn shut. The magazine in which Tim had found these photos lay open on the floor. The *Stern*, of course, although Benno could not recall noticing the article. He quickly left the room.

"You've got two minutes," he shouted a bit louder than necessary. "But I can't pick you up from school, you'll have to take the bus back home."

Tim followed him silently outside. Maybe Carolin's response to the incident yesterday had embarrassed him. He had shown his new friends a neat trick, had bragged with his illness. He had shown them something that only he was able to do, and his mother had ruined his performance.

It was a foggy morning, although the sun was already peeping out from behind the white mist. Tim wore a blue windbreaker, whose sleeves hid the freshly healed 'T.'

"It almost looks like a cross," he said.

"Do the Stroths go to church?"

Tim nodded. "Can I come with you?" he asked into the harsh rattle of the VW.

"Your mother . . ."

"Doesn't need to know."

"She'll be waiting for you at the bus stop." Benno didn't mind taking Tim with him to Lübeck, but Carolin wouldn't be thrilled. Even though they were married, Carolin insisted on making important decisions for Tim by herself. And there were no clear guidelines for the things that were important or unimportant, right or wrong.

"You can call and tell her that I felt dizzy."

Benno had to laugh. "And what about tomorrow?"

Tim sighed. "Please?"

The offices of the *Strandkurier* seemed transformed with Tim's arrival. The light appeared warmer, the colleagues more affectionate, and loud, rumbling Mr. Hecht almost seemed fatherly. While it wasn't a big city, Lübeck seemed a world apart from Strathleven. In Lübeck, nobody knew about Tim's illness, nobody offered them a huge marble cake. Last night, Carolin had carried it over to Mr. Cornelius' house, saying she didn't want a single bite of it.

Benno called the school, then Carolin, and no argument ensued. Maybe she was glad that Tim didn't have to sit in a classroom with Daniel and Jens. Instead, the boy was allowed to spread his things on the desk of an absent colleague, and Benno spent the morning trying to drum up more ad business. Together with Holger they went for lunch to a cafe that served *Labskaus*.

"That's disgusting," Tim said, poking his fork into the suspicious-looking mush.

"Not disgusting," Holger corrected him. "This is just how it is here. Like fisherman caps, marzipan, and shooting clubs."

"Shooting clubs?" asked Benno. He still remembered the club in the small Hessian town where he had grown up, the feathered hats, the festival around the time of the Feast of Corpus Christi and the hideous brass music.

"Jörg on the first floor is responsible for the coverage. They get really angry if we forget their board meetings."

In the afternoon the two of them went to a handball game in Bad Segeberg. As soon as they stepped inside the sports arena, they could hear the whistles and horns of the fans. Benno showed his press pass and then led Tim to the tables reserved for journalists.

Bad Segeberg lost terribly. Tim sat next to Benno, ate marzipan potatoes that Benno had bought in Lübeck, and cheered loudly for his team. From time to time, when the boy felt unobserved, he touched his arm and scratched at his new scar. And once or twice Benno caught the boy looking at him sideways, from behind his thick glasses and with his mouth half open. Every time, Tim moved slightly closer to him, and when Benno finally tousled his hair, he let him without protesting. When he later introduced Tim to the Bad Segeberg coach, he felt almost like a real father. "That's my boy, Tim," he said. Tim did not correct him.

In the early evening they drove back to Strathleven and stopped at the supermarket to buy sweet woodruff soda and red wine.

The owner, Mr. Johannsen, stood behind the counter himself and nodded at them. Benno wondered about the strong odor in the store. In Berlin, the supermarkets had smelled of glass and plastic wrap, but here, every packet of sugar, each tube of mustard and each bar of soap seemed to compete with the smell of stalks of celery, tomatoes, and coffee. Even the sliced cheese seemed to come straight from the cow, the canned stew still seemed to bear the fingerprints of the butcher. Benno did not trust the Bordeaux—where did this poorly printed label come from? What did the bottle truly contain? And the soda looked much too green.

"Plastic bag?" asked Johannsen and pushed the purchases past him.

"How long have you owned the store?" asked Benno.

Johannsen laughed. "Forever. My father already owned it when I was a little boy, but back then it wasn't a Spar market yet, and we still sold loose flour."

Tim looked at him skeptically, but Johannsen nodded emphatically. "There was no woodruff soda either, but we picked and ate the sweet woodruff at the roadside." Then he turned back to Benno. "This is the miracle boy, right?"

Benno saw Tim's grip on the shopping bags tighten.

"No 'miracle.' The doctors just don't know what it is," Benno said.

Johannsen nodded. "Doctors don't know much."

"Yes, you're right, of course," Benno said carefully. Apparently, Mrs. Stroth had spread the news of Tim's illness in the village. "By the way," he said, trying to switch topics as casually as possible, "are there any wolves around here? We thought maybe . . . we recently . . ." The shopkeeper looked at him strangely and he broke off mid-sentence.

"It's an evil spirit," Johannsen said. "Appears everywhere, but we cannot catch him. Lean like the devil himself. A bad omen if you ask me. Since he's appeared here, we've had nothing but hail and frost. And now it hasn't rained since June."

"Is he dangerous?"

"Rabid maybe. You should be careful with the boy. Rabies is no joke."

Benno nodded and took the shopping bags from Tim.

Before they stopped in front of the old school, the boy asked timidly, "Am I a 'miracle boy'?"

"Nah, you're not." Benno didn't want to encourage further experiments with the boy's skin.

"But what if I am?" Tim asked defiantly.

"Miracle boys don't eat marzipan potatoes and don't drink sweet woodruff soda," Benno replied, and knew immediately that his answer was wrong. Tim had been serious, and he had treated him like a small child.

"Never mind," Tim said and wouldn't talk to Benno for the rest of the night.

4

When he stepped outside in the morning, Benno discovered Manfred leaning over the hood of the Beetle. It was only six o'clock, but Benno had not been able to sleep because of the vinegary Bordeaux.

The fog had returned and made it difficult to see anything beyond the church. Manfred was wearing his gray suit and a white shirt and when he heard Benno's steps behind him, he hastily turned around. Still, Benno caught a glimpse of his reddish penis before Manfred could zip up his pants. Then the widow's son fished in his pockets for a white handkerchief and began to wipe the hood.

"What the hell are you doing?" asked Benno, but it was only sleepiness that made him ask. He had already understood.

"Nothing, you see, everything is clean," Manfred stammered.

"If I ever catch you at my car again, I'm going to talk to your mother."

"No, no, that won't be necessary," pleaded Manfred. "You see, nothing's left." He kept standing in front of the car, held the handkerchief in his hand and looked directly at Benno. It was a peculiar look, piercing and yet unfocused. "I won't touch your car again."

"Why mine?" asked Benno. "Why not that Ford?" Gustav Heintz drove an old Taunus, a special edition with yellow paint and black trim, black bumpers and sport rims.

"It's disgusting," Manfred said contemptuously and finally put the handkerchief back into his pocket. "You want to see something awesome?"

"Maybe some other time." Benno wasn't interested in what else Manfred kept in his pockets.

But the big, red hand had already come out again, and now held instead of the handkerchief a long Bowie knife.

"What's that?" Benno did not know whether he should laugh or be alarmed.

"I collect knives," Manfred said importantly and ran a finger over the wide blade. "I have twenty-three of them. This one has a hunting party engraved on the blade. It was quite expensive. From America. There are bison on it."

"I see," Benno said without looking, but Manfred seemed to have forgotten all about him. He took out the handkerchief once more and wiped his knife carefully, then turned without a word and disappeared toward the bus stop.

———

"They are quite harmless," Ms. Schmied assured Benno later that morning. "He finds them beautiful. He has never done anything to harm anyone. The knives are much too important to him. He doesn't want to scratch them."

What could Benno say in response? He was the newcomer. How could he explain to the widow that Tim had a rare disease and that a mere paper cut could disfigure the boy?

She might have read the doubt on his face. Maybe that was the reason why she invited her new tenants to Sunday worship. Or maybe she just saw an opportunity because Benno had mentioned earlier that he had nothing planned for the weekend.

"We are not very religious," he said, which he knew was an understatement. He had left the church at age 18, and Carolin hadn't even been baptized.

"Oh, none of us are." Ms. Schmied winked at him. "But we have fun."

The church had stood 500 years before it burnt down in 1619, along with large parts of the village. The new church, as the bronze plaque at the entrance explained, had been renovated in 1866 and the present church tower had been erected.

It was mid-September, and inside it was cool and smelled musty, just like the church Benno had frequented as a child. His parents had not believed much in God, but they were willing to worship the power of appearances. Attending service at certain choice times of the year had been a social necessity.

Pastor Cornelius greeted Benno and Carolin with a red, shiny face. His thinning hair was neatly combed, and he introduced them to his wife and children. One of the girls was in Tim's class; she had four other siblings, and all of them sang in the choir.

The service was simple. Instead of the sad drone of an organ, two teenagers were playing guitar, and even if the songs still sounded old and dusty, they were more tolerable than the half-heartedly sung hymns Benno remembered. The pastor did not deliver the sermon from the pulpit, but stood in front of a microphone next to the choir stalls and never spoke of eternal damnation.

"We still have a future despite Chernobyl and the neutron bomb. We must learn to guide our youth, rather than deprive them of all hope! Cynicism is not a virtue," Cornelius said at the end. "Maybe I'm old-fashioned. And if I'm to believe my children, I'm pretty uncool." The congregation laughed, the pastor beamed. "But cynicism is too expensive. It's the currency of the devil, and we cannot sell him the future of our children. 'No Future' is not the way, not the solution. And Jesus Christ teaches us that there is always a way."

"Even if it leads to the cross," Benno whispered into Carolin's ear.

After the service he just wanted to get up and go home—in his childhood, even staunch believers had left in a hurry after the last song—but nobody seemed to want to exit the church. Tables were set up and large thermoses full of coffee were carried in from the sacristy. Some women had baked and were cutting their cakes now. For the children there was orange juice and cola.

"Maybe we should . . . ," Benno whispered, but Carolin looked at him sharply and said, "Why are you in such a hurry? Be polite for once." And soon she was surrounded by a small group of women, praising the cake and listening to the protestations that it was so nice to meet the new family. Even Mrs. Stroth was there, and although she didn't smile as mildly as the pastor's wife, she didn't say a single word about the argument.

"How did you like it?" The pastor had suddenly appeared behind Benno. He had disposed of the black robe and was now wearing a plaid shirt and beige corduroy pants. He held a piece of cake in one hand, a cup of coffee in the other. "You play an instrument?"

Benno shook his head. "A good sermon," he said politely.

The praise seemed to flatter Cornelius. "We have a good congregation here. Not everyone is fond of our work in the village, but the ones who give us a chance, mostly stay."

Benno wanted to say something noncommittal, after all he was eating the pastor's cake, but all he could think of was, "How's your jogging?"

"It's going," the pastor said cheerfully. "At my age you have to pay attention to your beltline."

Benno nodded. Ever since meeting Carolin, he had trouble keeping his weight down. "Have the police contacted you again?"

Cornelius shook his head. "Vile thing. Vile, vile thing."

Benno often thought of the contorted body under the pastor's red jacket and wondered why Strathleven wasn't swarming with cops. Not even the Grevenhorster policeman had paid him a visit or asked him to come down to the station. "I was just thinking," Benno said. "We were witnesses, so to speak."

Cornelius' small eyes looked at him sharply. The many laugh lines around his eyes were suddenly wiped away.

"Just a thought," insisted Benno and quickly drank a sip of the bitter coffee.

"So you've been thinking a lot about it," he said, nodding slowly. Then his good cheer quickly returned. "Do you want to sing in the choir? We could use some more men's voices."

"A dog?"

"I can sell my bike if I you want me to."

The bike was now six days old, the new speedometer a mere three. Benno was home alone with Tim, and he knew that without Carolin, there were only wrong answers. "Have you asked Caro?" He still refused to say 'your mother,' which made him think of wet woolen socks, bean soup, and floor wax.

Tim shook his head. "She's helping out with the youth group."

"And you didn't bother to ask before she left?"

Tim looked down at his feet.

"We'll see." Tim's question presented one of those typical problems Benno knew mostly from other families. How does one behave as a father? What answer do you give a boy who mustn't get a single scar? Do you yell "No" until you are red in the face? His mother had preferred that approach.

When he had last seen his parents, Benno had visited that small town in Hesse with a new love in tow. Together with his parents they visited the cemetery to take care of the grave of his recently deceased grandmother. On the way back to the car, his father had taken the arm of Benno's girlfriend and walked ahead of the others to the parking lot. Suddenly his hand had come to rest on the girl's buttocks, as though it naturally belonged there. After that incident, Benno had broken off contact with his family and never initiated it again.

"You don't like dogs?" Tim asked timidly into the silence.

The question startled Benno, who had almost forgotten about the boy. "In Berlin I didn't like them," he said quickly. "All that dog poop on the sidewalks."

Tim nodded seriously. "Here it's different."

"Yes, maybe."

Carolin seemed to take Tim's wish in stride. Benno couldn't make any sense of her whims. What made her fly into a rage today, could leave her cold the next. "Yes," she simply said. "Maybe they can grow up together. The dog could protect him." They were sharing a bottle of wine in the kitchen, and Tim was in his room, probably too smart to show his face. He had made Benno promise to talk to Carolin about the matter.

It was getting dark, and they hadn't switched on the lights yet. Outside the window, the scrawny bushes moved in the wind, shaggy creatures scratching at the windows, as though demanding entry.

"Or he could bite Tim."

"You're too dramatic," she said.

Her calm irritated him, but maybe it was the drugs that transformed Carolin. Or maybe they saved her from more frequent or more intense crises. Three bottles always stood side by side in the medicine cabinet.

"You were against the bike."

"He won't fall off the dog," Carolin replied, laughing.

"How was the youth group?"

"Nice," she said. "I might invite the children over for coffee. Would be good for Tim if he had a few more friends."

"Even more?" asked Benno. He sighed.

Carolin looked at him through her thick glasses, and it was impossible to see what she was thinking. The next moment she slung her arms around his neck, pressing her lips to his. "You're sweet," she said. "I think you'll be alright with a dog."

"With a wife, a boy, a dog, and a youth group. You will eat me alive."

―――――――

Tim was careful to conceal his joy. "Cool," he said quietly at breakfast.

"You also don't have to sell your bike," Benno said, and after a quick glance at Carolin added, "I believe."

Later he asked Ms. Schmied if she knew anyone who might have dogs for sale. When she said no, he waited for Mr. Witte, the mailman, who delivered early in the morning. And when he didn't know anyone either, Benno stopped by Johannsen's store on his way to work. The owner had hung a corkboard in the store where farmers advertised fresh eggs and children tried to sell their model railways and roller skates, or offered to wash the neighbors' cars.

"Looking for something specific?" Johannsen's coat was still white and stiff, though by the evening it would be heavily stained.

"A dog," Benno said. "Tim wants one."

The shopkeeper scratched his chin and furrowed his forehead. "Farmer Reincke," he said. "He owns and sometimes sells dogs. It's the last farm on the road to Wengsten, it's a bit hidden, so you can see it only after you've already passed his driveway."

That same evening, Benno, Carolin and Tim made their way to Reincke's farm. Benno had called him from Lübeck, and after he had indeed driven past the entrance, he made a U-turn on Wengstener Straße and then bounced over potholes toward the low-slung farmhouse. To his right, Benno suddenly spotted something reddish brown and slimy hanging in a tree. He pointed with his finger, but Carolin shrugged. "Cow stomach?" She shook herself.

Reincke was already waiting in the yard, his hands in his pockets, a pipe in his mouth and a greasy cap on his head. His cheeks were covered with burst veins, his feet were stuck in dusty rubber boots. He relaxed only when Tim climbed from the back seat and politely stretched out his hand.

"The miracle boy," he said and spat. "Wants a dog." Without shaking hands he led the visitors behind his house to a series of cages. "I once had more of them," he said, as if he wanted to apologize. "Now I only have my Asta. Ran off and got involved with a Lab. That's what it looks like, anyway."

Asta was a German Shepherd, her offspring more black than yellow and with very short, dense fur. There were five pups, and Tim stared at them greedily. But when he knelt down to pet them, Benno heard a brief whimper that seemed to come from one of the cages in the rear. Reincke had also heard it, took his pipe from his mouth and spat to the side. "A stray that belongs to nobody. Full of worms and fleas. He's as good as dead."

Tim played with the puppies, let them lick his fingers and gave them the food that Reincke kept in a plastic bucket. The boy laughed at their rough tongues that tickled him, the teeth that nibbled on his fingers.

At last he stood up, his knees dirty and wet, and went over to the last cage. Benno followed him. The whining had stopped, and the stray neither seemed to pay attention to the noise nor to worry about the presence of the family. He was taller than Reincke's dog, and stood motionless in the cage and kept his eyes lowered. Tim's fingers clutched the wire, while he stared quietly at the dog's matted, reddish-brown fur.

"Last winter he showed up in town," Reincke said to Benno. "Nobody knows where he came from. Wouldn't let anyone come near him. He was too thin and weak to run away when I discovered him here at the barn."

Slowly, the dog lifted his head, sniffed, and turned to the boy, as if he remembered something from a long time ago. He whimpered softly and pressed his body against the wire. His left eye seemed almost black.

"This one here," Tim said, turning toward the adults. His cheeks were flushed. Then he knelt down in front of the cage and put both hands through the bars. The dog stood still, closed his eyes and let the boy pet him.

"Wouldn't you prefer another one?" Carolin asked. "The little ones are so sweet." She looked anxiously at Benno. The dog didn't seem to please her.

Tim shook his head.

"He's still sick. And he is quite wild. Who knows if he'll ever listen to you?"

"Your mother is right," Benno agreed. "And something is wrong with his legs." He pointed to the right front paw that looked crooked.

Only when the boy was close to tears, did Carolin give in.

"You can have him for free. You're saving me a lot of trouble." Reincke unlocked the cage, took a coarse rope that hung at the gate and tried to put it around the neck of the dog, yet the animal backed away.

Wordlessly, Tim took the rope from the farmer's hands and led his new dog to the car. The animal followed without resistance, but was too weak to climb into the back seat; Benno had to lift him into the car. Afterward his shirt and pants were smeared with dirt, and the stray lowered his head as though embarrassed. Quickly, Tim got in after him and hugged his dog.

"Do you have a name for him?" Benno said, as he climbed into the car.

Tim leaned over and whispered in Benno's ear, "It's the wolf. We saved the wolf."

5

For a week, the veterinarian in Grevenhorst kept him in her care. After three days, Benno went with Tim to the county seat to look at the patient. The dog came to the cage door to greet them, yet he displayed no exuberance, nothing that Benno could have recognized as obvious pleasure. Still, the dog's demeanor gave him the strange feeling that Tim hadn't found the dog, but that the animal had rediscovered the boy.

The farmer had been right: the stray had worms and was terribly emaciated. Only his thick coat hid the protruding ribs. Both ears were crusted with blood. Flies, said the doctor, the black spots would never heal. A front leg had been broken and healed incorrectly, the right hind leg was weak, maybe just a sprain. "But there is something very peculiar about him," she finally said.

"What do you mean?" asked Benno. Tim knelt in front of the cage and fed the dog treats from a large bag.

"I don't know what it is, but if I had found the dog, I wouldn't want to give him up again." She didn't even smile.

"And there's another thing," continued the doctor. "He has been shot, pellets were still in his flank. One hit him in the skull, bounced off a bone in the jaw and is stuck behind the eye. That's why the eye looks black—he can't see much with it, if anything at all. But around here, that's not necessarily something special. Maybe a farmer chased him off his property."

"Could he become dangerous?" asked Benno. "If Tim plays too rough with him or wants to take away his stick? Or, or . . ."

The doctor shook her head. "He's been through a lot. But no, not him."

Yet when Tim finally got up and stepped away from the cage, the dog's demeanor suddenly changed. He screamed and carried on like crazy. With horror, the boy watched as the animal bit down on the metal bars and rattled the door. Benno had to take Tim's arm and drag him out of the office, and when they finally sat outside in the car, they could still hear the dog howl.

One morning in early October, Benno got into the car and turned the key. On the fourth attempt the engine finally started, only to give up the ghost a few seconds later with a loud bang, which was followed by a violent clatter. The Ford dealer was the only repair shop in town, and the service department sent over a tow truck. Benno rode shotgun after he had been promised a loaner for the trip to Lübeck.

When Otto Friedrich called in the afternoon to tell him what the necessary repairs would cost—a new engine would have to be installed—Benno and Carolin decided to pay a visit to the dealer and look at his used cars.

"We have the best prices in the area," he said, and shook hands with them. His friendly smile bared long, brownish teeth. The front pocket of his suit jacket held a pack of Camel Filters. "And I'll make you a special offer as a welcome gift, so to speak. Have you settled in a bit in our backwater village?"

Carolin nodded. "Slowly we're getting to know everyone. Mr. Cornelius has taken us under his wing."

Friedrich laughed. "He's eagerly collecting souls. And up on that hill, you're a captive audience." He winked at her and asked, "What can I tempt you with? A quick Sierra or something larger? A Scorpio?"

"Maybe a Fiesta," Benno interjected. "There are only three of us."

"Don't forget the dog," Friedrich said with a grin. "All of Strathleven already knows that you have adopted the ghost dog. Nothing remains secret here." In a confidential tone, he continued, "Nothing ever happens here, so we welcome every bit of gossip."

"Have you ever met our predecessors?" Benno asked on impulse. "Christensen told me that they left in a hurry."

Friedrich shrugged his shoulders. "Christensen doesn't like anyone. Especially not people who are not from here. Don't take it personally. For your predecessors, the village was probably too small. What we call peace, they probably felt was just plain dull."

Together they walked across the yard. Friedrich seemed in his element, forcing Benno behind the steering wheels of cars that were much too large and much too expensive. "We really shouldn't buy a new one," Benno said, but seconds later he sank with a sigh into the leather seat of a Sierra. "I've read your articles," Friedrich said. "You're good. The previous editor was too conservative, you bring a bit of fresh air to the *Strandkurier*."

"Why doesn't Strathleven have a soccer team?" asked Benno. He couldn't help but feel flattered. "The place is big enough."

"We don't need it," Friedrich replied cheerfully. "All the others already have one. We have enough work with our shooting club. But that's not your department, right?"

Benno shook his head. "My colleague handles that."

"If you stay here, you must join us, absolutely. It's a great opportunity to get to know Strathleven, and we have a lot of fun."

"That's what the pastor said about going to church," Benno said and rolled his eyes.

Friedrich laughed loudly. "Hellfire is no longer enough. The children want to have fun, the church must be modern."

After an hour-long discussion, many concerns and doubts, and a generous trade-in offer for the old Beetle—Benno's first car ever had survived only six months—he agreed with Carolin on an almost brand new Escort. It was a show car, not even a year old. Light blue metallic with gray cloth seats. Four doors.

"You won't regret it," said Friedrich when Benno finally signed the contract. "This is a solid car. And it's under warranty." Friedrich's office was spacious and had a huge glass wall that looked out onto the showroom. On his desk stood a photo of his wife, another showed three children.

"Your daughters?" asked Carolin. "They are very pretty."

"They'll send me to the grave," sighed Friedrich. It was an old joke, and Benno was sure that Friedrich used it every single day of the week, but the dealer had an expression on his face that looked like real pain. Then the moment was gone and he grinned broadly. "If they don't eat me out of house and home first."

"How old are they?"

"Eleven, thirteen and sixteen. Difficult age. The boys are paying attention."

"They should come to our youth group," Carolin said eagerly. "We have a dance group, and even a band."

"My wife helps out there," Benno said.

"Yeah, sure." Friedrich beamed at her. He leaned in and whispered. "I'll send my daughters to the pastor and you'll get two tickets to the next shooting club ball."

"I don't know what the pastor would think of such a trade," Benno tried to joke. The thought of old men in loden and silly hats did not sit well with him. "Are you maybe the champion marksman, the king?"

"God forbid." The dealer leaned back in his chair. "That would bankrupt me. I'd have to buy everyone a drink. And not just one, these things always end in a binge. If you come, do what I do, aim a bit to the right." He paused briefly before he continued. "Anyway—who wants to buy a car from the king? People would start getting suspicious and not trust my prices. Am I not right? Why should I make my life unnecessarily difficult?" He winked before he pulled open one of his drawers and took out two tickets. "For our Autumn Ball at the end of the month. Absolutely free. I'm making your decision easy."

When they finally drove off the lot, Benno complained, "The car looks so dignified, "I feel so old."

For a moment, Carolin said nothing. Then it broke out of her: "Don't always badmouth Cornelius. He means well, and I think he does his best to offer the children a place where they belong. I like helping him."

"It was just a joke," Benno said. "The talk about hellfire."

"You always have to pick on him. Don't think I haven't noticed. Just because someone's trying to give our lives a bit of meaning."

Every day after school, Tim worked his way through encyclopedias, novels, and even the phone book. The night before they were to bring the dog home, he finally decided on a name. The stray would be called Rasmus.

"Is that stupid?" he asked Benno.

"How so?"

"He already has a name."

"But we have no way of knowing what it is."

Tim nodded slowly. "But what if he doesn't want to answer to his new name?"

Benno took his time with the answer. "Now that you're his owner, he will obey you."

"And if not?"

The next day, Benno walked into a pet store Holger had recommended, and bought a huge, red plush bed and a collar with a tag that the owner engraved in the store. Then he picked up Tim at home, and together they drove to Grevenhorst. Carolin had no time this evening, she was at a 'singing group' rehearsal—Cornelius apparently wanted to avoid the word 'choir.'

Rasmus trotted out of the cage and greeted them silently, but once Tim put on the new collar, he came alive. Whining excitedly, he bit into the leash and pulled Tim out of the vet's office. Benno paid the bill and got two bottles of medication.

"Take it slow with him. The dog is still weak. And come back in two weeks for a follow-up." She winked at Benno from behind her black-rimmed eyes. "I want to see him again."

This time, Rasmus climbed into the backseat himself, Tim only had to hold the rear door open. Then the dog pressed his face against the window and looked at the dark fields passing by and occasionally took a slice of sausage from Tim's hand. The road was almost empty, and white and yellow reflectors curved ahead of them and turned the night sky into a tunnel. It was a cool evening, and Benno had the heat turned on, and smiled happily because it really worked. In his old car it had only come on in the summer.

When they got home, the lights were on inside, and Benno could see Carolin standing in the kitchen. In the apartment next door, Manfred stood by the window, and when he saw Benno, he waved a bit too franti-cally. The church bell rang seven times. Rasmus peed on the flowerbeds and then trotted behind Tim into the living room, settled on his new bed and was asleep in minutes.

6

On Sunday Benno was awakened by Tim's voice coming from the garden. He sighed and stared at the ceiling, closed his eyes again. When he finally got up and walked to the window, Tim was just about to throw a stick. Rasmus looked expectantly at him, but then showed no inclination to retrieve the stick. His fur was clean and had gained some shine, but when he trotted after Tim, he was still limping. However, he seemed to instill fear in the people from the village, and even Mr. Heintz did not come too close to him. "He looks quite dead," he had said. "As if he had sprung from hell."

After breakfast Carolin insisted that the whole family attend church. "Don't you want to hear me sing?" she asked, batting her eyelashes.

"Sure," Benno said. "But I don't want to listen to Manfred. Or this woman with the hideous floral dresses. Your soloist."

"Elfi Krieg? You don't like Elfi?" Carolin laughed. "But her voice is as sweet as honey."

"Yes, exactly. And I really need to go to this soccer game in Timmendorf."

"This is more important than your wife?"

"You could come with me. Tim too. And they also sell decent brats there." While he was still going on about the fun they would have, he noticed that Carolin's face was slowly darkening. "Of course I'm coming," he reassured her.

That morning, Cornelius had invited a guest from Lübeck, a young pastor with short, black hair and a gentle smile. He was very slim, rather short, and looked like a schoolboy next to Cornelius with his belly and bright crimson face. Next to them, a cassette recorder sat on a small table.

Cornelius introduced the guest as Daniel Thomas, who had just returned home after a long stay in the U.S. and was now once again active in his home community. Today he would speak about the influence of British and American rock music.

Daniel Thomas had a pleasant, bright voice that suited his schoolboy charm. He reached behind the podium and came out with a Led Zeppelin LP. "Stairway to Heaven," he said. "Sounds good, right? A stairway to heaven? Don't we all wish we knew where it was? And so many young people are attracted to this music." He took a dramatic pause. "But the text is a satanic message. 'It's a feeling I get when I look to the west and my spirit is crying for leaving.' Played backwards, this means, 'I have got to live for Satan.' I have to live for the devil." Thomas stared at the congregation. Disgust was written on many faces. The teenagers looked fixedly at the young man in the black suit. He pressed the 'play' button and the next moment the congregation could hear a scratchy voice, which seemed to really say something, though Benno couldn't make out what it was.

But already the young pastor was holding up a new album. "The Beatles. They became famous in Hamburg, and are now considered one of the best bands that have ever played. Four cute guys, right? With mop-top haircuts. But their music glorifies drug abuse. 'Lucy in the Sky with Diamonds'? Have you ever wondered what that actually means? It stands for LSD. And 'Yellow Submarine'? Also a drug text. A song that will corrupt our youth. John Lennon once said during their stay in Hamburg, 'I know that the Beatles will have success like no other group. I know it for a fact—because I sold my soul to the devil.'" A smile spread on Thomas' face. "All the records devoted to Satan are built on the same principles. This includes the rhythm, also called beat, that evokes the movements of a sexual relationship. You suddenly have the feeling of losing your mind and going crazy. To have its fullest effect, a volume is chosen that is seven decibels above the tolerance limit of the nervous system."

The young people now looked intimidated, but their parents nodded, as if Thomas had only confirmed their own suspicions. "I recently received a letter from a good friend—an American Baptist. This friend had an encounter with a young woman possessed by demons. She was a skilled witch, took cocaine and heroin, drank large amounts of alcohol and was involved in ghastly sexual practices. This young woman asked my friend to help her drive Satan from her life, and my friend agreed. The demons that tried to oppose him made the same noise as rock musicians on stage. Adolescents who watched this battle were so shocked that they threw away their rock 'n roll records." Thomas took a second before stepping closer toward the congregation and said in a soft, caressing voice, "Anyone who wants to escape the shackles of rock music must break his records and destroy the tapes."

Benno didn't join in the applause that followed. The albums the pastor had mentioned stood on a shelf in his office next door.

The subsequent presentation of the choir was accompanied by three guitars and sounded neither dark nor satanic, only Manfred's dull voice had something uncanny about it. And yet, after Thomas' sermon, the hymns sounded strangely altered. He had heard Carolin practice all week, but now the songs didn't sound all that harmless anymore.

He craned his neck to catch a glimpse of his wife and spied her to his left, half hidden by Elfi, the soloist. He had rarely seen her so radiant.

Afterward, Thomas was surrounded by young people who asked him questions about their favorite bands. Were A-ha and Duran Duran of the devil? Were Depeche Mode and Spandau Ballet hand in glove with demons?

"Well, have you reconsidered my offer? About your singing career?" Pastor Cornelius came up to Benno. "Wasn't that something," he added with his usual enthusiasm. "You should write an article about it."

"I'm only responsible for the Sports section," Benno said defensively. "If you want to organize a football tournament, I'm happy to help."

"But this message about rock music must get out. Maybe one of your colleagues might be interested."

"Yes, of course. I can ask around."

"Oh, that would be great." The pastor's red face shone just as brightly as the teenagers.' "Could also be about Strathleven. What we are doing here. The good work our church is doing. Would be a nice task for you, a gift to your new community. Some kind of portrait of our town. What do you say?"

"Nobody's interested in what we're doing here. And nobody needs to poke his nose in our affairs." A scowling Gustav Heintz joined them. "People don't like it when outsiders come along and ask questions." He turned to Benno. "I don't have anything against you personally. I'm just saying. The dead woman was all the press we needed."

The pastor's blush intensified and he stammered, "Look, that's exactly why Mr. Diedrich should write an article about us, so that Strathleven is known for more than murder."

"We'll see," Benno said noncommittally. "But I cannot promise you anything. I'm still learning the ropes at the *Strandkurier*."

In the evening, when Benno mentioned the pastor's idea, Carolin just said, "Sure. It's quite easy for you to do."

"But what am I supposed to write about?"

"About our singing group and about me, my wonderful voice."

"Which didn't croak at all."

"About the good air and Tim and his dog and the youth group, and how engaging the pastor is, and the good air . . . you think about it! Why should I do your work for you? You could also score some brownie points in the village."

"Brownie points? What for?"

Carolin's face suddenly became serious. "For Tim."

"Why? Are Jens and Daniel after him again?"

"Not really. No, they're totally changed. Awfully nice. But . . ."

"But what?"

"Do you promise not to laugh?"

"Promise."

Carolin's eyes behind her glasses seemed even bigger than usual. "They're all . . . too nice. They look at him strangely."

"Who are 'they'?"

"People in town. The other customers in the store. Even when we run into somebody on the street."

"The miracle boy."

"Maybe this article isn't a bad thing. You can interview people, and if they have any questions . . . about us, about Tim . . . I don't know." She trailed off. "Maybe I'm just imagining things." After a pause she said, "By the way, I found a new doctor for Tim. In Lübeck. Dr. Warthmann recommended him. Specializes in skin diseases. He doesn't have a practice, only does research at the university. I made an appointment for next month."

Benno nodded. They both knew that it was hopeless, but that even so, Carolin would never give up. Benno was more and more convinced that her efforts at finding a cure for Tim's illness were about herself, not about her son. If they should ever find the right doctor, maybe a higher power would forgive her missteps during the pregnancy. Otherwise, she would never be able to forgive herself.

It was a rainy evening, and the wind was noticeable even in the narrow streets of the old town. Benno stood in the doorway to the *Strandkurier* offices and hesitated. His car was not far away, he could just go home and postpone his research a few days. He fumbled for his cigarettes, lit one and watched people hurrying past. Bank employees, school children, an old man with a fisherman's cap on his head and an extinguished pipe in his mouth. This last one didn't seem to mind the rain. Although he held an umbrella in one hand, he hadn't bothered to open it. Benno spread a copy of the *Kurier* over his head and walked to the public library.

In the reading room, he hung his sodden coat over a chair and rummaged through the catalog. His feet had gotten wet on his short walk over, but the rooms were well heated, the light thick and warm, and the bad weather had probably deterred most people from coming. Benno was nearly alone on the first floor of the building.

Since his graduation, he hadn't set foot in a library, and now as he pulled open drawer after drawer, looking for books about the area, he noticed just how much he had missed the atmosphere. Perhaps he missed the hours spent in university libraries even more than his bachelor life in Berlin. The eagerly bent backs, the slightly smudged glasses of students and their pale, serious faces. The smoking room at the Institute for Comparative Literature.

Benno wrote down the identification numbers of several books on Lübeck and the region, although he wasn't even certain what exactly he was going to write about. Did Strathleven really have a history? What could be an interesting hook for a small village with an eager Baptist congregation? Strathleven's church was pictured in some books, and its pagan origins were also noted, but the place itself seemed to have aroused little interest in amateur and professional historians alike. Shortly before the library closed, Benno selected six or seven books on the legends and mysteries of the Baltic Sea coast and made his way to the checkout.

"Oh," said the librarian when she looked at the first title. "Looking for something special about the area?" Her voice was a little scratchy. She was maybe in her early forties, very large, and had short brown hair with light-red streaks. Her face was finely cut, and her long earrings sparkled in the light of the desk lamp. She smiled, took out his loan slips, and asked Benno for his card.

"I don't have one, yet," he said.

She asked for his ID, but he still had the special, green Berlin one. And no, he had not thought of bringing a registration form with his new address. "I work for the *Strandkurier*. I'm still very new here."

"And you want to find out about Strathleven?" she asked.

Benno smiled, embarrassed. "Yes, it's supposed to be a kind of portrait. I moved there recently."

"The Wonder Beech. Is it still there?"

"Oak. Miracle Oak. And yes, I think it's still there. But I haven't seen it yet."

"If you have a disability, you need to climb through it." The librarian laughed, and her voice seemed to drop an octave. Benno wasn't sure if she was laughing at him. "Well then," she said, and laminated a card for him.

The rain didn't let up for Strathleven's Autumn Ball. The night before, Carolin had surprised Benno with a new dress. "I ordered it from a catalog. That makes me feel really old," she said laughing, turning this way and that. It was a simple, dark blue dress; her skin looked very white.

"Now only my stupid suit has to fit." But as much as he sucked in his belly, he wasn't able to button his pants. "But I haven't put on that much weight," he protested.

"You've widened," laughed Carolin. "And you're getting older. You're becoming a dirty old man."

When they arrived at the ballroom, which was located near the concrete plant and rather resembled a modern barn, half the village seemed to have already gathered. Benno was surprised to find that most of the faces he had never seen. On his walks with Tim and Rasmus, he had only spotted an occasional farmer on his tractor, or an old woman on her bike. He knew the store owner Johannsen and, of course, Otto Friedrich, plus a few people from the church. But who were all these men in dark suits, these decked-out women? Where had they been up until now? Benno himself had gone to Lübeck in the morning to buy a new suit for the event. He felt too old to wear jeans to a ball.

Otto Friedrich led them to a half-empty table. "Well, look at you," he said in a loud voice that could be heard over the music coming from the speakers near the stage. He introduced them to the other guests at the table, a couple called Wiesenknecht, and then excused himself. "I've got to take care of some business."

After ten minutes, the music stopped, and a man in a green suit and a large silver necklace made from coins carried a microphone onto the stage. He pulled a piece of paper from his pocket and began his introductory remarks. He was the treasurer of the shooting club, Henning Buhr.

"We shouldn't have come," Benno whispered into Carolin's ear.

"Why? It's quite nice here."

The first speaker was the president, and as it turned out, it was the Sparmarkt owner, Johannsen. His wet, thinning hair was neatly parted, and instead of his dirty apron he wore a black suit. "We had a good year," he said loudly. The whole shooting club burst into cheers and applause. "And tonight, we want to say thanks. Let us hope that the next year will be an even better one."

The Wiesenknechts looked rather sheepishly at each other. Somebody in the crowd shouted, "Are you going to be king?"

But Johannsen was not to be deterred. "Tonight we will celebrate and dance and have a great time!" When this found only lukewarm approval, he also pulled a note from his pocket and read the agenda. Finally, he asked the champion marksman, Andreas Wehrke, to join him on stage.

Benno hadn't seen the John Deere dealer before. He was a tall, thin man with a clear-cut face and a long nose that made him look like a bird. He wore a green fedora with several feathers stuck inside the band, and a gold chain over his suit jacket. "Tonight, we won't think of tomorrow," he said in a soft voice that didn't fit his appearance. The audience clapped eagerly.

"Dear President, distinguished guests, dear fellow shooters. I am not a born orator, so I'll be brief. And," he added with a grin, pointing to the instruments behind him, "the musicians are getting impatient." Then he began to talk about the history and tradition of shooting clubs. All the visitors at least pretended to listen with great interest.

"*Train eye and hand for the Fatherland!* This thoughtful saying was previously on our club banner and graced our clubhouse. Yet it has become rare nowadays. We have been in a phase of cutbacks and regression for years. We are misunderstood by the world. We have a reputation for being ridiculous and dangerous hillbillies. But shooters like ourselves don't cling to the old ways unconditionally. No, we are open to new ideas. But we demand that these new ideas be better than the old."

Applause could be heard, a few guests slapped the tables with their open hands.

"Strathleven has changed, but are the new things really better? There are those who want to leave our old ways of living, who want to forget who we were and who we are."

Silence spread after these words. Everyone was looking at Wehrke now.

"Yes, just like everyone else, we have become wealthy, we go to Italy on vacation, and our children attend university, but can we really forget our traditions? Do they really belong on the trash heap? Our village is faced with difficult decisions. Some people are no longer sure that we shooters have a place in society. Some say that we have nothing left to protect, and must give up our weapons. What will we decide?"

Wehrke had spoken very seriously, and now, while he was pausing briefly, no one dared to stand up or even cough. Benno looked at the worried faces around him. It seemed as though everyone in the audience knew exactly what the champion marksman was alluding to, and that only he could make no sense of the speech.

Then Wehrke grinned again, someone in the audience gave a sign, and seconds later somebody carried a glass of beer to the podium. Amid general laughter, the speaker took a long sip.

"Dear guests. I regret that I didn't live in the Middle Ages, because then I wouldn't have to pay any taxes for a whole year. Yet another custom has remained—the king invites his subjects for a drink. Shooters have always held their liquor, and I sincerely hope that this is still the case tonight. A word to the wives of our shooters: Ladies! Consider how important the maintenance of old customs is. Therefore, forgive our exuberance tonight, and merrily join us shooters on the dance floor. Let us raise our glasses to a long life of our fraternity and a beautiful, harmonious evening! Cheers!"

After the speech, the stage was cleared and within minutes, three musicians started to play "Fiesta Mexicana." Benno groaned, but Carolin laughed at him. "Come on, old man. You can dance with me."

But soon Carolin began to complain about his awkward steps. "You have to lead," she shouted in his ear. "The man must lead."

Painful memories of dance school lessons in the Hessian province awoke in Benno's mind. The next dance was too quick for him, and while all the other couples whirled around him, he stepped so hard on Carolin's feet that she almost fell over. While he was still apologizing, someone tapped him on the shoulder.

"May I?" It was Hubert Witte, the postman, almost unrecognizable in a dark blue suit and a red bow tie. In an instant he swept Carolin onto the dance floor. Benno returned to his table.

After ten minutes, he was still sitting alone in front of his beer. Carolin was now in the arms of a large, balding man, who seemed to have swallowed a broomstick, but she seemed to be enjoying herself tremendously.

"How do you like it in Strathleven?" Wehrke sat down next to him, without his felt hat and chain. "Otto told me that he had invited you. New in town, right?"

"It's very nice," Benno said and tried not to look for Carolin.

"Your wife seems to like it, too," said the champion marksman.

Benno wasn't sure how this last remark was meant. He just nodded. "The pastor is probably not a shooter?"

Wehrke laughed. "No, he's not from here."

"Do you have to be from here to join the club?"

"Oh no." Wehrke grinned. "But you have to appreciate your home country."

"And the pastor doesn't appreciate his home country?"

"Not the way we do," replied Wehrke and looked across the dance floor. "Your wife can dance. You should mingle with our people, have a little fun." He stood up and held out his hand. "Nice to have you with us."

Benno found his way to the bar, ordered a beer and then left the ballroom. It was still raining, but at least he could breathe some air that wasn't rank with hairspray and aftershave. After a few minutes a giggle came from one of the parked cars, and Benno wondered how and where teens could buy marijuana in Strathleven.

The chuckle grew louder, car doors were slammed, and a young man and a girl walked across the wet gravel toward Benno. The boy he didn't know, but the girl's pale face looked familiar. Yet they were not looking in his direction, and seconds later they had disappeared into the ballroom.

When he returned to his table his clothes were slightly soggy, and Carolin sat with the mailman and another man he had never seen. An almost empty bottle of champagne stood in front of them.

"There you are," Carolin said, laughing. "What happened to you?"

"It's raining outside," Benno said.

"And what were you doing out there?" She shook her head. "This is Bruno. Bruno is a club member."

"Bruno Maier. Allianz Insurance," the man said, extending his hand.

"Oh." Benno shook the very dry, very firm hand. "Have I seen you in church?"

Carolin whooped, "No, but he will come. He promised."

Maier gave an embarrassed laugh. "Maybe."

"No, for sure."

The man grinned good-naturedly. "Well then, for sure."

"But now I want to dance," she said and led the insurance agent onto the dance floor. Hubert Witte drained his glass of champagne, nodded at Benno, grinned, and excused himself.

"May I introduce you to my women?" Otto Friedrich had appeared behind him. Benno got up immediately. Friedrich's wife Martina was slightly taller than her husband, and not just because of her red, high-heeled pumps. Her face was very round, with slightly turned-down eyes. Her hair was shoulder length and straight, her hands small and neat.

"And my daughter Corinna. My eldest."

It was the girl he had seen at the entrance. Whether she recognized him, he couldn't tell. She smiled gently, but remained silent. She seemed embarrassed to be introduced to a stranger.

"Enjoying yourself?" Friedrich grinned broadly.

"Yeah, sure." Benno said. "But I'm not a great dancer."

"Me neither. I swear I have too many feet not to stumble and fall. But Corinna is fabulous out there. Ask her to dance!"

"I really can't do that to her."

Martina Friedrich smiled encouragingly. "Corinna turns everyone into a better dancer. Try it!"

There was no way to refuse without offending Friedrich and his wife, and although he felt like a silly curmudgeon, he grabbed Corinna's hand and walked with her to the dance floor. "I apologize in advance," he said. "You will regret this."

The girl did not laugh at his joke, and soon adapted to his rhythm. "Please don't tell my father that you saw us in the parking lot."

"Us?" asked Benno.

"Harald and me. Have you met Harald?"

Benno shook his head. "I don't have the correct sequence of steps, right? Harald is from Strathleven?"

"That doesn't matter. It's quite good." She smiled a little bit. "Harald is Mr. Wehrke's son."

"And why should I not have seen you? Because you were smoking?"

"That too."

The dance ended, but Corinna made no effort to move away from him. When the band started playing a more upbeat number, Benno tried as best as he could to avoid bumping into other couples.

"Move your upper body a little more, then no one notices what you're doing with your feet."

"Rhythmic standing?"

"Something like that." Her smile grew wider. Corinna was built stronger than her mother, she was broad-shouldered and had larger, clearer features. The more he danced with her, or at least pretended to, the more her pale face looked beautiful to him. Perhaps Carolin was right, and he was truly a dirty old man. At that thought, he looked around for his wife, but could not locate her.

"Why shouldn't your father know about Harald?"

"He's too old."

"How old is he?"

"Twenty. And he's going to college. My father thinks that he just wants to fuck my ass and then get rid of me."

Benno tried not to appear shocked at the girl's language. "And what do you think?"

"You're the guy who found the dead woman, right?"

Benno nodded. "Actually, it was the pastor." He looked once again for Carolin.

"Your wife is not on the dance floor." Corinna's face was oddly expressionless.

"Oh." He grinned, ashamed. "Why?"

"Why what?"

"Why did you ask about the dead woman?" Benno preferred talking about the corpse to talking about Carolin.

"Sybille told me everything."

"Sybille? Sybille who? What did she tell you?"

"Sybille Antler."

By a hair's breadth he avoided stepping on Corinna's left foot.

The girl laughed. "Her father's got a repair shop in Grevenhorst. She and a few friends found the body. I think one of them played around with the corpse. And I think one of the boys took a souvenir."

"A souvenir?" Benno paused, and a moment later received an elbow to his left kidney.

"Dance on," the girl said.

Benno obeyed. "What kind of souvenir?" he asked.

"She didn't know. Or didn't want to say."

The song was over, and now the guitarist of the group tried his hand at a Roland Kaiser imitation and belted out "Santa Maria."

"Oh, that's awful," Benno said.

"That he took a souvenir?"

"That too."

"It's okay for dancing, but you have to hold me more closely."

Benno did as he was told. He fervently hoped that Carolin would see him like that, with a young woman in his arms, and without committing any major blunder. Yes, he could have fun. He could dance if he wanted to.

"The miracle boy," Corinna said. "That's your son?"

"Yes," Benno said. "But he is not a miracle."

"You can't really hurt him, right? Like Siegfried."

"Who said that?"

"People," the girl answered vaguely.

"He can get hurt very easily," Benno said firmly, and to divert attention from Tim, he asked, "What is going to happen with Harald?"

Corinna looked directly at him, as if to make sure he had no ulterior motives, or wouldn't tell her father everything.

"It's not like he can do anything he's not already done. It's not as if I want to get pregnant and have his child."

Benno couldn't think of anything to say. "Patchouli," he finally blurted out.

"What?"

"Your perfume. That's what it is, right?"

She nodded. "Do I have your word of honor?"

"Where does Sybille live?"

"You can't say that I told you."

"Santa Maria" was over, and in the short break before the next number, Benno led Corinna to the edge of the dance floor. "Would you like something to drink?" he asked.

"Nah, that's okay. I should get back to my parents."

"Right." Benno hoped that he had not danced an inappropriately long time with the girl. "And about Sybille—I'm not going to rat her out to the police."

"That wouldn't get you anywhere."

Benno looked at her puzzled. "Why?"

"Oh, nothing," Corinna said quickly. "The Antlers live on Enge Straße. But don't tell her how you found out about the corpse."

"Word of honor." Benno took her hand and bowed slightly. "It's been fun to dance with you."

The girl wiped off her hand on her dress, and before turning away she said, "Your hands are all wet."

7

The bad weather continued. The leaves that had survived the fall until now landed on the ground and gummed up the streets. In Berlin, Benno had always felt melancholic and cozy during this time. Even when driving his taxi, the cold and rain hadn't been able to get to him, but in Strathleven he felt defenseless and soggy during the day until the early onset of darkness covered the puddles and rivulets.

At dinner, Tim was very silent, until he suddenly asked, "Is there anybody else like me?" His lips were smeared with grease and stood open. His third slice of pizza sat in front of him.

It was not the first time that he had asked that question. Benno and Carolin had done research, interviewed doctors, and scoured scientific journals and books for instances of Tim's illness, but they had never found an answer.

"No," Benno said. "You're a monster!"

Tim laughed, raised his greasy hands and curled his fingers into claws. His face was contorted, his tongue was stuck out. Rasmus barked, and Carolin laughed when the whole table began to shake. She was happy to watch her son's antics.

When the plate broke from the impact of Tim's elbow, Carolin screamed. Benno grabbed the boy and pulled him into his arms. All three were suddenly very quiet. Benno turned Tim's arm into the light. Together they stared at the narrow cut. The thin red line darkened quickly and disappeared, and in its place appeared a several millimeter wide bulge. There would be no scab, Tim had never had any. Benno and Carolin called them scars, but they looked just like slightly thicker, tougher, darker skin.

"Shit," Benno said. Tim wriggled from his grip and shrugged his shoulders a bit too calmly to convince his parents.

"We must be careful," said Benno. The spectacle of Tim's healing process still frightened him.

"You monster," Carolin repeated the joke, but her voice was shrill. Tim's mouth twisted and he began to cry.

He made it a habit to sit down at his desk every night, put on a record and read stories and articles about the region. He read of small creatures that were strong enough to move and arrange even the largest boulders. These beings could also turn themselves invisible or transform into all sorts of animals.

Benno had no idea how witches and superstition could help him with his article, but on cold autumn nights these tales made for good reading, and he also learned that the Goblins favored the shape of fat toads and sat under elderberry bushes, wearing small gold crowns on their heads.

Actually, he was more interested in finding out what Sybille Antler knew and what the boy had taken from the murder scene. But how could he find out about it? The girl didn't attend church, and he couldn't lie in wait in front of her house and then interrogate her. Even if the girl should talk to him, he was not the police.

Benno still hadn't found a hook for his story when he looked at the clock. It was after midnight. Tim had gone to bed at nine, and Carolin had said good night soon afterward. He had listened to the same Anne Clark album three times already, and finally he stood up to put on one last record and to drink one more glass of wine. His back and shoulders felt all stiff and when he went into the kitchen to open a new bottle, two cockroaches scurried toward opposite corners of the linoleum floor.

Armed with a bottle of Cahors, Benno made his way back to his office. The bushes outside were scratching at the windows. Perhaps it was this scraping noise that reminded him of the young pastor's sermon, or perhaps the stories of pagan gods he'd been reading all night were to blame, but Benno suddenly felt the need to listen to "Dark Side of the Moon" by Pink Floyd. What devil would he unleash on humanity?

He had never ordered his record collection, which consisted of maybe 150 albums and filled two long shelves. Benno's fingers slid over the backs of the sleeves, his eyes were tired and blurred the titles and band names. Again he went through his records, but no, even this time he couldn't find Pink Floyd. It had been a birthday gift from a former girl-friend, a girl with long fingers and a large nose. She had never removed her leather bracelets, not even in the shower.

Again, nothing. Benno took out every single sleeve, looked at each and every cover. No, it wasn't there.

Slowly he sat down on the floor and rubbed his eyes. The scratching of the bushes no longer sounded cozy. Spindly fingers asked to be let in, dark figures flitted around the house and looked for a gap, a small opening to squeeze through.

His fingers reached for the wine glass, and for a moment Benno remained completely silent in thought, thinking back to that little apartment in Wedding district, recalling friends and long winter nights with heat coming from the ancient tiled coal oven.

Then he sat up with a jerk. He had gone through his entire record collection, but had he seen his two Kiss albums? Once again, he went searching through them, but this time he was sure that the Eagles and Led Zeppelin were missing too. Benno drank his wine and looked outside the window to the shadows, as they turned and writhed. And all of a sudden he got the sinking feeling that they were rejoicing and applauding with their withered hands.

"Pink Floyd?"

"What Thomas played in church sounded really horrible. It scared me. And that can't be good for Tim." Carolin's face looked drawn.

Benno was still wearing his shirt and pants, he had slept on the sofa in the living room. "You're scared? That the devil is going to take over our lives?" He was tired and his lower back and sides were stiff and hurt.

Carolin put the toothbrush on the edge of the sink and turned her head to face him. "You don't take me seriously, you don't even try."

"You didn't ask me. Those were my albums. What did you do with them?"

"We're married. *Your* albums?"

Benno gasped in disbelief. "Where are they?" His voice was hoarse.

"I threw them in the trash." And as Benno was about to storm out of the bathroom, she added, "It was picked up yesterday. I didn't want to sell them and let them fall into other hands."

"Let them fall into other hands?" Benno's voice cracked. "That is complete nonsense. That pastor has a screw loose."

Carolin stared at him and then slowly lowered her head. But before he could continue to rant about the pastor, she began to cry. "Sorry," she sobbed, turned to him and grabbed his shirt. "I should've talked to you."

Her sudden change of mind let the air out of his rage. "Yes, you should've," he said in a low voice.

"I know. But I was alone in the house and I suddenly couldn't breathe. Thomas didn't make that up, and I don't want to have such things around me." She held on to Benno and pressed her face against his chest.

"It's just music," he said, trying to sound reassuring. "It won't harm us."

"Don't leave such things in the house. The pastor says you have to commit to the good, and that also means that you have to make sacrifices."

"And you sacrificed my records?"

"Not everybody understands this, and those who don't are the ones who tempt the true believers." Carolin was still crying. While he was stroking her hair and trying to soothe her, he wondered whether she considered him among the people who tried to tempt 'true believers.'

After Carolin had left the bathroom, Benno stood at the window and pressed his face against the cold glass. The driveway was full of puddles, and the old sand pit looked like a swimming pool. He saw Rasmus run out into the garden, pee on a rock in disgust and immediately trot back to the house. Even the dog despised the weather.

Benno slowly undressed, turned on the water in the shower. But when he reached down and grabbed a new towel from the small closet, a thought struck him, and he raised his head so fast that he caught the edge of the sink. The pain made him scream and fall to the ground. Cursing, he got up again and was greeted by his cheese-colored face in the cabinet's mirror. He opened the door and checked the contents. As much as he tried to locate them between Band-Aids and eye drops, he couldn't find Carolin's pill bottles.

The Miracle Oak stood in a meadow near the village exit, between Dorf-straße and Kambek. Benno had seen it every day on his way to work and never recognized what it was. The tree was near a small forest, and no cows were grazing in its vicinity. There couldn't be any doubt—branches and trunk were so severely knotted that two meters off the ground a nearly circular opening had been created, through which a person could squeeze with some effort. That's what Heintz and the librarian had been talking about.

Despite the rain, Benno stopped the car and decided to walk across the meadow. He tried to dodge the biggest puddles, but by the time he was halfway to the tree his shoes were soaked. Nevertheless, he hurried on. The oak's trunk was massive, the branches still wore a few brown leaves. If he got up on his tiptoes, he could reach the hole with his hands, but without climbing up he couldn't see through the opening. Benno walked around the oak and inspected it. Strangely, there were no nicks, no evidence of carved hearts, no lovers' names immortalized. At a mira-cle tree, he would have expected to find them in abundance. But the tree seemed untouched. Benno braved the rain for a minute or two longer. He hoped for an inspiration, a sign, or any special feeling of grandeur and awe, but he felt only wet. The tree didn't give up its secret.

In the evening he left the office early and walked over to the library. He looked for the librarian from the previous week and finally found her on the third floor behind a cart with books. She was taller than he remembered, and was wearing tight jeans and a sweater that made her look even bigger than on his first visit. Her many bracelets jingled, and Benno watched her as she took one book after another and placed it on the shelves. He had never seen anything special in this activity.

"Certainly an oak," he said as a greeting.

"Are you suffering from rheumatism?" She laughed, revealing coffee-stained teeth. "The opening. If you have rheumatism or asthma, you have to climb through in order to become healthy again. How did you end up in Strathleven?"

"It was cheap, I think. My wife found it. Short drive to town. Large apartment. Garden."

She nodded. Today she was wearing a nametag on her cardigan. Hanne Stein. She came up to Benno and put a hand on his arm. "Do you want to know more about your new home? More than soccer?"

Benno's face turned red, her hand was still on his arm, motionless and alive, like a small animal. Then he nodded and grinned sheepishly.

On the second floor, the library had a small reading room, and the built-in, wooden shelves were lined with books on regional architecture, old sailing ships, the Hanseatic League, Lübeck and its churches, and local cuisine.

"So what shall it be?" She turned to look at him and spread her arms wide. "Klabautermänner? Störtebeker? Pentecostal rites or Ghost Rider? Miracle Oak?"

Benno sighed. "Is there really something about the Miracle Oak?"

"Oh, of course." She rolled her eyes. "It's our specialty."

"I mean, I still need a hook, a specific angle. Something like 'Strathleven Throughout the Ages' or 'Miracle Oak Cures Frail Old Man.' What I have found so far makes no sense at all. A deity with four heads, witch hunts, shipwrecks and gold ducats—it's terrible nonsense."

The librarian furrowed her brow. She had a stronger chin than he did, Benno noticed, but this didn't make her face look harsh. To avoid being caught staring at her, he eagerly looked at the books around him.

"Wasn't Strathleven in the headlines recently? A month or two ago?"

"Yes," Benno said. "A woman was murdered."

"Do they have any suspects yet?"

Benno shook his head. "They don't even know who she was or why she was found in Strathleven. She wasn't murdered where she was found, but that's all they know. She was pregnant and was horribly disfigured, as if someone had stabbed her with dull knives and scissors."

For a moment there was silence in the paneled room, and Benno could now hear the rain beating against the window.

"That would be a good hook," the librarian said cautiously.

"But I want to endear myself to the village," sighed Benno.

"Then let's go back to the Miracle Oak. Or you can publish the article under a pseudonym."

Benno shrugged. "At the *Strandkurier*?"

"Of course. Haven't you noticed? Whenever they publish something iffy or sensational, they use a name that nobody has ever heard of. It's an open secret."

"Apparently not open enough."

Ms. Stein smiled. They returned to the small reading room with the coffee table and history books.

"I thought about barrows. Do they still exist?"

"Dolmens, megalithic tombs . . ." The librarian furrowed her brow. Then she seemed to have an idea. "There was something," she said, walking slowly up and down in front of the shelves.

She bent down and pulled out several books, but could not seem to find the right one. "Look," she suddenly said. "There's something from one of your new neighbors." She handed Benno a small book with a soft, pale brown cover. *The Children from Wodeberg* was printed in old-fashioned lettering, and the subtitle promised *The story of a Strathlevener family*. The author's name was Martin Wehrke. "Do you know him?" the librarian asked.

Benno shook his head. "Might be related to the champion marksman. No idea."

"I'll tell you if I find the book about the megalithic tombs. It was probably nothing important, but ask me about it next time. I have to go back down and guard the desk."

Benno sat down at a table and opened the thin book to a foldout family tree in the back. The author himself was the younger of two brothers, divorced, and father of an adult son. A photo of Martin Wehrke was printed on the inside of the book cover. He seemed to be thin, with a long nose, beard, and a bald head. A pipe was stuck in his mouth, and he wore a jacket and tie. Benno could not remember having seen him at the shooting club ball.

He made it just in time to the John Deere dealer before the store closed for the evening. Christensen's silent hostility was getting on Benno's nerves, and the lawn looked more chopped off than mowed whenever his neighbor was done with his handiwork. Buying his own lawnmower seemed inevitable.

There were only two cars in the parking lot, but one of them Benno recognized immediately. It was the black Jaguar Tim had fallen in love with a few months ago. Was this Andreas Wehrke's, the owner's car?

Unlike Otto Friedrich's glittering palace, the John Deere dealership was a more modest affair. Shabby linoleum covered the sales floor, where you could buy rakes, power tools, garden soil, and fertilizer. Two small tractors were parked in the blue and green-carpeted showroom, with extra pieces of carpet stuck underneath the tires.

"Can I help you?" An employee in a green coat approached Benno. He had a bald patch and seemed to have swallowed a broomstick.

"The shooting club ball," Benno said.

"Demnig." The salesman broke into a smile, which looked ugly because of his bad teeth. "Walter Demnig. Your wife, she's a great dancer. Full of energy."

"I need a lawnmower." Benno clenched his fists. He felt an itch to show this man what exactly he thought of him. "Is Andreas Wehrke here?"

"The boss? No, these days he's usually over at the concrete plant."

"Oh, I thought . . . the concrete plant also belongs to him? So that's not his Jaguar outside?"

"That's Junior's."

"He works here?"

"It's probably his winter break. And over Christmas, he's supposed to run the store." Demnig leaned forward and whispered, "We make sure that he doesn't mess up everything . . ." He wanted to add something else, it seemed, but suddenly straightened up and said, "If it continues to rain like that, you might still need the mower."

The reason for Demnig's behavior had just stepped out of a small office in back. Harald Wehrke wasn't wearing a green coat, but a black velvet jacket that matched his car's coating. He was almost as tall as his father, and even slimmer. His dark hair was curled and reached almost to his shoulders.

"Nice car," Benno said loudly enough that Harald could hear it. "My boy loves it."

An involuntary smile appeared on the young man's lips, but quickly disappeared again. He nodded at Benno. "Is Walter helping you?" he asked. "Or is he trying to talk you into buying a tractor to cut your grass? Walter loves his tractors."

Demnig turned red, but bravely held on to his smile.

"We'll find the right mower," Benno said. "Thank you."

Harald slowly walked back into his office and closed the door. Through the glass window Benno could see the young man put his black shoes—adorned with straps, silver buckles and studs—on the desk and light a cigarette. One perfect smoke ring after another escaped his wide-open mouth.

8

It was mid-December when Benno stopped for a second time at the Miracle Oak and ran out into the field. Fortunately, the rain had taken a break. They'd had their first night of frost and the grass crunched under his shoes. Benno was as happy as a little boy—he had even thought to bring gloves and a wool hat.

From the car he had seen something hanging in the now leafless branches, and since he had left the house early enough, he allowed himself the little detour. That something had probably been red or brown originally, but was now covered by a layer of frost. It had no shape at all, and looked like a big, half-filled plastic bag. With an old branch, Benno poked at the strange thing, which turned out to be still soft and not fully frozen.

Suddenly he remembered the night when they had picked up Rasmus. "Bovine stomach," Carolin had said, and really, whatever it was that had hung in Farmer Reincke's tree had looked like the innards of a large animal.

Benno hastily ran back to the car and pulled his camera from the glove compartment. His fingers were so cold that the camera almost fell out of his hands. He couldn't make any sense of his find, but he'd figure it out one way or another. He would develop the photos in the darkroom of the *Strandkurier* and show them to people in the village. But to whom? For a moment he paused. Mr. Heintz maybe? Yes, that was a possibility. Or better yet Martin Wehrke? If he had written a whole book about Strathleven, he would also know stories about the oak tree. He had to be listed in the phone book.

———— ————

Even Corinna Friedrich, whom Benno had never seen in church before, stood with some friends at a booth and sold cookies and cake. It was the second weekend of the Advent season, and Pastor Cornelius had announced during his sermon that the proceeds of this year's Third World Bazaar would go to a cooperative in Colombia.

Benno was wearing a Santa hat, which Carolin had bought for him at the table of her youth group, and picked up small bags containing marzipan or almond biscuits, before eyeing a tin can filled with cinnamon cookies.

"Tell me," he said to Corinna. "The story about Sybille and that boy . . . you know, the story about the dead woman." He hadn't been able to shake the image of one of the boys taking a souvenir from the murder scene.

"Yes?" Corinna asked slowly. She stepped closer toward him, so that the other girls wouldn't be able to overhear their conversation.

"Has Sybille told you anything more about that day?"

Corinna shook her head. "That hat is too small for you." She took hold of his Santa hat and adjusted it. Her hands brushed his ears. "Yeah, that's better."

"Have you found out what the boy stole that day?"

"No idea."

"Who else knows about it?" he asked. When the girl only stared at him with vacant eyes, he added, "What's up with Harald?"

"What should be up with him?"

"Are you guys still . . ." Benno hesitated.

"It's none of your business, but yes, I'm still fucking him. Are you going to buy those cinnamon cookies or are you just going to stare at them?"

Benno quickly produced his wallet, and after he paid and left the table, he could hear the girls snickering behind him. He hoped that it was only because of his silly hat.

"Old wives' tales," Mr. Heintz said cheerfully when Benno stopped at his table and asked him about pagan rituals. Before him lay an assortment of wooden figurines.

"No black cats? No witches' dance in Strathleven? Where are the Miracle Oaks?" Benno pointed to the colorful figurines: the Christ Child in the manger, the Three Kings, obese Santas and small angels in white robes, playing the flute or harp.

"They don't please Cornelius. Not holy enough. But really, if we go back two or three hundred years, every village was still burning witches at the stake." His ring of white hair was oiled and lay plastered against his skull.

A hand touched Benno's shoulder. He turned around, expecting to see the pastor's face. To his amazement, it was Andreas Wehrke who stood before him.

"Well, that's a surprise," Mr. Heintz said. His face seemed to try on different expression yet proved unable to decide on a particular one. Suspicion and fear seemed to mingle, and then suddenly made room for a vigorous grin.

Wehrke was wearing a light wool coat, a suit that looked too shiny for this little town, and he smelled a bit too strongly of aftershave. "Oh, you have to support good causes. And when you're even allowed to drink wine . . ." He smirked.

"Lawnmower," Benno burst out.

"What?" Heintz stared at him in astonishment.

"Oh, sorry, but I've just bought a new mower. My first. If it keeps raining this way, I'll still need to trim my lawn by New Year's Eve." Then he turned directly to Wehrke. "I've been meaning to get in touch with you."

"Well, well," Heintz said, as though this concerned him.

"With me?" asked Wehrke.

"Yes, with you and your brother. I'm working on an article about Strathleven, and I thought, I mean, as the champion marksman . . ." Benno began to stutter.

"Have you seen my son?" Wehrke asked, without addressing Benno's remark.

"Harald? No, I haven't."

"He wanted to help a friend. Sorry!" He shook Benno's hand. "Just stop by the store sometime."

Benno watched the dealer as he walked through the crowd. Maybe it was just his imagination, but it seemed to Benno as though the members of the congregation backed away from him. No one seemed to want to talk to him, and many turned this way and that to avoid eye contact. Probably people were just being polite and simply did not want to bump into Wehrke. He was a businessman and the champion marksman, he commanded respect.

"He doesn't come here often," said Benno and turned back to Mr. Heintz. "Doesn't seem to be too happy either."

"Ah, nonsense, he's just . . . he's just a Wehrke."

"Are they something special?"

Heintz shrugged. "They've been here forever."

"I have a question about the Miracle Oak," Benno said. "There was something strange hanging from the branches."

The old man had sat down in a folding chair and now he opened the *Lübecker Nachrichten*. "You're ruining my business," he said dryly.

"What?"

"You're standing in front of my table and blocking the view."

Benno blushed, mumbled an apology and looked around for Tim and Carolin, but couldn't find them in the crowd. He joined Heintz behind the table, once again asked about the oak and fished two of his photos from his pocket.

Heintz looked at the pictures with narrowed eyes, then took a pair of reading glasses from his jacket. "An old dragon, perhaps?"

"There was blood on it and it almost looked like a bovine stomach. Maybe. I can't be certain."

Heintz shrugged. "Some monkey business. Probably some kids who hung it there."

"I saw something similar at Reincke's farm."

"You didn't grow up here. It's terribly boring in Strathleven. A bovine stomach or an afterbirth is a lot of fun here."

Benno said goodbye, without having learned anything new. And now he had to hurry. Lübeck would play this afternoon against TSV Kiel. He kept looking for Tim and found the boy at a table that was heaped with old junk. Braided juice bottles, Macrame hangings, a camera, and old dishes were inspected, but apparently not purchased, by the villagers.

"Have you seen Carolin?" asked Benno.

Tim shook his head.

"I have to go. Please tell her that I'll be back for dinner."

The boy looked at him pleadingly. "Can I come?"

"Not today. You're needed here." Benno took off his Santa hat and pulled it over Tim's head. "Next time."

He ran into Carolin near the exit, next to the old baptismal font which was used to collect money after the service. She had a petition lying before her on the table and was collecting signatures and sipping coffee. "Do you have to leave already?"

He gave her a kiss. "Call of duty."

"Can you let out the dog once more?"

At that moment Pastor Cornelius appeared in the doorway. Benno had not seen him since the rock-music sermon, and his face was bright crimson. He was not wearing his wire-frame glasses, and Benno was able to see the man and not his office for the first time. Cornelius was strongly built, and his face did not exude its usual shiny goodness. Without his robe, he was an intimidating presence, bigger and probably stronger than Benno. Yet the pastor did not seem to notice him. Without wiping his mud-caked shoes, he marched past Carolin and Benno.

"Damned insolence," he hissed and was gone the next moment.

"What's got into him?" asked Benno, but Carolin seemed too shocked to answer.

When he stepped outside, seconds later, he saw a black car drive off slowly. It was raining cats and dogs, but Benno stood and stared after the car. The black velvet coating he recognized immediately. It was Harald Wehrke's car.

―――――

Lübeck lost as expected, and after talking to the players and the coach of the TSV Kiel after the game, Benno stopped by the offices of the *Strandkurier*. Advent wreaths hung in the newsroom, and it smelled like cinnamon rolls. The whole town was festively decorated and looked like a Christmas fantasy. Only the snow was still missing. Even though it was already after five o'clock and dark outside, two of his colleagues were still sitting at their desks. Even Jochen Hecht, the publisher, was in his office, and Benno seized the opportunity and knocked on the open door.

Hecht looked up from a stack of bills and smiled. He might have been about sixty years old, and his skin was leathery and wrinkled. The eyes behind the thick horn-rimmed glasses were reddened, his voice was loud and smoky. "Diedrich, why aren't you with your family?"

Benno shook his head. "You're not home either."

"Divorced. No child custody. Girlfriend. Too young and not interested in the business. The holiday season is just lousy, but for New Year's we're going to Sylt." Hecht always seemed cheerful. "Got anything on your mind?"

Benno sighed. "Not really."

"Really?"

"I don't know. We're slowly settling in, and I thought . . . I thought maybe I could write an article about Strathleven."

"Cattle and grain prices?"

"More like a portrait of the place, maybe a bit of history, profiles of some people."

"Who put that idea in your head? The mayor?"

Benno laughed sheepishly. "No. It was the pastor."

"Oh, the Anabaptists?"

"Baptists. They take that seriously."

"I don't want to curb your enthusiasm," Hecht said, taking off his glasses and rubbing his eyes. "But every new employee comes into my office with such a story, and I have to reject them all." Without his glasses his eyes seemed twice as large. "There are always people who think, 'Oh, maybe now we get into the news.' It's a minor miracle that you haven't asked me earlier. We are not the *Hamburger Abendblatt*, but not a week goes by without random people stopping me in the street and suggesting I write an article about their mothers, nieces and great-grandchildren."

Benno just nodded his head.

"But if you dig up any dirt, then of course we will print that. Eight-legged calves, unsolved murders and ghosts. Have you already visited the old insane asylum? I think we did something on that . . . oh my goodness, fifteen, twenty years ago."

"Insane asylum?"

"Yes, a private clinic. Quite posh. But at the time they were housing young drug addicts there. The whole area was in a state of panic. Drug addicts!" Hecht laughed and leaned back in his chair. "You want some coffee? I think Kerstin just made some." He stood up, put his glasses back on, and together they went to the small kitchen. Hecht took two mugs from the cupboard and poured Benno some of the pitch-black liquid. "Half-pot Kerstin we call her," he said in a low voice and chuckled. "Filter full to the brim, but only half a pot of water. One day my heart is going to explode."

"So if I find something . . ." Benno tried to steer the conversation back to Strathleven.

"Yeah, sure. Violence and murder are preferred. But that's probably not what your pastor expects. But the people there will still be proud to be in the paper." He paused for a moment. "How's your wife?"

"Good. I think, anyway. She enjoys country life. She . . ." Benno was about to mention Carolin's medication, but he swallowed his remark. He realized that he hadn't spoken to anyone about Carolin, hadn't confided in any of his colleagues. In Berlin there had been friends who had listened to his every sorrow and heartbreak, but here he didn't know anybody.

Perhaps Hecht interpreted Benno's silence correctly, because he said, "You should bring your wife to our Christmas party. It can get awfully lonely in the country." He nodded and left the kitchen. Benno stayed behind, drank the bitter, burnt liquid and thought about driving home and joining Carolin, Tim and the dog. But instead he leaned against the cupboard for several more minutes thinking about what Hecht had said.

Then he put the cup in the sink and walked quickly to his desk, took out the phone book and opened it to 'W.' Wehrke—there were four of them, but only one Martin. Benno looked at the clock; it was almost seven, not yet too late to call.

9

Monday morning Benno dropped Tim off at school. "I'll be home by five clock," he promised the boy, "and take care of Rasmus." Tim and Carolin were going to participate in a peace demonstration in Lauenburg, together with Pastor Cornelius and other members of the congregation.

Benno parked on a small side street near the police station in Grevenhorst; Strathleven was too small for its own precinct. He hesitated at the entrance to the building, which looked like a repurposed villa. The bricks were painted pastel yellow, and a showcase was filled with wanted posters and other official announcements. Finally, he pulled himself together and climbed up the stairs and pushed open the door.

At the reception he asked for the officer who led the investigation in the murder of the unknown woman, and was sent to the first floor, to Sergeant Gruber.

It wasn't only on the outside that the police station looked like a mansion. Although the walls could have used a new coat of paint and the hardwood floors a new finish, the high ceilings and ornate balustrades were still impressive.

"And you are?" asked the uniformed officer who tore open the white-painted door after Benno's third knock. His shirt and jacket were wrinkle-free.

"My name's Diedrich. I live in Strathleven."

The officer nodded. "Gruber." He had short mousy hair, a red face, and was a head taller than Benno. Benno was sure he hadn't seen him in the summer. He could not have been present during the initial investigation.

"I work for the *Strandkurier* in Lübeck, but that has nothing to do with why I'm here."

"So you work for the *Kurier*," replied Gruber, stepping aside to let in his visitor.

"I was the one who found the body in the summer."

"What body?" Gruber asked suspiciously and closed the door.

"The dead woman, the one no one has identified yet. The pastor and I waited for you at the crime scene."

"For me?"

"For the police."

Gruber nodded and offered Benno a seat. The office was spacious, with large windows that looked out onto the main road. Gruber sat down behind his desk, which was empty except for two family photos and a penholder. Benno couldn't discover any overflowing files, reports, letters or speeding tickets. It smelled of dill pickles.

"Jochen Hecht still the publisher?"

Benno nodded. "You know him?"

"Who do you really know?" Gruber gave back half-philosophically. "But I've had the honor." His lips were cut thin and sharp, and now they narrowed even more.

"You don't particularly like him."

"Back then he accused us of police brutality."

"When was that?"

"When the junkies came to Strathleven. I hadn't been here long, and sometimes the patients escaped from the asylum and appeared in Grevenhorst. One weekend there was a big fight in town, right over at Ulli's Pub. We had to intervene, and some fool photographed everything and later sold the snapshots to the newspapers. People wanted to sue us. And your Mr. Hecht compared us to Hitler's storm troops." Gruber's tone was meant to challenge Benno, and an ugly smirk appeared in the corners of his mouth, but his eyes seemed expressionless.

Benno didn't take the bait. After all, what could he say about the incident? All this had happened long before his time at the *Strandkurier*. "What became of the drug addicts?" he finally asked.

"Building code. The clinic had been built for other purposes. The rooms were overcrowded and a short time after the brawl, several patients contracted jaundice. The health department intervened and after two weeks, the whole operation was shut down." The sergeant paused, looked up from the toe of his shoes and out the window, then fixed his gaze on Benno. "But you're here because of the corpse."

"Yes. I thought because I was at the scene . . . that the officers would contact me. Because I was a witness."

Gruber nodded thoughtfully. "And?"

"Nothing."

"You know that we handed over the case to Lübeck's homicide department?"

Benno shook his head.

"If they don't contact you, that's not our problem." Gruber spoke fast, loudly, but almost without emphasis. Was he upset that he had lost his case to Lübeck?

"They still don't know who she was, right?" asked Benno.

"Is this what you want? Get a great story for the *Strandkurier*?"

"No," Benno said, and sharply added, "But I don't find a corpse every day."

Gruber stood up and left the room without a word. After ten minutes he still had not returned. Benno stood up, unsure if he should leave. From somewhere came the clatter of a manual typewriter.

Then at last the door opened again, and the sergeant appeared with a file in his hands. He took no notice of Benno, sat down noisily behind the desk and began flipping through the rather thin file.

"Dreadful scrawl," he said softly. He pulled open a drawer and put on wire-frame glasses that seemed much too small for his massive head and began reading. "It doesn't mention you." He looked over the rim of his glasses, half questioningly, half accusingly.

"How can that be?" Benno asked confused. "That's impossible."

"Impossible?" Gruber laughed out loud. "My good man, you almost had me convinced. Does the *Kurier* want to interfere with police matters again? Are you trying to advance your career? Because the stupid police cannot do their job?"

"But I was there. I drove the pastor to where the corpse lay." Benno stopped. He sounded almost as if he wanted to confess to the crime. "I mean, after the pastor came back to the village, he asked . . ."

"The pastor," interrupted Gruber. "Yes, his statement is in here. And according to him, he discovered the body alone."

"Yes, initially," Benno said. "But really." He paused. He had almost mentioned the children, but just in time he remembered his promise to Cornelius. The children must not be drawn into the murder case. Sybille Antler and the boy who had taken the souvenir.

Gruber stared at him wordlessly.

"But I waited with him for the police and paramedics to arrive. I was there." Benno swallowed; he knew his protestations simply sounded embarrassing. Not even he would have believed them.

"Did you notice anything strange? Did you find something at the scene and take it with you? Did you know the deceased?"

Benno shook his head.

"Ingo must have been sure you didn't."

"Who?"

"Officer Schmoeh. He grew up in Strathleven, you should know him. He was in charge; I spent the week in Ibiza." Gruber's eyes looked up and inspected the ceiling. "I've been with the Grevenhorst police for over twenty years. And when our first murder case breaks, I'm in Ibiza. With the wife and children." He looked sadly at Benno. "And now Lübeck has taken it away from us."

"But the report has to mention me," Benno said. "I was even in the newspaper."

Gruber shook his head. "Either you're lying or Schmoeh messed up." The sergeant's face turned red. "I would prefer the former. If you're right and you were actually at the scene . . ." He looked at Benno with narrowed eyes, but did not finish his thought. Instead, he said, "But you were only the driver. So to speak."

"The driver? Is Officer Schmoeh here? You can ask him."

"He's making his rounds. But as I said, this is no longer our case." Gruber paused, sighed, and added, "If you want, I can give you the number of Lübeck Homicide. You can complain to them about your missing testimony."

Nothing. He had accomplished absolutely nothing and instead antagonized the police. Benno cursed on the way back to his car. But what did the omission in the report mean? Had the officer simply forgotten to add his testimony? He had been in the newspaper, and the whole village had known about his involvement. How could Schmoeh have forgotten that?

He hit his faux leather-wrapped steering wheel. He had been acting like a complete idiot. Or was it Gruber's fault? You couldn't talk sense to such a pig-headed cop. Even if he was still mad at Jochen Hecht—what did he, Benno, have to do with it? He was only the sports editor.

Outside of Lübeck, a tanker truck lay overturned at an intersection, blocking the road. Benno sat frustrated behind a bus and cursed Gruber, Hecht and especially Pastor Cornelius. And Carolin found him 'charming' and 'wonderful.' Now she even joined him at a peace demonstration. Such an old fool!

The pastor! Benno had enough of the pastor. It had been his idea to protect the children and not drag them into the murder case . . . But just like the traffic in front of his windshield, Benno's thoughts screeched to a halt. The children. What had the children really done with the body? When exactly had they found it? Gruber had asked him if he had seen something special—maybe Corinna was right, and one of the boys had taken a souvenir and now didn't want to come forward. Or maybe the pastor had his own reasons for not getting the children involved? Perhaps he had asked Officer Schmoeh to leave Benno out of the report? But why? Had Cornelius known the dead woman after all?

But as much as he struggled, he couldn't get anywhere with his thoughts, and half an hour later the road had been cleared and he was still angry. Angry and confused.

"To hell with the Grevenhorst police," Benno said to himself. "To hell with Cornelius."

As promised, he came home in time to let out Rasmus. Whenever Tim was there, the dog followed him around the house. But when his master was in school, he slept all day on the carpet in front of the door, apparently worried that Tim would not return. When Benno unlocked the door, the dog rose quickly, and the hair along his back stood up in a kind of Mohawk. It wasn't Rasmus anymore, but rather the devil dog from Reincke's cage. The black eye was full of suspicion and his cross-eyed gaze appeared demonic. Yet after a few seconds the dog turned back into his normal self. His hair smoothed out and he again hung his head.

Benno petted the monster, but Rasmus didn't make a sound.

"God, you're really stubborn. Or depressed," Benno said. "But I know the magic word: chow." The dog immediately sat up and cocked his head, as if to make sure he had heard correctly. Then he jumped ahead of Benno into the kitchen and drooled happily on the linoleum floor.

While Rasmus wolfed down his dry food, the phone startled Benno from his thoughts. Friedrich was on the line, he had just received the floor mats that Benno had ordered for the winter. "It's almost closing time, but if you don't turn me in, you can pick them up tonight. I'll still be here until seven."

"Oh wonderful," Benno said. "The carpet looks quite awful already. In this weather."

Normally Benno would have left the dog behind, but tonight he felt sorry for Rasmus. Without Tim, he just looked too pathetic. As they stepped outside, Mrs. Schmied arrived on her bike.

"Are you not with the pastor?" asked Benno.

"I'm too old for something like that." She got off her bike and extended a hand to pet Rasmus, but he didn't seem to notice her at all.

"That's how he is," Benno said. "His master is at the protest."

"Oh," Mrs. Schmied said. "Isn't he too young to . . . ?" She paused. "I'm sorry, I don't want to tell you how to raise your son. Manfred is waiting for his food, I should be going," she added, pushing her bike past Benno and Rasmus.

When they drove onto the car lot, Friedrich was standing with a customer at his door and then came slowly walking toward them. Obviously, he didn't keep regular hours.

"Is that the stray?" He pointed to the backseat while Benno was getting out of the car.

Benno nodded, but when Friedrich came up to the car, the dog wouldn't have it. His hair stood up again, and he jumped into the driver's seat. He had never barked at anyone, but now he bared his teeth and snarled. He looked frightening.

"Sorry about that." Benno slammed the door shut.

"I'm not possessed." Friedrich stepped back from the car. Then he led

Benno to the service department, where he handed him the floor mats. "With such dogs you never know. You can't trust them."

"I'm really sorry."

"Don't worry. But keep an eye on him for your son's sake. Make sure Tim's not doing or saying the wrong thing."

"Oh, Rasmus worships the boy."

"Really?" Friedrich looked at him questioningly. Then he smiled. "If you say so."

Benno stared at the gray rubber mats in his hand. Friedrich's suspicions didn't sit well with him, but after Rasmus had acted so peculiarly, he could understand the dealer's reaction.

"I wanted to ask you something."

"Do you want to switch to a Sierra? I told you so."

"No, no," laughed Benno. "The Escort is just fine. No, I'm working on an article about Strathleven. Or maybe not." He scratched his head; the episode with the Grevenhorster police had discouraged him, and he was not so sure about Cornelius' motives anymore. "The pastor suggested it, and I thought . . . I thought that this might be an opportunity to ask you about the shooting club. And about everything else."

Friedrich looked at him with slightly narrowed eyes. "Shooting club? Of course. We have a long history. But what is 'everything else'?"

Benno hemmed and hawed. Could he really tell Friedrich that he wanted to write about witches and pagan rituals? "Well, you know this place. I'm not sure what I might be looking for. Dark secrets, rumors, ancient legends?" He laughed, and the dealer joined in.

"Sure thing. Spells and old wives' tales. Of which we have many. But all that happened such a long time ago." The laughter subsided, and Friedrich's face turned serious, with only a strange smile playing about his lips. "The time hasn't stood still here, Mr. Diedrich. We may seem strange to you, strange and behind the times. You have lived in Berlin and might still feel very suave compared to us."

"I didn't mean it that way," Benno said quickly, but Friedrich interrupted him.

"I know how you meant it. But we are decent people here. Strathleven is not stuck in the Middle Ages." Friedrich paused, and his tone was getting friendlier. "But if you want to write something about our village,

I'm of course happy to assist you." He put a hand on Benno's shoulder and escorted him to the door. "If you'd like to order winter tires . . ."

"Do I need them?" Benno was happy to step out of the stale air of the service department.

"You never know. You don't want to slide off the road here. Too dangerous." He winked. "The slush can be pretty disgusting." He turned around and disappeared behind the fireproof metal door.

———

After eight o'clock, Carolin and Tim came home wet and chilled to the bone, but at least Carolin seemed overjoyed. Before he could ask about her afternoon, she threw herself into his arms. Tim seemed to be tired, and did not even take notice of Rasmus' joyous barking.

"Are you hungry?" asked Benno and began warming up some soup, while Tim and Carolin changed clothes.

When they were all sitting around the dinner table, he realized how much he had missed his little family. "Rasmus was worried about you," he told Tim. "He's pretty depressed when you're not here." Friedrich and the dog's strange behavior toward the dealer he didn't mention. "How many were you?"

"Fifteen. Cornelius rented a small bus."

"No, at the protest. Did many come out?"

Carolin looked up from her onion soup. "Maybe two hundred people."

"All the others didn't want peace?"

Tim shook his head.

"No police? No fights?"

"Police were there, of course." Carolin's skin was still flushed, and she'd put on a shirt of his. She looked tired and beautiful and happy. "They didn't interfere. We wouldn't hurt anyone—at a peace protest." she added quickly, and looked at Tim as if she was waiting for a confirmation.

"Exactly," he said, and stuffed a large piece of bread into his mouth.

Later in the bedroom, Carolin pressed herself against Benno and whispered, "You smell good." She leaned on one elbow and looked at him in the darkness. Then she leaned down and kissed him quickly. "You're so sweet. So sweet. Sometimes I'm not as crazy as I look." Then she took a deep breath and said, "I've been drug-free for exactly eleven days now."

"I know," he whispered.

"Have you been snooping?" she asked indignantly, but Benno could hear that she wasn't serious.

"Nah," he said, laughing softly. "But I'm a reporter. I keep my eyes open."

"Aren't you proud of me?"

"How are you feeling?" asked Benno. "Do you think it was the right decision?" He tried not to sound too suspicious.

"Yes. I feel . . ." she stopped to think, "as if I had finally woken up. I don't feel so . . . dead anymore."

— 10 —

Martin Wehrke was the older brother of the John Deere dealer, as well as the village historian. "Not officially, of course," he added. "We have no archives in Strathleven, and as far as I know, people do not keep diaries here. If they did, they probably wouldn't admit it, and take their doodles to the grave. Very North German."

"North German?" asked Benno.

"Cool on the outside, but deep down they are very passionate." Wehrke laughed, but Benno could see that he was serious. "Very deep down."

Wehrke lived in an old farmhouse, whose stables he had torn down. Inside, too, he had left very little in its original state. Several walls had been eliminated to turn the small rooms into one large one with integrated kitchen. Larger windows and bamboo floors gave the house warmth and light. Wehrke had hardly any furniture, but some Japanese woodcuts and a few Tibetan wood panels covered with paintings of tigers accented the emptiness.

Wehrke might have been fifty-five and looked as lean and leathery as in his author photo, but he was a bit shorter than his brother. He was wearing a sports coat, jeans, and Birkenstocks, and his socks were made of coarse wool.

"You are welcome to smoke," he offered Benno, and dug out a pipe. "I think you are the first to ask me about my book. My brother Andreas has read parts of it, and maybe one or another person in the village has leafed through it. But it's not . . . a bestseller. It was meant to be a family history."

"Self-published."

"I wanted to spare myself the search for a publisher. When I taught at the university, I had some contacts with scientific publishers, but most of them are now retired. And the book may be interesting to only a few people. The copy you borrowed I donated personally. Pure vanity. A book belongs in a library."

Benno didn't quite know if Wehrke was modest or just played the part, but his slightly hoarse voice and his even delivery made him appear trustworthy. His unhurried gestures did the rest.

"Do you live here by yourself?" he asked.

"At the moment, yes," replied Wehrke.

"Sorry." Benno turned red. "Stupid question."

"Don't worry about it. So, you're doing research on witches and pagan rituals?"

"Something like that. But I've already stepped on some toes." He told Wehrke about Friedrich's indignation. Although it was unprofessional to talk about other sources, he had the feeling that Wehrke wouldn't take it the wrong way. "And somehow I can understand his reaction. I come along and try to dig up something ghastly about this town. His town."

"Yes, that wasn't very polite of you." Wehrke smiled. "But your editor probably won't print an article about the quality of Ford vehicles or Strathleven's god-fearing people."

"Exactly."

"And what makes you think that I'm going to spill the beans?"

"Your book. According to you my house was built on a *Thingplatz*, the ancient meeting place for the court and civic assemblies."

Wehrke filled his pipe with an earthy-smelling tobacco, which he took from a leather pouch. He had trouble lighting it, but finally succeeded and sank back into his chair. "You live on Wodeberg. Sure." He paused for a moment. "Wotan was very important in this area, but over time worship blended with other gods and rites. Of course, the meeting place itself was taken over by the church. A few people in the village wanted to set up a memorial for the *Thingplatz*, but the pastor was against it. The Miracle Oak is probably the most obvious remnant of Wotan worship."

"I've recently seen something hanging in its branches. Looked like cattle stomach," interrupted Benno.

"Horse placenta," replied Wehrke. "It's supposed to bring fertility."

"But that's superstition."

"We just don't know who really rules the afterlife. We like to believe in God, but we don't want to upset Wotan, witches, or the devil. We are timid creatures."

"And the other legends?"

"There are, for example, the *Rauhnächte*, the Twelve Nights. There are only two weeks left until the Wild Hunt."

Benno looked at him questioningly. He had never heard of a Wild Hunt.

"It's sometimes called the Journey to Asgard, and is led by Wotan, although that is disputed. Depends on where you grow up. Sometimes the leader is called Hell Hunter or Ghost Rider, sometimes historical figures are pulled into the mix. But here it is Wotan who leads the souls of people who have died before their time through the night. And you better keep quiet if you listen to the Wild Hunt. Otherwise, death might take you as well."

"Why does Strathleven not have a soccer club?"

Wehrke laughed out loud. "Do we need one?"

Benno shrugged. "Not even a handball team."

"If it makes you happy—we once had one. Soccer club. Long time ago. But I think there were brawls after the games. Must have been back in the 50s. Friedrich's father, I believe, was the goalkeeper."

"Did he build the dealership?"

Wehrke nodded. "But Otto didn't rest on his dad's laurels. It's not easy to keep a business going in such a backwater village. His methods are not always subtle, but he has worked hard for his success."

"Subtle?"

"He has a reputation for talking his customers into buying cars they can't possibly afford. They take out loans, fail to make payments, and then Friedrich repossesses the car."

"But that doesn't seem to hurt his business."

Wehrke shook his head. "I bought one of his cars, too."

"And the old Friedrich is now in retirement?"

"Dead. Otto was maybe twenty or twenty-five years old when his father committed suicide. I think he wanted to study Mechanical

Engineering. At the University of Kiel. But then he came back home to run the business and take care of his mother. Got married and found out that he was a born businessman."

"Why did his old man kill himself?"

Wehrke took his time with a response. For a few seconds he stared blankly at Benno, then he let his gaze wander over the carefully stocked bookcases and finally come to rest on the window overlooking the garden. Dark clouds took up the entire sky. "I'm a lousy host. Will you have a whiskey with me?"

Benno nodded. "Certainly." While Wehrke shuffled in his Birkenstocks toward the kitchen and took a bottle and two glasses from one of the cupboards, Benno took the opportunity to look around a bit. He loved this house. His own—with the smorgasbord of Ikea furniture, old carpets, and framed posters—looked like a college dorm in comparison.

"What are we drinking?" he asked as Wehrke poured two glasses.

"Suntory. From Japan. Probably lousy whiskey, but it agrees with my stomach. Can't deal with the other stuff anymore."

The liquid was slightly sweet. "Not bad."

"The thing about Friedrich's suicide," began Wehrke, "is that the circumstances are a bit strange. It happened a long time ago—I was in my mid-thirties, had just divorced my second wife. Lived in Hamburg at that time and wanted nothing to do with Strathleven. My own father was still alive, and my share of the company was large enough to pay the rent and travel around the world. Nothing fancy, but agreeable." Here he paused, took a sip of whiskey. "As I said, I didn't live in town, but from time to time I visited my mother. My father had had other plans for me, I was his elder son and should have taken over the store and the concrete plant."

"But you didn't want to," interrupted Benno.

"I wanted to study anthropology—but he thought that was nonsense. Concrete, tractors, those you could touch, see, sell. Anyway, when Friedrich's father died, a jolt ran through the village. I was here for the funeral, and his death was a big deal. I mean, he was one of the pillars of the community. And suicide is always an unpleasant thing. Fortunately, the old pastor was still here. The church was still Lutheran, but they shut it down a few years later—our souls were not numerous enough."

"Fortunately?"

"Oh, yes, Pastor Daum didn't care how Friedrich had died. The new one, Cornelius—I don't think that he would have given Friedrich a resting spot in his cemetery."

"As a suicide."

"You were buried in the far corner or outside the cemetery."

"How did he . . . I mean . . ."

"That was just the strange thing. I hadn't come home to attend the funeral, that was just an accident, so to speak. But I distinctly remember the open coffin in church, and the pastor gave his eulogy and talked about the tragic death. The widow cried, and Otto sat beside her and tried to calm her down. Daum did not use the word suicide, of course, that would have been tasteless." Wehrke fell silent, as if his memories had carried him away from his living room and his visitor. Raindrops hit the windows and made Benno suddenly feel lonely and uninvited. He should have brought Rasmus, he thought.

"What was peculiar about it?" he asked into the silence.

Wehrke startled out of his reverie. "He was said to have hanged himself," he said. "In the old psychiatric hospital. At the end of the fifties it had gone bankrupt. Or maybe nobody had wanted to take over operations. The whole building was empty, and a farmer who had his cattle grazing on the property found Friedrich by chance. He hung from the balcony over the main entrance. Hanged himself with a white sheet. That alone would have been strange enough—because the farmer didn't see Friedrich's car in the driveway or anywhere else and it was later found at his home. But as I sat in church, I could see how disfigured Friedrich's face was."

"It must have been bloated."

"Sure, sure. But I sat in the third row and later went past the coffin, and despite the makeup and the meticulous work of the undertaker, Friedrich looked atrocious. He had bruises on his face, cuts. If I'm not mistaken, he also had stab wounds on his neck." Wehrke shrugged. "My life at the time wasn't focused on Strathleven. I had no right to walk around and ask questions."

"Have you ever talked to Friedrich, to Otto . . ."

"No, this is water under the bridge. Impossible. But back then . . . how should I say—I had my own reasons for visiting Strathleven."

"Love?"

"'Affair' is probably the better word. But because of it I came in contact with the undertaker in Grevenhorst. Long story. After the police released the body, he was responsible for . . . preparing the corpse. And apparently his whole body was covered with wounds."

Benno sank back into his seat. "How . . . how . . ."

"Exactly. I've often asked that myself. As I said, I was living in Hamburg, and my affair broke off a short time later. I had no time and no desire to meddle in the affairs of the village. But since then, I've often wondered—if you want to kill yourself, why stab yourself like crazy beforehand?"

The rain beat against the windows, and although it was not yet four o'clock, the room lay in darkness. Benno slowly took his whiskey glass and stared into the now seemingly gray liquid.

"What I meant," said Benno, "was, if that undertaker was right, Friedrich must have looked just like the dead woman this summer."

Wehrke looked at him directly. He didn't nod, didn't even seem to breathe. Something in Benno warned him that he might have gone too far. "Why did you return to Strathleven?" he asked as casually as possible.

Wehrke shook his head and then chuckled. "I was valedictorian. I was young enough not to have to fight for the Nazis during the war. The people expected great things from me. I went to college, lived for five years in Bougainville to write about the natives and their garden cultivation. And then I must have lost my way. My first marriage broke up—my son still refuses to talk to me—and for a long time I let my work slide. And during the time in which I should have accomplished something great, I had a secret affair in Grevenhorst." He broke off, but continued after a few seconds." I think I eventually understood that my life here would be more peaceful and generally better than in Hamburg or anywhere else. My father has been dead for years, so I don't have to contend with his accusations. Maybe I just gave up. I have money enough."

Wehrke fell silent. Benno waited a few moments before asking, "Do you think that Pastor Cornelius has kept the records of his predecessor?" He had to repeat the question before his host finally answered.

"That would be a miracle. I think he wants to deal with the old church legacy as little as possible. And I do my best to keep out of his way."

"You don't like him?"

"He quotes God as though he were going bowling with him. And I think he's quite happy about my absence."

"Have you had a falling out?"

"Oh no." Wehrke smiled. "Nothing dramatic. But he won't like to see me in church."

"Why's that? Are you atheist?"

"Worse. Atheists can be converted. With gays it's not that easy."

He had received only approximate directions, and there were no signs to point the way to the clinic, but Benno had no difficulty finding the place. He turned right on Hökerstieg and then drove north on Glasbuscher Strasse. The old mental hospital was to his left, its blackened brick walls surrounded by bushes and shrubs. He could see the gable of the main building and a huge smokestack at the forest's edge. The sight of the smokestack, its bricks covered with moss, frightened him.

He was encouraged and yet disappointed with his visit to Wehrke. The man was certainly interesting, but he hadn't given Benno much. The strange death of Otto Friedrich's father was a good story but had little to do with his research. And anyway, at the time of old Friedrich's funeral, his death must have been investigated and too many people had seen the body to raise any serious doubts about the suicide.

He parked the car and got out. The wrought-iron gate was worthy of a steel magnate's 19th century mansion, but it was held together only by a bike lock. Yet it wouldn't budge, no matter how hard he pulled. When he caught his breath, Benno saw that a few steps to the left was a small door set into the brick wall, and it opened easily.

Benno waded through dead leaves, which were completely soaked by the recent rainfall and their colors had degenerated to a uniform brown. What might have been a sizable park once, now looked unkempt and ugly. The building itself, which was still quite impressive, seemed to have been vandalized by burglars or adolescents. The doors had long since been broken, the locks had disappeared.

Inside it smelled musty, and mold crept up the walls. Benno slowly climbed up a broad staircase, which led to a lobby. His shoes squeaked on the old linoleum floor. Behind the reception was chaos—phone books, notepads and blank registration forms were lying scattered, half burned books littered the floor. Files had been ripped from metal cabinets, and their innards had been strewn in the lobby. The clinic was too far away from the city to attract the homeless, but addicts had left their drug paraphernalia lying about. Small, empty plastic bags lay on the ground, along with small pieces of aluminum foil with telltale black spots. Two syringes.

Benno remained silent for a moment, listening to sounds from the upper floors, then he slowly moved towards the staircase and went up to the second floor. He entered a small room with two bunk beds and four small metal cabinets in it. He had hardly any space to move. According to Jochen Hecht the building had stood empty for more than a decade, but open suitcases and duffel bags were lying around, and the beds were littered with clothes, as if the occupants had suddenly fled the building.

Benno hurried into the next room and found it in similar condition. The clothes were strewn on the beds and the floor; someone must have lived here a short time ago.

Who had left such a mess? In the main lobby, the walls were moldy, but the stuff in the rooms had no spots and still looked very dry.

Benno climbed the stairs to the third and last floor, but even there he found the same inexplicable chaos. Unfortunately, he had left his camera in the car, but he vowed to ask around in the village. Someone had to know what was going on.

He went back down the stairs and found several small rooms on the first floor, which had probably once been used for the treatment of patients. They had been vandalized, but otherwise they seemed unused. Nobody had stayed here.

In the basement, Benno looked around the large kitchen. There were broken dishes, dented pots. The dining room had several long tables but there were no chairs.

It was completely silent down there and Benno almost wished to hear a suspicious noise or to come across a squatter. But nothing happened, nothing at all. Only the rain had begun to fall again and pattered against the barred windows. Benno made his way toward the main entrance, but he took a wrong stairway and suddenly found himself in a hallway he hadn't noticed before. His hurried steps were too loud, echoing through the building, announcing him to whoever had found shelter there. Finally he began to run and arrived at last at the reception and from there stormed down the stairs. But he did not stop to catch his breath outside the entrance and didn't turn around until he arrived at his car. When he opened the driver's door, he suddenly felt foolish. But who could have observed his panicked exit? Benno looked all around him, but no, no, there was nobody in sight. What the hell, he was an adult. He could run away whenever he felt like it.

11

During the week before Christmas, the temperature held steady at five degrees Celsius, and the courtyard in front of the old school turned into a huge mud puddle. Tim was obligated to clean Rasmus' paws after each walk with a towel, but even so the carpet in the hallway appeared brown rather than off-white.

On December 21st, the day of the Christmas party at the *Strandkurier*, Benno had already been in the newsroom since six o'clock. It was a Wednesday, and he was busy with sales ads and special offers, but that mattered little to him. He enjoyed working in Lübeck, and the times he spent with Carolin became ever more exhausting. In the morning she was irritated and scolded him for every little thing; in the evening, she was introverted and unresponsive. Benno was worried about Tim, but at least the boy had Rasmus, with whom he could play and hang out. Benno only had his work.

Margit Scholl, the accountant who was rumored to have had a long-standing affair with Jochen Hecht, came to his desk around noon. Even without looking up from his files, Benno would have recognized her perfume.

"Do we finally get to see the wife tonight?" she asked with a smile that probably tried to be friendly, but looked rather dangerous.

"No, unfortunately not," replied Benno. "The drive is long, and she has to practice the Nativity play with the children."

"How many do you have?"

"Just one, but Carolin is very involved in the church."

"Oh my goodness. Poor you!" sighed Scholl. "I'm rounding up willing victims. Have you had lunch yet? We need a firm foundation for the party tonight." She winked at him.

Together with Scholl, Holger, and two other colleagues, Benno made his way to the Bourgeois, a restaurant a few streets away from the news office. It didn't look very inviting from the outside, with its yellowed curtains and withered plants, but it served an excellent pork roast with red cabbage and croquettes.

It was the first time since the summer that Benno saw Jörg Ottermann, the reporter responsible for articles on the local and regional shooting clubs.

"I didn't see you at the Autumn Ball," he said, trying to keep up with the thin man.

Ottermann lowered his head and looked at him over the rim of his glasses. "I wasn't there." Then he quickened his pace.

Margit pushed closer to Benno. "They don't want him. They aren't registered or whatever you call it, and don't belong to any association. I believe during Jörg's last visit twenty years ago, it came to blows."

"It came to blows?"

"They also sliced his tires. Not that anyone would have admitted it."

Inside the restaurant, Benno sat as far away as possible from the accountant and her perfume and ordered a beer before he went to the restroom. Here too, the restaurant was far behind the times. It smelled musty and if you wanted to dry your hands, you were forced to use a dirty, wet towel next to the sink. Above the urinals hung the headlines of the *Lübecker Nachrichten*, and Benno skimmed over what the competition had to say.

Seconds later, he apologized to his colleagues, paid for the beer and ran out into the street. He could feel a dull pain at the back of his head as he ran through the streets to the nearest newspaper store.

He ignored the line of lottery players, put his money on the counter, and ran out of the store and opened the paper.

The lines only made sense after the third and fourth time he read them, so overwhelming was his agitation. The dead woman's name was Irina Sobieski, she had been a Polish citizen and had come to the West as an undocumented immigrant two years ago. She had worked as a waitress in Lübeck—the police had received the tip from a former colleague. Out of fear of being deported, she had kept silent until now.

"What did she want in Strathleven?" asked Benno and only then realized that he had spoken the words aloud. He stared at the woman's face smiling into the camera, as if she and the photographer shared a secret. But the short article revealed nothing more about her, and Strathleven wasn't even mentioned by name. The general population was asked to help, and the telephone number of the Lübeck police was printed underneath the photo.

Benno felt the urge to run to the next phone booth, call the number and say, "I found her. I was there." But he remembered his talk with Sergeant Gruber all too well. Of course, the Lübeck police would think he was just after a story.

He stood on the small cobblestone street, surrounded by Christmas lights and the smell of grilled sausage and cinnamon. It was so long ago that he had found the dead woman. Why should he care about her? His face turned into a grimace; he couldn't do anything about it. Ashamed, he stared at the lightly soiled clouds above. His face was wet, and for a moment Benno thought that he was crying for the dead, but then he lowered his eyes, and he seemed all alone on this narrow street, with the newspaper in one hand and a lump in his throat, and stray flakes fell around him. They seemed as clueless as he was, seemed to look hesitantly for a spot to land. Benno followed their course and didn't move, didn't want to get in their way.

———

At four in the afternoon, most of his colleagues were already tipsy and fingering the gifts that lay in piles next to the Christmas tree. Benno couldn't miss the party, especially not Jochen Hecht's annual speech, in which he praised individual successes and sometimes even rewarded employees with cash.

Hecht was in top form and climbed on top of a desk. In one hand he held a glass of cognac, a cigarette in the other. He spoke vividly of Margit Scholl and her twenty-two years at the *Strandkurier*, Holger's award for a series of articles about migrant workers in Lübeck, and

Torsten Mayfarth's success in raising ad revenue. When he finally mentioned Benno, he smiled and said that he had never received so many complaints about the sports section. He paused and took a long drag from his cigarette. Music blared in the background, but the room was strangely silent. "Two. From the same subscriber. And he is convinced that you are taking kickbacks from TSV because Lübeck always comes off so badly in your articles. I quote: 'If he ever pulls his head out of his ass, maybe I'll give the *Kurier* a second chance. Until then, it's not even suitable as toilet paper!'"

Everyone else burst into laughter, but Benno's face burned uncomfortably. Hecht jumped off the table and was now making the rounds to distribute the red envelopes and even Benno got one.

"Good work, Diedrich," the publisher said, patted him on the shoulder and went to refill his glass.

When the party turned raucous around half past seven and someone began to play Torfrock, Benno stole away. The snow was falling more heavily now. In the last week before the holidays, some stores were open longer, and so he strolled through the streets, not knowing what he was looking for, enjoying the cool night air and the glittering lights. His stomach felt completely screwed up from skipping lunch and drinking bad champagne. He pulled the red envelope from his jacket pocket, opened it, and took out the two hundred-mark bills.

In a candy store he bought a box of brightly painted marzipan figurines and had them wrapped. Of course, she wouldn't be waiting for him, he told himself. And even if she was at the library, she would rebuff him.

But Hanne Stein stood at the door when he reached the library. She had just locked it from the inside and now stared at the approaching figure. A smile showed Benno that she had recognized him. The smile widened when he invited her to dinner with a little pantomime. She opened the door a crack, and he handed her his gift.

"I still have to finish up something, you can wait here in the foyer."

Benno sank into one of the leather chairs and watched Hanne disappear into a back room. Only a few lamps above the checkout were still on, and from his position he had a good view of the street and the snow that was picked up by gusts of wind and whirled around the houses. He had no idea what he was doing at the library or what he wanted from Hanne Stein, but he was glad to have caught her. He shook his head, as though he could shake off thoughts about Carolin like so many drops of water.

"And where are you taking me?" asked Hanne when she reappeared after twenty minutes, wearing coat and hat.

Benno hadn't given it any thought. "I know almost nothing here. Maybe you could decide?"

Together they left the library and walked towards the cathedral. The hotdog stands were still open, and men and women with huge shopping bags stood in front, drinking grog and mulled wine. "Do you have plans for the holidays?" the librarian asked.

"We just bought a tree. This is our first Christmas as a real family."

"Frightening, isn't it?" Hanne Stein laughed.

"Yes, a bit," Benno admitted. "What are you going to do?"

"On the 24th, I'll visit a café in the morning and watch the crowds. I have already purchased and sent all my gifts, so I can take my time and regret my fellow men. In the evening I'll take myself to a fine restaurant and the rest of the holidays I'll spend in bed, on the couch, or on walks through the snow."

"No family?" Benno asked. "Not that it's any of my business . . ."

"Mother lives in Kiel, my father in Munich, my sister in Italy, my brother in France. No, I'm staying here. And I will visit my grave and set up flowers."

"Your grave?" Benno stopped in his tracks. Hanne turned to him and smiled. "I have adopted a grave. The cemetery is not far from my apartment, and the grave looked very neglected, so I adopted it. In the summer I sometimes visit with my picnic basket and read there."

"Who is buried there?"

"Hubert Stolzenburg."

"Was he anyone special?"

Stein shrugged. "I've never tried to find out anything about him. He's just my Hubert." She smiled.

The Indian restaurant was only half full this evening. Red light chains running along the ceiling created a pleasantly cheesy atmosphere. The waiter led them to a table by the window, from which they had a view of the street. Cold air was coming through the cracks and made the candle on the table flicker wildly.

"Are you cold?" asked the librarian, but Benno shook his head. "The food is excellent," she added. Then she rolled up the sleeves of her blouse, revealing a number of tattoos that were joined together so that no bare skin was left. Hanne saw Benno's look and laughed. "I could not let them come down quite as far as I wanted. And the neckline," she said, "had to remain white too. I'm still in public service."

Benno could make out a figure that reminded him of a Buddha, but who grinned mischievously. On her left arm he saw the rays of a sun half hidden by the sleeve. "That must have been painful." He couldn't think of anything else to say.

She nodded. "A little bit. If my customers saw it, they'd probably run away screaming. Or propose on the spot."

Benno was no longer sure that the invitation had been a good idea. He realized that he didn't know Hanne Stein at all. To conceal his silence, he immersed himself in the menu. "Any recommendations?" he asked.

"The lamb is excellent. If you're not vegetarian. How's it going with your article?"

Benno looked at her in silence, unsure of where to begin. Finally he said, "You remember the dead woman?"

"Which one?"

Benno smiled involuntarily, then he told Hanne that the woman he'd found in the summer had finally been identified. "I don't know. It shouldn't concern me, I had only just moved there and still didn't know anyone, but when I read her name today it made everything worse."

Hanne nodded.

"And then this guy—the one who wrote the book you showed me— told me that the father of Strathleven's car dealer was stabbed in the same gruesome manner more than twenty years ago, and that his death was declared a suicide. And Tim, my son, has this strange disease, and my wife is making friends with the Baptists." He told her about his fruitless search and about Sergeant Gruber's distrust of reporters. When he was finally finished, he did not feel better, just empty. "Sorry," he muttered.

"Come closer to the candle. Closer still." Hanne's voice was quiet but determined. "Let me use a bit of magic." She grabbed his hands and held them for a minute or two. His hands were cold and clammy, but hers felt dry to the touch. They looked padded, and the nails were painted dark purple. Grinning at him from her forearm was the demonic Buddha, and the sun now showed itself in its entirety. Benno sighed deeply and realized that he had held his breath for quite a long time.

Hanne took a small bag from her purse, extracted something that looked like grated basil and sprinkled a pinch into the flickering flame. It crackled pleasantly, and small sparks flew in all directions. It suddenly smelled of the summer days he'd spent as a boy about town, of dry branches, tall grasses, and the bark of birch trees that you could peel off like paper.

"What is this?" he asked.

"Sage. Cleans the atmosphere. But don't look around now, we don't want to attract any attention. Not everyone appreciates magic."

Her serious face convinced Benno that she wasn't making fun of him. "Magic?"

"I won't turn you into a toad," she replied with a smile.

Benno shifted in his chair and looked at the candle flame in order not to look into Hanne's face. Magic? Here at an Indian restaurant in Lübeck?

She laughed. "You're doing research on superstition, and a bit of sage intimidates you?"

"It's just . . ."

"That reasonable people don't do such things?"

Benno grinned and shook his head. "My wife, Carolin . . ." He trailed off. He thought of Pastor Cornelius, the young pastor and his sermon on rock music. How could he explain to Carolin that he had left the Christmas party to have dinner with a strange woman who had cleaned the atmosphere at their table with sage leaves?

"Men can be so stubborn. That's why I work mostly with women."

"Work?"

"I sometimes give seminars. My family didn't get along very well, and I spent summers with my grandmother. She collected herbs and made teas and tinctures. You would never have called her a witch, but that's what she really was. She sometimes sold herbs and powders at local markets."

Benno nodded.

"Everything you send out comes back threefold. Good or evil. So you should think carefully about what you do and how you behave towards other people."

"But that has nothing to do with magic, right?"

"Magic just means that you manifest something. If you believe in something, then opportunities will open up."

"And the tattoos? Are they magical too?" he asked.

"No, those are expensive."

The food came and interrupted their conversation. Benno's stomach growled loudly, and both had to laugh. "It's about time, it seems," she said, handing him the bread that was as big as a balloon and shimmered with grease.

The food was really excellent, and it seemed to Benno that rice, raisins, nuts, and lamb exorcised the uncertain fear he had felt since noon. "I miss Berlin," he said, without thinking about it.

"Even the Wall?"

"Even the Wall. My God, I sound really whiny today," Benno said apologetically.

"Strathleven is quite a change. Have you finally visited the Miracle Oak?"

"They hang horse placenta in the branches. It's supposed to bring luck. And Mr. Wehrke went on about the Twelve Nights and the Wild Hunt, which will travel through the village."

Hanne nodded.

The snow had picked up outside. Benno watched it being blown against the window, then he said, "Maybe I'm just not ready for this whole family thing."

"Is that the reason why you invited me tonight?"

"No, no," Benno said quickly, but felt caught. How much easier it would be to follow Hanne home, accept stoically the inevitable row with and separation from Carolin, and then live as a bachelor in Lübeck.

"No, you don't want that," Hanne responded, as if she had read his mind.

"And if I do?"

"I would have to agree first."

———————

After they left the restaurant, snowflakes blew into their faces. The street was almost deserted now, with only a few pedestrians hurrying past, keeping close to the walls of houses.

"Are you able to drive?" asked Hanne. She had pulled her hat low over her forehead.

He nodded. It was time to return to Strathleven.

"Do you have far to go?" he asked. "Shall I drive you home?"

"It's faster if I walk," she said. "Thank you for the invitation. And the marzipan. I think I have never been given marzipan before."

"Thanks for coming. And for the magic."

They remained quiet for a moment outside the restaurant, the reddish light from the interior lighting their faces. Snow melted on Benno's nose and flew into his eyes, but he did not even blink.

Hanne leaned forward, grabbed his hair and pulled him close. A moment later, the kiss was already over. "Just wanted to see what I'm missing out on," she said, turning away quickly. After a few seconds she had disappeared in the snow.

Benno trudged back to his car and wiped off the windows with his bare hands. He felt miserable and yet oddly comforted. It was just a kiss. Just a kiss. But the warmth he felt in his chest and in his belly betrayed him. "She wants nothing from me," he said aloud. It was the second time that he had spoken to himself out loud that day. Maybe he was finally losing his mind.

The roads looked almost untouched; the wind was erasing all traces tonight. The snow seemed to slide off the windshield so that he didn't even have to turn on the wipers.

Benno had switched on the heater, and after hours sitting near the drafty window, he was finally getting warm. For the first time he realized how much he had really drunk. In order not to fall asleep on the short route to Strathleven, he searched for a radio station with Christmas songs, and to Bing Crosby's "Little Drummer Boy" he drove past white fields and dark farmhouses.

Before arriving in Strathleven Benno slowed down, looking for the Miracle Oak. When he finally spotted it, he pulled over. He switched off the radio, opened the glove compartment and grabbed his camera. While he was still looking for the small flashlight he had placed in the car yesterday, it happened. He did not understand what was going on, and only when he slipped out of his seat and his head bumped against the passenger door, did he realize that the car had just slipped into the ditch.

"Shit," Benno said loudly, and as if the car felt insulted, it made a second, smaller jerk, and something outside seemed to break. Benno cursed a second time. In the upper part of the front passenger window he could still see snow-covered bushes, but the bottom was completely black. After the heavy rains of the past weeks, the trenches were still full of water.

Cautiously, he tried to sit up and lift his legs over the shifter. The car groaned, but did not slide down farther.

To open the door was relatively easy. To keep it open, however was much more difficult. Both hands on the doorframe, he pulled himself up, his legs pushing against the passenger seat. Then he lifted his upper body out of the car and finally clambered up the ditch to the road.

Around him was only silence. He let the door fall shut, locked it, and without a flashlight but with camera in hand, he began to walk toward the village. Yet after a few meters he stopped. The damage was done, and a few minutes more or less wouldn't hurt the car. Benno didn't know if the alcohol was making him do it, but he felt suddenly very sober, and without further thought, he jumped across the ditch and ran through the snow to the Miracle Oak.

Only a few lights from the village shone across the fields and made the white bustle around him visible. The cold penetrated his clothes and wiped Hanne's kiss from his lips. He stopped and howled like a wolf, paused, and then howled a second time.

He suddenly heard a noise beside him, quietly, as if someone was sucking in the cold winter air. Quickly he turned around, but there was nothing. Only snow.

Cautiously he strode towards the tree, whose branches appeared even more massive and majestic than usual. A second sound, this time a crash, made Benno stop once more, and this time he crouched and knelt down in the snow. Was someone hiding in the branches? Or crouching behind the huge trunk? Yet as much as he stared, trying to discern any shadows or movement, no one seemed to be near him. But something hung from the lower trunk, and Benno hoped that it wasn't horse placenta again.

At first he could not even make out what had been tied with barbed wire to the tree, but as he approached, his stomach turned. Two dead ravens hung there with spread wings that moved in the wind. Over their heads hung a simple cardboard sign. Benno wiped the snow away and read: The King Must Die.

"The king must die?" he asked, as if the tree or the ravens could give him an answer, but all he heard was the faint whistling of the wind. He ripped off the cardboard sign, and then tried to untie the barbed wire, but only managed to cut his fingers. He took a picture of the ravens, but without a flash the pictures would probably only show black night.

With the cardboard sign in hand, he headed for Strathleven's lights. The snow stabbed his right cheek and temple. From somewhere came the rattle of a motorcycle.

———————

He had slid off the road while trying to avoid a deer—that would be his story, he decided as Carolin opened the door.

"You're finally here," she said, and pressed herself against him.

"Yes, finally." He seemed to melt in the warmth of the house.

"You want something to eat?" she asked.

He shook his head with a smile. "We need to call Friedrich."

A short time later, a tow truck drove up to the house. The driver, who introduced himself as Günther, was very young, maybe in his early twenties, wore his hair short in front, long in back, and was working on a mustache.

"You're in luck. I just came back from another job. And a few seconds after your call the next two came in. It's going to be a busy night with all the snow. People underestimate the weather or overestimate their driving skills."

Benno nodded.

"Are you related to Friedrich?" he asked.

Günther laughed. "No, he has enough to do with his three daughters. When he comes home, four women are waiting for him. No, I am the son of Rudolf Dithmann. If you drive down the state road, you can see our farm on the right side. You've probably met my old man in church."

"Oh, yes," Benno said, but couldn't remember a face to fit that name. "Sure thing. Your mother too, right?"

Günther shook his head. "She died four years ago."

"I'm sorry," said Benno and wished himself far away. What a pathetic liar he was.

"It's alright. We miss her. My old man especially. I don't think he would have joined the church otherwise. Couldn't stand the pastor at first."

"The old pastor was different."

"Yes, he was good friends with everyone. Often dropped by for a *schnaps*. You should wear a hat."

Benno had left the house without a hat. Gunther, however, wore a cap lined with fake fur.

"Yes, probably."

"I even wear a hat in the summer," the driver said with emphasis. "Read that the brain works better when it's kept warm. You just have to keep it warm . . . Is that yours?"

They had arrived at the Miracle Oak and Günther opened the door. The diesel engine rattled like a can full of pennies and Benno got out too and walked over to his car. He handed the young man his key.

Günther unlocked the driver's door and swore under his breath. "You landed right in the water."

"Is it bad?" asked Benno.

"Could be worse, I think. But you didn't dodge a deer, right?"

Benno could feel himself blushing in spite of the cold.

"You put on the handbrake."

"I couldn't see the shoulder clearly," Benno mumbled in reply.

"What were you looking for? In the middle of the night?" But Günther wasn't looking for an answer. He released the brake, then ran back to his truck, made a U-turn and brought it into position.

After a few minutes, the Escort was back on the road.

"Can I drive it home?" Benno wanted to know.

"You'd probably be safe," Günther said and walked a second time around the car. "But I wouldn't recommend it. The axle could be bent, you could possibly make matters worse. I'll take it to the dealer, and in the morning a mechanic can look at your car."

Benno nodded.

"What did you want out here at the Miracle Oak?"

"I didn't realize I was at the Miracle Oak," Benno lied without thinking. He couldn't explain it, but it seemed inappropriate, even dangerous, to mention what he'd been after. As if he had discovered something that hadn't been intended for him to see.

"Not a good place to stop."

"Why is that?"

The young man looked at him thoughtfully, scratching his mustache, which was now full of snow. "You haven't been here all that long . . . but if you have to take a leak, or want to smoke, you'd better stop behind Johannsen's store." He laughed. "Everyone else smokes and pisses there."

"Why?"

"No idea. It's just the right spot." With a push of a button, he lifted the front end of the car, and secured the wheels with chains.

"No," Benno said. "Why shouldn't I stop here?"

Günther stood up, and looked at him with narrowed eyes. "It's not a good time to hang around here," he finally said. "Today is the first of the Twelve Nights."

— 12 —

"Nothing bent, just scratches in the paint and a small dent in the door. The side mirror is gone, but we need to order it."

The snowfall from last night had given way to gray clouds and a fine rain, and the road to the garage was slippery and full of puddles. Carolin had asked Benno to take her to the city—it was Tim's last day of school, and she wanted to go shopping in Lübeck. Mrs. Schmied had promised to warm up the boy's food.

Carolin's chin looked wrinkled from gritting her teeth. Ever since the alarm had sounded earlier that morning, she had avoided him.

"What do we owe you?" Benno asked the car dealer.

Friedrich shook his head. "We can do the repairs under warranty. Not quite legal, but it's Christmas, for crying out loud. Bring the car after the holidays, when we're not swamped. You only have to pay Günther."

Benno thanked Friedrich and shook his hand. Carolin said nothing, only nodded briefly at the car dealer on her way out and walked next to Benno toward the car.

"He just wanted to be nice," he said.

"I was nice."

"You didn't even look at him. What has he done to you?"

"What do you want from me? He only does what's good for his business."

From the left, the car still looked like new, but the dents on the right were not quite as small as Friedrich had said. Benno felt saddened when he looked at the damage. He didn't want to be reminded of last night's misadventure.

Carolin stared at the passenger side, at the black stump, where the side mirror had once been. "We haven't even paid it off yet," she said and slid her fingers over the jagged plastic. "Good thing nothing happened to you."

In silence they drove to Lübeck. Benno suppressed the impulse to tell Carolin that the dead woman had been identified. Irina Sobieski was now associated with the Christmas party, with Torfrock, Hanne and her witchcraft, and he didn't want to give himself away. Nothing had happened, but how could he explain that to Carolin? It was better not to mention last night.

At his desk, several packages and bags were waiting for him, gifts from business people and sports clubs. Pennants and jerseys that he would give to Tim, a bottle of rum, and a lot of marzipan.

The premises of the *Strandkurier* hadn't been cleaned yet, the bins were overflowing, and champagne bottles and glasses stood on the photocopier and in the restrooms. Holger told him with bleary eyes that Margit Scholl hadn't gone home at all, and that instead she'd eaten breakfast with him and two others at six o'clock in the Hotel Störtebeker. "Well, we didn't have much to eat," he added, and opened one of Benno's marzipan bars and took a bite. "You can have one of mine," he mumbled.

Benno waved his offer aside. "Do you have any plans for the holidays?" he asked.

"Visit my folks in Schleswig, let my mother cook for me." Holger grinned broadly. "And do my laundry. And you?"

Benno shrugged. "Nothing, I guess."

"No parents?"

"Not exactly. Say, do you have Twelve Nights in Schleswig?"

"Do we have what in Schleswig?"

"*Rauhnächte*. Twelve Nights. The Wild Hunt? Wotan and his un-dead companions riding through the night?"

"Zombies?"

"Something like that."

"Never heard of them. Does it have something to do with Strathleven?"

Benno shrugged. "No idea."

"Hey, they have identified your corpse." Holger had finished the marzipan, crumpled the golden paper and threw it toward the trashcan. He missed by half a meter.

"I know," Benno said. All of a sudden he wished Holger far, far away.

"Have you actually wondered whether the killer might be one of your new neighbors?"

"She was naked."

"And?"

"She wasn't killed there. The murderer probably took her from the trunk and dragged her into the bushes."

Holger pushed back his glasses with his index finger. His nose shone greasily. His wavy hair stood up in all possible directions. "He could have killed her there and then pulled off her clothes and stuffed them into a garbage can somewhere else or he could have burned them."

"He?"

"The murderer? She was raped."

"Why would someone from the village put her in the trunk and unload the corpse almost at his own doorstep? That's nonsense," he hissed.

Holger didn't seem to notice Benno's mood change. "Maybe that was his intention."

"What?"

"To make it look stupid."

"Do murderers really think around that many corners?"

Holger ran his fingers through his hair, grabbed a second marzipan bar, and said, "Probably not. If the dead had been found in Schleswig, who would ever dig around in Strathleven?"

"Exactly."

"But have you ever thought about it?"

Benno shook his head and reached into the box of marzipan himself. "How should I know how someone who is stabbing women with knives and forks thinks?"

Carolin came at half past four into the newsroom. Her face was red, her eyes shining, and her arms were hung with bags and packages.

"The others are already in the car," she chuckled and beamed.

"Did you leave anything for the other shoppers?"

She shook her head happily. "Want to see?"

"Later," he whispered, "I need to look busy for another hour."

"Should I wait for you at a coffee shop?"

"Nonsense!" Margit appeared behind them and smiled at Carolin. She looked rested, as though she hadn't stayed up all night. Her hair was perfect, and she even wore fresh clothes—she had to have stored them in her office. "Would you like a glass of champagne? We still have a bottle or two."

Within a few minutes, a group had gathered around Benno's desk. After five, Holger also joined them, and even Jochen Hecht, who had appeared late in the afternoon, came over.

"I've met Tim. He looks exactly like you," Holger said and looked suspiciously at the glass of champagne that Margit handed him.

Carolin smiled. "We have to get back soon. We left him in the care of our neighbor."

"The one with the mongo?" asked Holger.

Carolin turned around to Benno. "Are you talking like that about Manfred?" she asked heatedly.

Benno sighed, and Holger, who had noticed his mistake immediately, said, "No, I didn't mean . . . that was just . . ."

"Manfred is a wonderful boy . . ." Carolin's anger vanished quickly. "He can't help it. And he's not a mongo."

"He collects knives," Benno interjected, without quite knowing why.

"We really should get going." Carolin smiled at Margit. "And maybe if you are interested," she opened her purse and took out a stack of photocopied handouts, "we have a wonderful Christmas service in Strathleven."

"Yes, we must go," Benno said a little too loudly, a little too cheerfully. He was glad to have his hands full of packages. Holger gave him a meaningful look, but fortunately kept his mouth shut.

"How nice," Margit Scholl exclaimed after she had inspected the flyer and hugged Carolin. "You have to stop by again."

"That was so nice," Carolin said in the car. They bumped over the cobblestones, the streets still wet and muddy. A few snowflakes could be seen in the headlights. "Your colleagues are really nice. Even Holger." She sighed. "I miss work."

"At least you have the pastor. Or rather, the pastor has you," Benno said.

"That's not the same."

"It's not," Benno admitted. "Did you carry around that flyer all day?"

"Cornelius asked me to."

Benno nodded. "I think they have enough churches here in Lübeck."

"Did I embarrass you?" Carolin asked.

"No, of course not."

"I want to work again," she said.

"And you will."

"But how?"

Benno looked at her. "What do you mean?"

"We'd need two cars."

Benno thought about that. "You're right," he finally said. "Unless you can get a job in the village."

"As what?"

"Milkmaid."

Carolin didn't laugh at his joke and for the next few minutes said nothing more, before she suddenly burst out, "You're not taking me seriously. You think that you can make fun of me because I don't work and only sit around at home. And because you think I'm sick."

"I . . ."

"Crazy. Just because I don't want to take my medication. Because they numb me. When we sleep together, I can feel almost nothing."

They had reached the main road, and the traffic declined steadily. The asphalt was almost dry here, but the snow fell heavier again.

"And now? That you don't take them anymore?"

"Do you want to hear what a great lover you are?"

Benno moaned softly. After the first three months of their relationship, Carolin had tried to quit her drugs for the first time. "You're better than drugs," she had said, and he had been flattered. Benno, the great lover, the savior, the one and only. But after a few weeks, Carolin broke into a thousand pieces, and only when she slapped Tim several times and yelled at him, did she return to her doctor.

"You're insanely great," she said now, and licked her lips. "You fuck like a god."

Benno slowed the car, ready to stop. "I didn't mean it that way," he said. "You want to work again. If you can't find a teaching position, where else are you going to apply?"

"Don't pretend you're interested. You like the way things are: the woman stays at home, and you can drive around in the area and watch handball games and then get drunk with friends. What happens to me, you don't give a shit about. Cornelius is right."

"What?" Benno could feel anger rising up in him.

"There are people who are not good for you, who want to steal everything from you, everything that's dear to you. I feel safe at church. It feels so good to live with people who believe in something, but for you it's all just a joke. A hoax. You should have seen your face when I distributed the flyers. Hatred. Pure hatred. Your wife embarrassed you."

"Stop it," Benno said. "This is complete nonsense."

"Oh yeah? Do you think I didn't see Holger rolling his eyes? Oh, poor Benno, he is married to a Jesus-lover."

"You're imagining that."

"That's exactly what Thomas and Cornelius have said. Once you tell people the truth, they say you're crazy. Once you commit to something, others want to destroy it."

Benno took a right into a dirt road, and hoped fervently that he would not end up back in a ditch. "When did you see Thomas again?"

"Jealous?" Carolin laughed. "Of a pastor? Because you know that you could never keep me if I weren't damaged goods? Because my husband can only hold on to me by stuffing drugs down my throat? Because he can't satisfy a woman without drugs?" Her voice was pure fire. For a second she paused before she stated with shining eyes, "You're a hyena, Benno, a cowardly, misshapen soul. Too cowardly to believe in anything in this world. You've got to hold on to soccer results, that's all you've got. You've stolen my family because you could never raise and keep your own. No real woman would even look at you. You don't dare approach a real woman."

Benno put on the hand brake and got out, leaving the engine running. He ran aimlessly along the small path until he stepped out of the headlights and into the night. Then he ran, ran farther and farther into the darkness.

— 13 —

He stopped only when the cold night air began to hurt his lungs. He bent down with his hands on his knees and stared at the woods in front of him. He had no idea where he was.

Behind him he could see the headlights of cars along the county road, white lances racing toward one another.

"Shit," Benno cursed. He'd acted stupidly. What was he thinking running toward the woods? Did he really think Carolin would run after him and ask for forgiveness? His wife was probably already home.

The night sky was opaque, only to his right a single star peeked through a hole in the clouds. Snow cooled his face, and now that he had exhausted his anger, Benno noticed how wet his feet were. He wore simple dress shoes, and the leather was completely soaked. Slowly he stumbled back along the dirt road. Yet even when he had come within a few hundred meters of the county road, he still couldn't make out the headlights of his car. Carolin had really left him.

"Benno?" Her voice was squeaky, very thin. "Is that you?"

And then he felt her strong arms grabbing him. She pulled his face down to hers and covered it with kisses. "You can't just run away from me. Don't run away! "She reached under his shirt and put her hands on his back, dug her fingers into his skin. He did not cry out. He let himself be dragged to the car, pressed down on the back seat, which smelled of Rasmus and was full of shopping bags. Then she was on top of him, around him, tugging at his shirt and his pants. "May I?" she whispered.

He knew that this would only be a short phase, that Carolin would later hate herself for her weakness and greed, and that this hatred would be eventually directed against him.

He knew all this, but at that moment it didn't matter. Perhaps she was crazy, but he had never felt so loved.

She clutched him, buried her face in his neck. "May I?" she begged. "I want you in me." Her face was wet, whether from tears or snow, he couldn't tell. "May I?"

―――――――

"Oh, I'm so happy that you made it home safely," Mrs. Schmied greeted them. "I thought I would have to call the police. After what happened to little Sybille."

Carolin's hand was still in his, her face relaxed, flushed. "We really need to apologize to you," she said. "We weren't able to get out of the city. An accident in the old town, everything was gridlocked."

The lie came so easily to her. It was credible too, because Carolin didn't even try to come up with a better one. Her voice was casual, solicitous, and not interested in the widow's opinion. Benno's pant legs were wet, Carolin's were stained. And yet he couldn't help but wonder about Carolin's response. What had Benno told her yesterday? He had dodged a deer? How many lies did they tell each other in a day? In a week?

"Why? What's happened to the girl?" he asked.

Tim ran toward them happily, Rasmus whimpered softly. Benno stroked the broad head of the animal, and the dog let him. Manfred stood up from the kitchen table and held out his large hand. He had taken off his suit jacket, wearing a winter sweater with a pattern of snowflakes.

"Hello," he said. In the other hand he was holding a half-eaten cookie. Rasmus turned his attention away from Carolin and focused with his good eye on the cookie, sat down in front of Manfred and looked silently up at him.

"Here you go." Manfred grinned as the dog tenderly took the cookie from his hand and then gulped it down. "We are friends," he said. Indeed, the devil dog looked quite tame in Manfred's presence.

Benno turned around again to the widow Schmied. "And Sybille?"

The widow sighed deeply and cleared her throat. "She was found this afternoon in the forest. Half-naked." She paused and looked around with a mixture of sadness, anger and satisfaction. The girl had been hitchhiking home from Lübeck—even though her parents had strictly forbidden it—and came to a few hours later in a wooded area near Wengsten. She had no idea how she got there. Or so it had been told to Mrs. Schmied by Mr. Witte, the mailman, with the urgent request not say a word to anyone. The parents were too ashamed.

"If you ask me, she brought this on herself," Mrs. Schmied said. From the Antlers' neighbors she had heard that the girl had taken drugs with the driver. "I'm not saying that I wanted this to happen, but look at the girls nowadays. They run around as though they want to get assaulted." Whether Sybille had been raped, she couldn't say, but the evidence pointed to it.

"Awful," Carolin said. "Just awful. We need to pray for them."

When Benno walked toward his office to put down his bag, he saw light behind the half-open door, and a moment later Mr. Heintz came out with a slip of paper in his hand.

"Oh," he said when he saw Benno.

"I made him come over," the widow said quickly. "We were worried."

"Sure," Benno said hesitantly, and looked at the paper in Heintz' hand. Why hadn't the old man joined them yet? They had been home for ten or fifteen minutes already. What was he doing in the office?

"What is this?"

"I was looking for your work number."

"The phonebook is in the hallway."

"Really? I didn't notice it." Without another word, Heintz walked past Benno and joined Mrs. Schmied.

"Would you like to drink a glass of wine with us?" Carolin took off her coat and Benno could see that her black shirt was buttoned the wrong way. "Tim, shouldn't you be in bed?"

"Oh, thank you. But we must go home," the widow said.

"But it's only seven. And I don't have to go to school tomorrow," Tim begged.

"Thank you again." Carolin's voice was still hoarse. She closed the door behind the neighbors, leaned against it, smiling.

Tim said, "Can we make mulled wine?"

She nodded, but winced when there was a knock on the door behind her. It was Mr. Heintz, who almost pushed her out of the way and approached Benno, as if he were in his own home.

"Can I have a word with you?"

"But you were just . . . maybe tomorrow morning," Benno said.

"Only takes a minute," the old man said and walked casually through the apartment and into Benno's office. Benno had no other choice but to follow after him.

"What's this?" he asked sharply, after closing the door behind him. Mr. Heintz waved his question away, as if it were a waste of time.

"Where did you get that?" he asked, pointing at the cardboard sign that Benno had leaned against the wall the night before. *The King Must Die.*

"What business of yours is that?"

Heintz seemed not to have heard the question. "When did you find it?"

"Last night."

"Here at the house? Or *inside* the house?"

"No."

"Good, excellent. That is excellent." For a moment he seemed lost in thought. He was still wearing a suit, including a red, plaid shirt. "So?"

"What?" Benno's voice broke. He was at the end of his patience. "It was kind of you to take care of Tim, but . . ."

"Have you even looked at this?"

"I can read."

Heintz looked at him sharply. "Yesterday, right?"

"Yes, at the Miracle Oak."

"What were you doing there? Who else did you see there? Something evil is coming our way."

"Get out!" Benno opened the door, and to his surprise the old man left the office without another word. With as much determination as he had entered the house, he went to the entrance door, opened and closed it gently behind him.

"What was that?" Carolin had opened a bottle of Bordeaux and poured it into a saucepan. The smell of wine and spices spread throughout the kitchen and living room.

"I have no idea." Before Benno joined Tim and Carolin, he went back to his office one more time and picked up the cardboard sign. Last night it had been wet, and now it was wavy, the black letters had run. After today's events—the car, Holger's remarks about Irina's murder, his row with Carolin—he had completely forgotten about it. 'Something evil is coming our way.' What did that mean?

When he came back into the kitchen, he felt that the last shred of this evening's feeling of security was gone. He thought of Sybille Antler, whom he had wanted to talk to just a few days ago. Other things had occupied him—the identification of the body, the Christmas party—and now he wouldn't be able to ask her for quite some time. In the summer the girl had found Irina Sobieski, and now she had fallen victim to rape. Was the killer after her? Because she had discovered something on or near the body? Did the killer live in the village, as Holger had suggested? Or in Lübeck? But why hadn't he killed the girl?

What had Heintz to do with all this? And why had he behaved so strangely tonight? Was the old man more than just a carpenter?

Benno shook his head and looked around the brightly lit apartment. All the lights and lamps made the darkness in front of their house completely black. Whoever might be standing outside the windows would remain unseen.

———————

The next morning Benno and Carolin spent in their pajamas. Tim and Rasmus were outside, romping through the snow. Benno had never seen the dog so alive, he seemed like an entirely different animal. He chased after Tim's snowballs and then looked in vain for them on the ground.

Although Benno had only drunk a little mulled wine, he felt hungover. The cardboard sign looked just old, ugly and stupid this morning, and he threw it into the kitchen trashcan. The newspaper reported nothing of Sybille Antler's abduction.

Carolin had gotten out of bed before him and wrote Christmas cards to friends and relatives in Berlin. They wouldn't arrive in time for the holidays. Benno made more coffee and went into his study, looked thoughtfully at the pristine garden behind the house. Although he had now been living almost half a year in this house, he had never ventured there. It seemed impossible to access the garden from their side of the house, or maybe only the widow could get to it. But he had seen neither Mr. Heintz nor Manfred outside his window, and the garden was largely overgrown. The old Christensen had never cut the grass.

Benno had typed two pages of his article, but they'd been lying on his desk for weeks now, and looked at him alternately stern and disappointed. Hecht had been right—there wasn't anything newsworthy in Strathleven. Benno would have to disappoint the pastor.

After lunch, which consisted of all sorts of leftovers and old rolls, Benno left the house under the pretext of needing to run some final errands, got into the car and drove over to the old clinic. The death of Friedrich's father couldn't have left any permanent traces, and yet he felt he had to visit the building again.

To his surprise, the side door of the building was locked, and the bike chain at the main gate had been replaced with a proper padlock. Benno trudged through the snow around the walls of the clinic, but the only other gate, a service entrance, was blocked off.

When he came to the east side of the property, he stopped abruptly. According to Wehrke's description, Friedrich had hung himself from the main balcony. Now a white sheet hung from the balustrade on the second floor, and shifted uncomfortably in the wind. The black, untidy letters read *The King Must Die!*

The lights in the house were already on when Benno drove into the yard. Two cars were parked there. Wehrke had to have guests.

"Sorry to bother you," Benno said, as the door opened. Wehrke wore a sand-colored suit and held a glass of wine in his hand.

"It's you. Come on in."

"I really don't want to disturb you, but I wanted to ask you a question." Benno entered, took off his wet shoes and placed them next to a pair of expensive-looking leather boots.

"You're not disturbing me at all," Wehrke assured him and led him into the living room. A man in white trousers and a red knit-sweater was sitting on the couch and greeted Benno with a nod. "A friend of mine from Hamburg, Thomas Hutter." The man stood up and shook hands with Benno. He might have been in his forties, and wore a neatly trimmed beard and gold-rimmed glasses. His voice was deep and pleasant and had a strong Hamburg accent. "Nice to meet you." He could have been a radio announcer.

"I just came back from the clinic," Benno said, taking the glass of wine Wehrke offered him. The room was lit by only a few lamps, and in one corner stood a Christmas tree. It wasn't a spruce, but something that looked like an oversized coat rack. Chromed metal rods stuck out in all directions, and were furnished with strangely thin, silver needles.

Benno sniffed his wine and took a tentative sip. The liquid spread over his tongue, and although Benno understood little of wine, he realized that compared to this, the Bordeaux he bought at Johannsen's store was pure vinegar.

"California Syrah. Here, of course, people still turn up their noses."

"Oh," Benno said, trying to find a suitable facial expression, but only managed a grimace. "I went over to the old clinic again, after what you told me about Friedrich's death." He couldn't possibly talk about wine now.

Wehrke frowned. "You don't think . . ."

"If you're thinking what I'm thinking, no, no, of course not," protested Benno, all the more because it was a lie. "The last time I was there the building was full of clothes. All the rooms were . . . full of clothes and not even moldy."

"What clinic are we talking about?" asked Wehrke's guest.

"Oh, I'm sorry. The old mental hospital," Benno said.

Hutter looked at Wehrke. "Do I know it?"

He shook his head. "Nothing special. A stupid old box. Creepy family history. What you saw," he turned back to Benno, "were the remains of the ill-fated attempt to use the old hospital as a transit camp for refugees."

"Refugees?"

"Asylum seekers," Wehrke explained. "You can imagine how people responded here, when they showed up in the village."

Benno shook his head. "Not really."

"They locked their doors. Were afraid that the strangers would steal something. Everything."

"When was that?" Hutter asked. He poured himself more wine and sat back down on the sofa.

Wehrke followed him and offered Benno an armchair. "Last winter. The camp in Lauenburg was overcrowded, and the state was looking at other options. Hostels were converted, and finally they came across the clinic. And then people came from all over the world into the Schleswig-Holstein winter. Didn't have winter coats, sweaters, or boots. Had no money, no one to look after them. What you saw might have been donations."

Benno nodded. "What happened then?"

"There were cases of syphilis, then lice, and then the clinic, just like before, had to close. After only five weeks, it was all over."

"An epidemic?"

Wehrke shrugged. "Let's say the sanitary conditions were lacking."

Benno was silent and took a sip of wine. "The people here weren't happy about the refugees?"

"Of course not," said Wehrke. "Imagine nearly a hundred people from Africa, Asia and the Middle East, strolling into Johannsen's store and walking along the aisles. The shelves are filled and they have no money. Everyone in the village stares at them."

"Was there any violence?"

"Wasn't necessary," Wehrke said ambiguously. "Didn't stay long enough." Then he grinned broadly. "Strathleven is certainly not a village full of angels, but people immediately started collecting clothes for the refugees. Friedrich had a large container on his lot and delivered the packages himself. Nevertheless, that doesn't mean that people weren't pleased when the refugees were gone."

"The sheet," Benno said suddenly.

"The sheet?" echoed Wehrke.

"With which the old Friedrich hanged himself."

"Yes?"

"It was hanging from the balcony? Above the main entrance?"

Wehrke nodded. "And?"

Benno told him of his find. After he had finished, there was a sudden silence in the room. It was so quiet that Benno heard the refrigerator spring to life in the kitchen. "You know what that means? '*The king must die*'?"

Wehrke looked at him probingly, at least Benno had the feeling that his host's expression became more serious, suspicious even. Hutter, however, seemed perplexed, amused maybe. He looked at his clock.

"Do you have to leave? I'm sorry I just barged in." Then he asked, "Is this connected with the Twelve Nights? Two days ago I found two dead ravens tied to the Miracle Oak."

Wehrke also looked at his clock and nodded. "We have to make a show," he said apologetically. "The king must die," he repeated. "Two dead ravens?" Then he shook his head. "Someone is showing very little sensitivity."

He saw Benno to the door. The shoes seemed to be even more soaked than before, and Benno reluctantly headed back out into the cold. He liked how quiet Wehrke's house was, loved the absence of toys and dog hair and cheap Bordeaux. It was the absence of things that allowed him to breathe.

"Keep me posted" Wehrke said. He was still standing in the doorway, when Benno had reached the county road and turned toward the old school. He needed to get back to his own life with toys, dog hair and cheap Bordeaux. At least the car heater worked.

— 14 —

Carolin was ready to go to a final rehearsal for Christmas Mass and kissed him quickly goodbye. After Benno had put on dry socks—thick gray socks from Berlin, three pairs for ten marks—he, Tim, and Rasmus took a stroll through the village.

They went to the former mill pond, which now consisted of a water hole for the Grevenhorster fire department. The little stream winding through Strathleven was partially frozen. Only distant children's voices reached them, the streets lay deserted. Snowmen stood sweating in front of decorated windows, sleds rested unloved in front yards. Benno had made Tim promise to keep Rasmus on his leash at all times, even if the dog wouldn't leave his side anyway. The episode at Friedrich's dealership still gave him pause. He was convinced that Rasmus would never hurt Tim, but in regard to strangers he wasn't so sure.

Yet today, the dog behaved perfectly normal. He sniffed eagerly at lampposts and hydrants, leaving yellow snow behind for the other dogs in the village. A group of children came running across a yard, stopped in the street to look at Benno and Tim, and then ran away laughing.

"Your friends?" asked Benno.

Tim shook his head. "They don't talk to me."

Benno was taken aback. "Why?"

The boy shrugged.

"Have you guys quarreled?"

"No."

"And what about Daniel and Jens?"

Tim didn't answer. He stared straight ahead and didn't even notice that Rasmus had stopped to lift his leg. He pulled impatiently at the leash and Rasmus lowered his leg and trotted after the boy without having relieved himself. "They have other friends now."

Benno stopped in front of Johannsen's store and looked at piles of candy and champagne for 9.99. That was all the Christmas cheer Strathleven had to offer.

"Are you guys playing together at all?"

When Tim didn't answer him, Benno turned around to look at the boy. He and Rasmus stood rooted to the front of the store and looked at a couple who crossed the street carrying plastic bags and colorful packets. When they were only a few meters away, they slowed their steps.

"Hello," said Benno in a friendly way. He didn't know the couple, and it seemed that they hadn't noticed him until now. They quickly turned to face Tim and Rasmus.

"Merry Christmas," the man said, nodded, and walked in a wide circle past Tim. Rasmus appeared to have grown, his back was completely straight and he began to growl softly.

"Here you go," the woman said, put a bag down in the snow and dug out a gift wrapped in gold foil. She approached the boy slowly, as the dog seemed to intimidate her. She nodded, handed Tim the package and then hurried after her husband.

Benno was puzzled. "What the hell was that?"

Tim held the package in his hands and looked directly at Benno. "I also got one yesterday."

Benno shook his head.

"Sometimes they want to touch me," Tim said with a mixture of pride and indulgence.

"Sometimes? When?"

"When I go for a walk with Rasmus."

"How do those people know you?"

Tim shrugged. "Word gets out," he replied precociously.

"About what? Your skin? The miracle boy? Does Carolin know you're getting presents?"

Tim didn't seem to like the question and averted his eyes. "She doesn't understand," he said with certainty. "Can I keep it?" He raised the golden package, shook it.

"Sure," Benno said. "Is that the reason why no one wants to play with you anymore?"

The dog whined, and Tim let himself be dragged away. Rasmus did his little dance and then deposited his business in the snow. Since the two didn't wait for him to catch up, Benno sighed and ran after them.

———

Benno had insisted that decorating a Christmas tree was men's business, and while Carolin was still rehearsing, he carried the tree into the living room. He screwed it into the metallic-green stand he had bought in Lübeck, and then called out to Tim.

"What was in the package?" he asked as casually as possible.

"A toy car," Tim said just as casually. He seemed unimpressed.

"Will you help me?" Before Carolin returned, he wanted to ask the boy a question, and he did not want to sour the mood with useless admonishments.

The bulbs and tinsel were new since they hadn't brought anything from Berlin. Without memories of past Christmases, the decorations seemed strangely out of place.

"Tim," Benno began when he lifted up the boy to let him put the star on top. "Was Thomas, that young pastor, at the peace protest?"

Tim's face seemed to contract. He was on his guard.

"You remember, the protest in Lauenburg."

"Yes," Tim said slowly. It sounded more like a question.

"Was Thomas there too?"

The boy remained silent, his eyes fixed on Benno.

"Was he with you?" Benno tried to sound unconcerned, but something wasn't right here. "How many people were actually at the protest?"

Tim shrugged. "Fifty perhaps. There was another church with us."

"Only you and the other congregation?"

For a moment, Tim's face remained expressionless, then he nodded.

"Pastor Thomas' congregation?"

Tim nodded slightly.

"Do you have any leaflets left? The ones you were handing out?" He felt shabby. Maybe Carolin had been right. Maybe he was a weasel. No, she had called him a hyena. Yes, maybe he was a scavenger. A coward.

Tim stood up and walked upstairs to his room. A few minutes later he came back. He held a blue flyer in his hand.

"Thanks," Benno said, and smiled at the boy. The flyer was simple, its message written on a typewriter, all capital letters. Benno stared at the slogan. He tried to maintain a semblance of a smile. He couldn't show his feelings to the boy.

"Are those real babies?" asked Tim.

Benno shrugged. "Depends on what you mean by 'real.' Because people don't agree on that definition."

"But that's bad, right? To kill a baby?"

Benno sighed and handed back the flyer. 'Abortion is Murder' was written on it. 'God loves all children.' "Maybe," he said evasively, and began to pick up the empty cartons and boxes and put them in a large plastic bag. "That's pretty complicated."

He didn't know what bothered him more—that Carolin was ready to stand in front of a clinic and protest against abortion, or that she hadn't told him and asked the boy to keep quiet about it. But when she came back home from choir practice, and stood before him with dark circles around her eyes, Benno just warmed up some soup, without saying a single word about the flyer. On the one hand, he couldn't betray Tim's confidence, and on the other he had his own secrets. How could he complain about Carolin and at the same time tell her lies about the scratches on the car?

Silently they sat at the kitchen table, spooning the soup, and only when Tim got up to lie down on the sofa with Rasmus, did Carolin notice the decorated tree.

"Had a bad rehearsal?" asked Benno.

"No. Why?"

"For good luck," Benno tried to joke. "Bad rehearsal, good performance."

"We're not 'performing' anything. You still don't understand."

"Explain it to me!"

She dropped the spoon, and a splash of pea soup started running down her blouse. Carolin stared at Benno, her eyes large and wide behind the thick glasses. "So you can make fun of it?"

"I'm just trying . . ."

"The hell you are trying." She got up and left the kitchen. He could hear her steps first on the stairs and then above his head in the bathroom.

Benno turned around to look at Tim, but the boy seemed to have fallen asleep on the sofa. Only the dog looked at him attentively, but he seemed only interested in the crust of bread in his hand.

Above him the Milky Way spread. In front of him shone a single star, and when he stopped to admire it, Benno saw that the glowing spot was moving. Low aircraft noise reached his ears.

At the bus stop, Manfred sat in a black fur coat and an old-fashioned fur cap under the light of a street lamp. He had placed his thick mittens beside him on the bench, and nicked a branch with a Swiss Army knife.

"It's almost Christmas," Benno said. Nothing else would come to mind.

"Hmm," grumbled Manfred.

"What are you still doing here?"

"Uncle Gustav's mad at me."

"Why?"

Manfred lowered his head. "I've broken his pyramid."

"His pyramid?"

"The one with the little angels. I just wanted to have one of them. It no longer turns."

"Oh." Benno stared after his visible breath. "He's certainly not mad anymore. You shouldn't sit alone in the cold."

"He doesn't want to see me anymore," Manfred replied emphatically. "I don't want to be bumped off."

"By Uncle Gustav?"

Manfred nodded eagerly. "He can do that."

"What does your mother say to that?"

"She's afraid of him too." The pocketknife looked very small in Manfred's hand, like a silly toy.

"What do you want for Christmas?" Benno asked.

"A knife." A smile contorted Manfred's face.

"What kind?"

Manfred's voice dropped to a whisper, but was still so loud that any passer-by could have heard it easily.

"I already have it. I found it yesterday. But you mustn't say a word. Promise?"

"Promise."

"Otherwise I have to stay in the basement."

"The basement? But you don't have a basement." Benno was sure he'd asked the widow before moving in. He had been relieved—basements had already intimidated him as a child. He'd never gotten over his fear.

Manfred reached into his coat pocket and pulled out a gently curved dagger. The handle gleamed whitish.

"Genuine Ivory," he said. "From Egypt. Very expensive."

Benno nodded. Was it possible that this seemingly peaceful giant could stab a woman? Was there anything that would drive him to madness? Fear of his mother, or of Mr. Heintz? Was the old man really powerful enough to intimidate him? "You should probably return it," he said. His toes started to go numb, and his nose ached uncomfortably.

"But it's mine," Manfred said with a grin. He could neither call him a boy nor a man.

"Merry Christmas." Benno left him at the bust stop and ran down to the village to revive his toes. The snow still looked brand new, dirt and slosh would come later.

When he arrived at the main road, which lay almost deserted, he could hear the sound of a loud, running engine, and behind Johannsen's store, where, according to the tow-truck driver, everyone smoked or peed, he saw the black tail of Harald Wehrke's Jaguar. He wasn't eager to talk to the young man, but then he heard a woman's voice cry out. He quickly ran toward the back of the building, and as soon as he turned the corner, he saw Corinna Friedrich hit her boyfriend with her fists. "You weren't allowed. Not that," she cried. "Why? Why? I trusted you. Get lost, get lost already!"

"Harald." Benno wasn't sure if he was witnessing a lovers' fight, or whether the young Wehrke had turned violent, but he felt entitled to intervene.

Harald turned to face him, his face flushed, either in anger or shame. "What are you doing here?" he asked harshly, but the girl wouldn't stop hitting him. Blows rained down on his back. "Get out, you snoop!" he cried angrily, but now Corinna started to kick out, and he ran around the car and opened the driver's door. "We are not done yet," he hissed, and a few seconds later he was gone. Only the roar of his car could still be heard.

"Are you okay?" Benno asked.

Corinna, who had gone to her knees, weeping, now shot up and spat at him. "Go away! Why do you get involved in all this?" She kept crying, even as she yelled at him. "You don't understand a thing."

Benno raised his arms, as if to defend himself. "I'm leaving," he said and went back to the main road. Although he had done nothing wrong, he felt like a monster.

He wandered through the village, hoping not to encounter the two young people again, and after half an hour he was so cold and his body so numb that he could finally shake off the ugly scene. He didn't know why the two had fought, but he had acted properly. At least he hoped he had.

In the lighted windows he could see decorated trees, the icy snow crunched under his feet, and when he stopped and looked around it felt like Christmas for the first time this year. The roofs glittered in the starlight. Benno finally pulled out the bottle of vodka he had slipped into his coat pocket before leaving the house, and screwed off the cap. "Merry Christmas," he said loudly and took a deep swig. The cheap alcohol burned his mouth and throat. When he stopped coughing, his eyes fell again on Johannsen's store. Because of Harald and Corinna he hadn't paid any attention to the store window. With black paint, somebody had written across its entire width, *The king must die.*

15

Lunch consisted of sausages and potato salad, and Tim spent the afternoon watching TV. Benno's new suit, the one he had worn to the autumn ball, was a bit tight now, but Carolin made sure that he wore it. After dark, they went together to the Christmas service. He still hadn't mentioned the "peace protest," and when he entered the vestibule of the church and saw the four fir trees that the pastor had set up in the interior, they looked neither peaceful nor solemn. The pastor himself—just like Benno, he wore a white shirt and black suit—did not look friendly and engaging anymore, but overzealous and intimidating. Perhaps Friedrich, Johannsen, and Wehrke didn't attend services for good reason. Perhaps they were right in their opinion about Cornelius. Maybe he really was a self-righteous bully. Benno wondered if the pastor knew that Carolin kept certain things from her husband.

Although he would have preferred to sit far back, Carolin led Benno to one of the front pews. The peace at home was perhaps only a tacit agreement not to spoil the holidays with quarrels.

Tim couldn't sit still, constantly scratching his neck where the starched collar pinched his skin, and he was making whining noises. "But afterward we'll exchange gifts, right?" he asked.

"Dinner's first."

"We need to eat first?"

"And wash the dishes." At least they wouldn't send Tim to his room and make him wait for Santa Claus, the way Benno's parents had done in his youth. Carolin had raised Tim without Easter Bunny and Santa Claus. He'd first learned about them in kindergarten.

Benno had not been to church since the bazaar, and he looked discreetly but curiously around him. It might well have been a hundred people, and he knew many faces. But as small as Strathleven was, the last six months had not been long enough to know who sat behind him constantly blowing his nose, who was the woman with the antiquated beehive hairdo, or whose children were sitting in a row like organ pipes.

Then the lights dimmed, until only the Christmas trees were ablaze, and the choir was already singing as its members emerged from the sacristy. After they had taken up position in front of the altar, the choir director gave the sign, and "Silent Night" began. Despite his anger, despite their ugly dispute, Benno couldn't shake the peculiar effect the singing had on him. He closed his eyes and felt a grin spreading across his face.

The congregation sat in silence when Benno thought he heard the distant clatter of hooves. Astonished, he opened his eyes.

"What is that?" Tim whispered in Benno's ear.

He shrugged. He would have loved to stand up and move past the believers in his pew to rush to a window and see what was going on outside. But the choir could not be deterred, even when the noise came closer and loud voices could be heard.

Benno now saw shadows flitting across the walls. Light came from outside the church, it seemed to flicker and pulsate, and a terrible howling began. Finally, the choir stopped, the director stepped aside and lowered his head. After that, it was completely silent in the church. The entire congregation held its breath.

Then Benno saw Cornelius standing by the altar and waving his arms. "Light," he cried. "Light. Damn it!"

A woman's voice mingled with the howling outside, a voice full of rage and anger, but Benno couldn't understand a word. Cornelius shouted angrily, "We're not afraid."

Seconds later a window shattered. Something landed two or three rows in front of Benno and some people jumped up in terror.

"You helped us chase," the shrill female voice cried, "now also help us gnaw."

And then the voices of her male companions started their ruckus again. The clatter of hooves and the neighing were so loud that Benno was afraid the door might fly open and the riders would storm into the interior. But finally the noise faded as the horses seemed to gallop toward the center of the village.

Benno took advantage of the confusion to climb over two pews to the front and pick up the package that had broken the window. It was wrapped in butcher paper and a lot harder than it looked. A stone.

Then suddenly the light went on, and Benno looked around. No one had followed his example. He alone stood before the congregation and the pastor, who with a reddened face approached him. "Hand it to me," he thundered. "Give me that!"

Benno did as he was told. The pastor seemed to become aware again of his office, thanked Benno loudly enough that the churchgoers could hear it, and held the stone high in his hand. "A stone," he cried, "cannot put fear into our community. A stone cannot break our faith."

Through the broken window to Benno's left cold air penetrated the church, and the altar candles flickered more wildly than usual. After a brief look at the damage, Cornelius asked the choir to gather again, and two minutes later, the congregation once again sat in near darkness, listening to the song "Es ist ein Ros entsprungen."

Benno took his seat next to Tim, but his hands were shaking. He didn't know what was more terrible, the noise of the horsemen, or the disheartened singing of the choir in front of the Christmas trees. And only he and the pastor knew what else the package had contained. Only he and Cornelius had seen the bloodied raven head.

———

The congregation dispersed very quickly after church, with only a brief nod in the direction of the pastor. Cornelius and his wife couldn't find any takers for biscuits and fruit juice.

"What was that?" Tim asked.

Benno looked at him but didn't have an answer. "Maybe an old tradition," he said.

"With horses? Where did they get them?"

"No idea, but the farmers must have some." After the service he had tried to run after Mr. Heintz to ask him a few questions, but he hadn't been able to catch up with him. He could have sworn that the old man had noticed him and sped up.

"What did your choir members say?"

Carolin did not correct him this time, did not tell him that it was a singing group. "Nothing," she said, and outrage made her voice sound hoarse. "Just nothing. They disturb us during the Christmas Mass, and everybody just shuts up."

Benno enjoyed that she was mad at her church members. It might have been shabby of him, but he felt closer to her.

Once they were home, he poured more red wine and got a new bottle of sweet woodruff soda for Tim. The three of them sat at the kitchen table, opened a bag of potato chips and then got some pizza from the fridge.

"Can we exchange gifts now?" Tim finally asked. "We don't even have to do any dishes."

They switched off the light in the kitchen and went into the living room. Benno had insisted on real candles, and walked around the tree with a lighter in his hand. In his childhood, this had always been the big moment, and an echo of that time was still noticeable.

For a few moments they sat quietly until Tim couldn't take it anymore.

"What should I unwrap first?" he asked.

"Always the biggest first," Benno said.

"No, you must save that until the end," Carolin replied with a grin.

Tim stood irresolute beside the tree. The pleasant smell of the needles spread in the house, and Rasmus stood wide-eyed next to Tim and sniffed at the wrapping paper. Finally, the boy rushed to the largest of the packages and ripped it open.

"A race track," he said breathlessly, and opened the colorful box. Soon he was buried under an avalanche of paper.

Benno had bought Carolin a new, thick bathrobe.

"I've got something for you too," she said, and reached for the smallest package under the tree. Excitedly, she watched as he unpacked it. It was a brown box from a jeweler in Lübeck. Benno carefully opened the lid. Under a layer of cotton wool was a small silver cross.

"I hope you like it," Carolin said softly. He nodded. He had expected nothing of the kind, and felt paralyzed. "Thanks," he said, and then had the presence of mind to ask her to put it around his neck.

Her smile told him that it was the right answer. She stood up quickly, came up behind him, and locked the chain.

"Well?" he asked, and unbuttoned his shirt in front.

"Splendid," she said proudly, and gave him a kiss.

"Disgusting," Tim said.

A noise at the front door interrupted their laughter. A few seconds later Benno stood at the entrance and peered through the small glass window. There was no one there.

He opened the door and stepped into the night. The yard lay dark and deserted before him. From the main road only an occasional car could be heard. Everyone in the village was probably busy unwrapping gifts. Or maybe not everyone. Because at his feet lay a package wrapped in brown paper. Tim's name was written in large letters on it. It was very light, not a lot could be in it.

He walked slowly back inside. Tim stood in the hall and looked at him questioningly.

"Did I get anything?"

"Seems so," said Benno and wondered how many gifts from complete strangers Tim had actually received. It hadn't even occurred to the boy that the package could be for someone else. "Let's unwrap it together."

He went into the living room, blew out the last candle on the tree and led the way into the kitchen. "Careful," he warned the boy. "We don't know what it is."

With serious faces, they all sat down at the table and pushed aside the potato chips. After what had happened in church, Benno expected the worst. "Let's do it," he said softly and tried to smile.

"Shouldn't we . . ." Carolin tried to interrupt, but Tim had already torn the paper and was opening the cardboard box inside.

"Oh." The boy made a long face. "That's stupid—a crown!" Then he put it on the table. "That's something for girls."

It was made of sheet gold, unadorned and without stones. Still, it wasn't shabby, and the five points had been carefully honed and polished.

"Yes, that's for girls. This is really stupid." Benno took the crown and placed it back in the box. "Okay, who wants some hot chocolate?" He stood up and went over to the stove. His hands trembled and almost dropped the pot. He looked out the window into the night, only not to look at the table and the crown again, but all he could see was a pale face that, he realized after a moment of shock, was his own. The features were blurred, his eyes were sunken in their sockets. It looked anxious and afraid, this face. He mustn't let Tim see it.

When he was little, the first day of Christmas had belonged to relatives, the second day to friends and acquaintances of his parents. It had been boring, but Benno had received gifts for two more days. Here in Strathleven they had no relatives or colleagues, and he was grateful for this new kind of boredom, which was interrupted only by walks, old movies on television, and new candles on the tree.

On the afternoon of the 26th, the doorbell rang, and Benno was surprised to see the pastor. Cornelius was wearing jeans, sports shoes and an oversized sweater that appeared to be hand knitted.

"I really must apologize to you." In the gray daylight and surrounded by thawing snow, he did not look like a pastor at all. "I shouldn't have yelled at you on Christmas Eve."

Benno nodded. He had not expected an apology and would have preferred not to get one.

"Who were the people outside the church?" he asked. "It was the Wild Hunt, right?"

"Ah, old superstitions. I behaved childishly." Cornelius probably intended to look contrite, but he did not succeed. For no apparent reason, he seemed to enjoy the memory of that incident. "A few stupid folks who wanted to play a prank on the man in black."

"Who's the king?" Benno asked, before realizing that they were still standing outside the door. "You want to come in?"

"Oh no, thank you." Cornelius said quickly. "I wanted to invite you. You and Mrs. Schmied and her son. My wife has been baking, and we thought . . . we're neighbors. I'm not here as your pastor. Would four o'clock work for you?"

Benno could have imagined a more agreeable afternoon, but he knew Carolin would insist. He nodded.

"Do you know him?"

"Who?"

"The king?"

"What do you mean?" Cornelius looked at the sleeves of his sweater, which were much too long and made his hands disappear.

"Have you not seen the slogans in the village?"

For a moment it looked as if the pastor might burst into tears, he seemed so concerned all of a sudden. Then he quickly said, "At four, then," nodded, and walked over to Mrs. Schmied's door.

"Do I really have to go?" Tim looked almost as unhappy as his dog. Then he glanced in Carolin's direction and immediately surrendered.

"They'll have cake," Benno tried to comfort him, but after days of jelly stars, dominoes and marzipan potatoes, Tim seemed unconvinced.

Mrs. Schmied and Manfred were already there, and the whole Cornelius family seemed to have gathered in the living room and kitchen. The TV was on, Mrs. Cornelius was wearing a dark red dress, and the pastor was still buried in his too big sweater.

"Come on in, come in," he said in his strained baritone. "Sit down and please don't touch the cookies. Feel at home—at home you're on a budget as well."

"Don't listen to Walter's jokes," his wife said, rolling her eyes. "If he has nothing to do, he's simply intolerable."

It was the first time that Benno heard the pastor's first name and it felt inappropriate, as if his wife had made a dirty joke.

"Anita mostly finds me intolerable," the pastor said, grinning broadly.

"Shhh," said one of the girls. She was watching television.

"We can turn off that box," threatened the pastor.

While Tim joined the children, Cornelius took their coats and led his guests into the kitchen. It was a large, yellow-tiled room, with a table that could have seated twenty people. The table and chairs looked shabby and the walls above the tiles were in need of fresh paint.

Biscuits were on the table, and Mrs. Cornelius had just made fresh coffee. Her short hair was gray and looked a lot like thick wire.

"Beer?" asked the pastor. Benno turned his eyes away from Mrs. Cornelius and nodded.

"Wine for the ladies?"

Mrs. Schmied smiled. "But only a tiny glass."

"I shouldn't offer you any alcohol," the pastor stage-whispered. "But the flesh, even a pastor's flesh, is sometimes weak."

"Is Mr. Heintz coming too?" Benno asked.

"He can't," the widow said quickly. "His hip is giving him trouble."

"Age is not a cakewalk," said the pastor, grinning incessantly.

"Have you ever seen the Wild Hunt before? Does it ride through the village every year?" Since the pastor wasn't by himself and had to be polite, he hoped to get answers this time.

"Not for a long time," the widow said with a sigh. "When I was a young girl, it still came through the village every year, but those were the bad years. I was hoping never to see them again. It's a shame."

Mrs. Cornelius put the coffee on the table, cut the cake and put large slices on everybody's plates. "Beer and cake." She frowned.

"Heaven!" her husband said and stroked her arm.

"And have they always attacked the church?" Benno asked.

"No," said Mrs. Schmied. "That was the first time."

The pastor looked worried. "The window will cost a few hundred marks."

"Do you know who the riders were?"

An uncomfortable silence ensued. Mrs. Schmied and the pastor chewed with devotion. Only Manfred hummed to himself.

"Will you go to the police?" Benno received a worried look from Carolin, but he wouldn't back down. "You must have recognized the woman's voice, right? Someone must have recognized it."

The pastor took a sip of beer, licked his lips, then said, "It's a small village. We are a small congregation. Many people are not especially fond of us. We don't go around pressing charges."

"The stone could have hurt someone."

"You should be happy that nothing happened," Mrs. Schmied said quickly. Then she looked at the pastor for help.

"It's just a bit of glass," Cornelius said. "We want to show love, not hate."

Benno thought of Martin Wehrke, and what he had said about the pastor's abhorrence of homosexuality, of the so-called peace protest and the ugly leaflets. But he sat at Cornelius' table and didn't want to make a scene in front of Tim and Carolin.

"What does all this have to do with the king?" he asked instead.

"Oh, just listen to you." Mrs. Schmied might have wanted to sound more conciliatory, but her tone was sharp and even Manfred stopped humming and stared at his mother.

"Someone walks around and sprays slogans on people's houses. The king must die. Don't you find that strange?"

The widow looked at him directly. "Stupid talk. There is no king. Who should it be? There is only one king, and that is our Lord!"

"Amen," said Mrs. Cornelius and got up from her seat.

The rest of the afternoon Benno tried to fix the damage his questions had done. Which for the most part meant that he kept his mouth shut. But as much as he struggled to remain polite, Carolin refused to acknowledge him. When she finally got up from the pastor's kitchen table, he had the vague feeling that he would spend the night on the sofa again.

It was pitch dark outside. Benno had forgotten to turn on the light over their door, and so they walked cautiously on the half thawed, half frozen snow, trying not to trip. Carolin remained silent, and after he had unlocked the door, she walked past him into the kitchen without another word.

Rasmus was overjoyed to see them again, jumped up at Tim and nearly threw him to the ground. "We have to take him out for a walk," Benno said. He wasn't ready to face Carolin yet, and so the two of them made off with Rasmus. The sidewalks had only been partially shoveled. Even the road was slippery.

"Mom is mad at you," Tim said matter-of-factly.

"True," Benno said.

"Why did no one answer your questions?"

"Were you listening to us?" Benno shrugged. "If only I knew. Were the kids nice to you?"

"I guess," he said undecided. "Am I the king?"

"Why do you ask?"

Tim groaned. "I'm not stupid."

Benno nodded. "I don't know why you got the crown."

"It wasn't meant for a girl, right?"

"Why?"

"It belongs to the king. Angela said that."

"The pastor's daughter?"

Tim nodded. "Do I have to die now?"

"Of course not," Benno said firmly. "This is silly nonsense."

"But you asked about the king yourself. You don't believe it's nonsense."

"I know that you're not a king. Kings have horses and servants. And you have nothing. You only have a dog."

"And the gifts?"

"That is really weird," Benno admitted. What else could he do? "But surely there is a simple explanation for everything." But he wasn't so certain. The reaction of the pastor had done nothing to alleviate his fear. What did the people conceal from him? "Let's go home before Carolin gets really pissed off," he said.

They turned around toward the old school and cleaned Rasmus' paws extra carefully. Before closing the door, Benno saw Mr. Heintz stepping out of his entrance and crossing the front yard. With firm steps, the old man hurried down to the village. His hips didn't seem to give him any trouble. Whom in the village would he pay a visit?

— 16 —

On 27 December, a Tuesday, Benno had to go back to the office. Hecht was still with his girlfriend on Sylt, and the atmosphere in the newsroom on Hüxstraße was generally sleepy. The small kitchen was full of *stollen*, cinnamon stars and other sweets, and in the afternoon, Holger pulled a bottle of cognac from his bag and poured some in everyone's coffee.

Benno was sitting at the desk working on his January schedule. He checked the games he would attend, and got up from time to time to stretch. He had indeed spent the night on the sofa, and his left side was still sore and numb. His neck was aching. He buried his head in his hands and closed his eyes.

"Is everything all right? Or is this a bad moment for a visit?"

Benno sat up abruptly. He stared at his visitor with wide eyes and shook his head. "No, it's okay," he said at last.

"You look pretty horrible." Hanne's short, red hair glistened wet, and raindrops ran down her coat. "Should I come back another time?"

"Nah, that's alright," Holger, who appeared behind her, said. "All he needs is some cognac." And he soon returned with his bottle and two glasses, and Benno introduced Hanne.

"Do you have time for a coffee?" he asked and smelled the amber liquid. That alone was enough to clear his head. Disgusted, he put the glass on the desk.

"Thank you," Hanne said in Holger's direction, "but I still have to work."

"Shame." Holger poured the contents of her glass in Benno's and took a sip. "Ghastly stuff," he said, and slipped away with a wink.

"Coffee then," Hanne said.

In the rain they hurried through the streets, and sat down on the first floor of a cafe on Königstraße, with a view of St. Catherine's Church.

"Returns," Hanne said as she caught Benno staring at the countless plastic bags of two women near them.

"Better than Christmas."

"Are you happy? That I visited you?"

Benno looked at her far too long. "Yes," he finally said.

"At least it sounded convincing."

"Good," Benno said.

"But you wouldn't have come back to the library."

"Maybe not."

"The kiss?"

He shook his head. He wasn't even sure what or whom he was trying to avoid. "Maybe I don't really trust myself."

"Is that kind of a compliment?"

"Somehow. Yes." He grinned sheepishly.

The coffee came, and Benno paid. Suddenly he felt the desire to spend the night in Lübeck. The two women at the next table showed each other their new acquisitions, laughing from time to time at he didn't know what.

"What scares me most is that Tim doesn't want to be healthy."

Hanne looked at him questioningly.

"I think he enjoys the attention. And the people in the village offer him gifts, they treat him like a minor celebrity." He told her what had happened in the days before Christmas, about the crown, the riders in front of the church and the sprayed slogans. "I really believe he thinks he is a king. And that he's in danger. But he takes everything so stoically. I can't make any sense of the situation."

Hanne nodded, and he was grateful that she had no advice for him, no empty phrases.

"What does your wife say?" she finally asked.

Benno sighed. He didn't want to talk to another woman about his marriage. But who else could he confide in? Hanne was the only person he knew and who had nothing to do with his work or his family. Almost a girlfriend.

"She . . . she doesn't pay the king or the horsemen any attention. I think she thinks that this is all just a bad joke. To annoy the pastor. For being a Baptist and overzealous."

"And you?"

"No idea. But it scares me. I grew up in a small town, and I knew all the people, but nobody ever offered me toy cars and chocolate."

"But you didn't have any scars."

"That only makes it scarier. I have no idea what they want from Tim. It's rumored that he's invulnerable. There's just no end to this, as if the village were waiting for something to happen. That Tim blesses them or heals them all and makes them rich." Church bells began to ring, and Benno looked at his clock. It was 5:30.

"Don't you have to go back to work?" he asked.

"I'm not working today. That was a little white lie." She laughed at him. "I just came by to see you."

"You're not returning any gifts?"

"What I gave to myself cannot be returned." She winked.

"Oh," he said.

"But I can't show you here."

He grinned, looked into his half-empty cup. The coffee was bitter and sour, only Holger's cognac might have saved it.

"Are you going to visit me again some time, or should we say good-bye here?" Hanne asked into the silence.

He looked at her, let his gaze wander over the made-up eyes, her rouged cheeks, the full and yet somehow small mouth. Her ears had the roundest lobes he had ever seen. He didn't want to find her beautiful. With an ugly woman he could have coffee, with a woman who would never kiss him and whom he didn't want to kiss. No, he didn't want to find her beautiful. "Yes, I'll visit again." He wondered if it was the truth.

New Year's Eve fell on a Saturday, and even in a small town like Strathleven Benno heard firecrackers all through the day. When he stepped outside in the afternoon, he even thought he smelled gunpowder in the air.

The temperatures had dropped further and the icy air penetrated his clothes. Firecrackers and rockets had been off-limits for Carolin since Tim's early childhood. In Berlin, they'd only had champagne together and listened to albums or watched television. She had refused to leave the house after five o'clock in the afternoon. The risk was too great for Tim.

For this night they had nothing planned, and it was okay with Benno. They hadn't received or given any invitations, and anyway he didn't feel in the mood for a celebration. Around ten o'clock they went to bed, despite Tim's protests. "I want to see the rockets," he begged, but Benno and Carolin refused. Within fifteen minutes he was asleep, and a short time later they switched off the lights in their bedroom.

In his dreams, Benno heard the church bells ring, and a fraction of a second later he was sitting up in bed. The ringing didn't stop. What time was it? Had a fire broken out? Was it only a New Year's greeting?

He switched on the light. When he saw that it was still ten minutes to midnight, he put on his clothes.

"That doesn't sound right." Carolin was still looking for her glasses. "They've never sounded like that."

She was right: it didn't sound like the ringing on the hour, nor like the bells before Sunday mass. It was louder and more hectic than usual.

Benno ran barefoot out into the hallway. Tim's door was open, as always, but light came from his room, and when Benno checked on the boy, the bed was empty.

"Hurry," he called to Carolin, and ran down the stairs.

Tim stood in coat and winter boots in the front yard, Rasmus by his side. Under the coat he was wearing his pajamas, and he stared up at the bell tower. The dog pulled frantically on the leash, and Tim had trouble standing his ground. In the dark, Rasmus looked twice as large, and he barked without pause. The sky was full of shredded clouds. Fireworks could be heard from the village and from surrounding farms, even through the ruckus of the church bells.

In the belfry, Benno saw a light. It flickered on, seemed to go out, only to reappear seconds later at a different angle. Benno could see dark figures moving about the narrow space. The place seemed to swarm with them. At that moment the pastor came storming out of his house.

"The ladder," he shouted in Benno's direction. "Pull away the ladder!"

"Go back inside the house," Benno told Tim, but the boy made no move to leave his observation post. "Well, don't leave this spot!" Rasmus wouldn't let anyone touch the boy.

"They've come to get me," Tim said.

"Nonsense." Benno rushed towards the steeple, at the heels of the pastor, who ran around the tower to the north side of the church. And really, there was a ladder leaning against the wall, extending up to the roof. As Benno and the pastor approached, four figures materialized in front of them. Where they had come from, Benno couldn't tell—maybe they had been hiding in the shadow of the church wall or in the cemetery. All four raised their arms, and Cornelius exclaimed, "Why have you come here? This is a house of God."

Laughter answered him. Two of the figures were carrying axes, one was holding a scythe, and the fourth a pitchfork. Their faces were smeared with soot, and they wore ski masks and caps.

"We'll call the police," shouted Benno, but that earned him only more laughter. He pulled on Cornelius' sleeve, wanted to drag him away, but the pastor wouldn't have it.

"You won't get away with this," he said in a trembling voice. "What have I done to you? What is this supposed to mean? I am not your enemy. I want to make peace." When the four men took another step toward him, he didn't back away. "God's kindness is everlasting, he will crush your old world and wash it away." Cornelius was only a meter away from his attackers. The bells were barking above their heads.

One of the men shouted, "Your God has no say here." The voice was hoarse, but Benno thought he'd heard it before. He did not immediately remember when or where, but it was an unpleasant memory, of that he was certain.

"Come on!" Benno grabbed the pastor, but just when he thought Cornelius would follow him, the pastor pushed him away and walked with his raised hands toward his attackers. Benno saw the blunt end of an axe come down on Cornelius shiny head, causing him to sink to the ground without a noise.

Benno ran. Scornful laughter followed him. He had to call the police, he had to carry Tim to safety. The pastor was beyond his help now, he told himself.

When he had rounded the tower and again stood in the front yard of his home, Tim was nowhere to be seen. 'They have come to get me.' Had the boy been right? "Carolin," he shouted and stormed into the house. There was no one in the living room or the kitchen. "Carolin," he shouted once more, but received no answer.

He picked up the phone and dialed the emergency number. When, after the sixth ring, no one had answered yet, he hung up and ran outside again.

"Come over here," hissed a voice from the adjacent door. It was Gustav Heintz, who waved him inside. "Your family is with me."

Benno walked cautiously toward the dark entrance. "What is all this?" The church bells still rang, and they sounded now as though somebody were hitting them with hammers.

"Come already. I don't want to stand here forever."

"The pastor . . ."

" . . . is a fool. Will you finally come inside?" The old man stepped out of the shadows and pulled Benno into the house. "Don't be stupid, my goodness."

Everyone had gathered in Heintz' small kitchen. A candle on the table threw flickering shadows on the frightened faces of Mrs. Schmied, Manfred, Tim and Carolin. They all stared at the newcomer with concern.

"The police . . ." said Benno.

" . . . know exactly what's going on."

"They have killed the pastor," he said. "At least he's unconscious."

"As I said, he's a fool," Heintz said bitterly. "He knew exactly what he did. Such a moron. Well, at least they didn't get to you."

"What's going on out there?" Benno asked again.

"Do you still not understand?" snapped Heintz.

"Gustav," admonished the widow.

"But it's true. How often do I have to tell him about the Twelve Nights? And this year it's different, almost like old times. People stay home, don't go out at night. Especially when they're living next to this silly church."

"Gustav," the widow admonished him again.

"Yes, yes," he muttered to himself. Then he turned to Benno again. "You want a drink?"

Benno nodded. "And who exactly is out there? I think one of them was the young Wehrke."

Heintz seemed not to have heard him, or maybe he simply chose to play deaf. He said, "Someone. It's nothing."

"The pastor was attacked in front of my eyes, and it shouldn't concern me? Harald Wehrke strikes Cornelius, and everything is fine because it happened during the Twelve Nights? Have you called the police?" Benno was getting furious. What was this old man up to?

"The phone is in the hallway," Heintz said curtly and handed him a full glass.

Benno stood up, angry at Heintz and his Twelve Nights, but Tim's voice stopped him.

"Don't you see that they've come to take me away?"

Everyone stared at the boy, whose face was completely white except for his cheeks glowing crimson. He didn't look at anyone, just stared down at the table. "I'm the king, and they'll soon be here and they're going kill me."

Carolin was about to put a hand on Tim's shoulder, but he dodged it. "Stop it," he shouted at his mother. "You are all blind. I got the crown and I am the one who has to die." He flung the words at the adults, and no one contradicted him. Rasmus yelped. Even Heintz seemed to have forgotten the bottle of liquor in his hands. All of a sudden Tim's body began to tremble, and seconds later he burst into tears. This time he let his mother put her arms around him. "Nothing will happen to *you*," he wailed. From outside, the sound of the bell reached them.

"You're safe here," said Carolin in a shaky voice, but her words did nothing to soothe Tim.

"Nobody's going to hurt you," Manfred said, furrowing his brow. "Isn't that right, Mom?"

"Of course," Mrs. Schmied said firmly.

Only now did Heintz remember his bottle, poured himself another drink and emptied it. With a brief nod he suggested Benno follow him into his workshop.

"Close the door," he said as he turned on the light and sat down on a roughly hewn stool. "You want another one?"

Benno held out his glass. "Are we safe here?" he asked.

"From what?"

"Those people out there."

"As long as you don't venture outside." Heintz frowned and poured himself another shot. He thoughtfully looked at the clear liquid, then emptied the glass and poured some more. "You don't know the village."

"And?"

"Some people take the old customs very seriously. Perhaps too seriously. For a few years it might look as though we may forget them, but then they come back. A bad harvest, too much rain, a drought—and suddenly the old ghosts rise again. There's little to be done about it."

"The police in Grevenhorst . . ."

". . . don't give a damn about us. They tried that in the sixties. Thought we should join in what they said was progress. Two of the officers almost died. After that, they never bothered us again."

"In the sixties."

"Doesn't matter now."

"The year Friedrich's father was killed?"

Heintz looked at him with narrowed eyes. "In March of 1965. What do you know about that?"

Benno drained his glass and held it out again. The old man refilled it without hesitation. "It wasn't suicide?" He sipped his *schnaps* and turned to inspect the walls with the many hand-painted figurines, which all seemed to stare at him. He thought of the pastor and wondered if Cornelius was still lying on the ground. And how strange it was to be here in the carpenter's workshop and drink liquor and not intervene, while a few hundred meters away a crime had been committed. Wasn't it normal to call the police and to provide first aid?

"Do you have a basement? The . . ." Benno broke off; he didn't want to betray Manfred to his 'uncle.'

"What should I do with a basement?" Heintz was visibly irritated.

And while Benno still thought of the dark figures and the weapons in their hands, he realized that he had just noticed something unusual among the wooden figurines. He was dizzy for a second, but then discovered the desired one, took it off the hook and held it out to Heintz. "The Brothers Grimm write nothing about this one." The figurine showed a young man in a fur-trimmed coat. In one hand he held a scepter, in the other instead of an orb, two ravens. On his head sat a simple gold crown, which Benno recognized as the one Tim had received on Christmas Eve. "Who is the king?"

Heintz slowly opened his mouth, clicked his tongue, and seemed about to give an explanation, but then he shook his head. "The hell you know."

— 17 —

There was no mention of the New Year's Eve attack in the local paper. In Grevenhorst a man had lost his hand to an M-80, in Lübeck, a car had burnt out. The pastor was now wearing a bandage around his head and a felt hat to cover it as well as possible.

Benno went back to work, and Otto Friedrich kept his promise and repaired the car for free. The Ford looked as good as new.

The bustle in the office of the *Strandkurier* made Benno happy. He could focus again on handball, basketball, and hockey. Restaurants wanted to advertise with coupons and department stores announced their winter sales.

But after a week, his curiosity returned, like a small, persistent, and ugly creature. He could still hear the hoarse voice of one of the attackers. 'Your God has nothing to say.' Benno was certain now that he recognized it as Harald Wehrke's. What did he have against the pastor? And what had happened during the bazaar? What had enraged the pastor back then? Had the young man been seeking revenge?

Also, the old Friedrich's suicide still occupied him. Heintz hadn't given him any more details on New Year's Eve, but Benno was convinced that Friedrich's death had made headlines. And if his neighbor's story was true, and two police officers had almost lost their lives, then somebody must have reported it.

"That didn't take *too* long," Hanne said slowly when Benno visited the third floor of the library. Today she sat behind the information desk, multiple stacks of bound journals spread around her. "A friendly visit or a request for help?"

"Both?"

"Help then." She laughed at him. "What can I do?"

"Newspaper archives. From 1965. Microfiche, hopefully."

"A specific paper?"

"All the local ones."

A separate room had been set up on the second floor, with three Microfiche readers. The folders of the *Lübecker Nachrichten* stood on the shelves, and Hanne promised to send for the *Grevenhorster Anzeiger*. "We close at seven o'clock today," she said. Benno looked at his watch. It was only half past five, so he still had an hour and a half.

"I need to be at a hockey game later," he said.

She looked at him curiously, as if he had said something inappropriate, and Benno didn't know himself why exactly he had mentioned it.

One folder contained the year 1965, but if Heintz had been right, he could focus on March. If the news had reported the incident, it had to be in the East Holstein section. At least he could start his search there.

A Jack Russell Terrier had been abandoned in Eutin, hail had caused property damage in Malente, and mayoral elections in Glasau had been moved to an earlier date. Long after six o' clock he had only managed to look through half a month, and the two policemen from Grevenhorst had not been mentioned.

About twenty minutes later, just as he was looking at March 22 on the grainy screen in front of him, Hanne returned.

"The *Anzeiger*," she said, and put the folder on the table. "Any luck?"

"What was your Christmas present to yourself?" he asked. He didn't want her to feel used, but it felt good to play this little game. To feel that someone was interested in him. Not as breadwinner, father or reporter, but interested in himself, his thinning hair, his thin arms.

"You serious?" she asked, as if he had just revealed his thoughts.

"Yes." He could hardly take back his question. Didn't even want to.

"Got time for a visit?"

"Sounds dangerous."

"For you?"

"For you?"

"Do you really think of me? Or more about what you could lose? Or about the possibility that you're not really serious? That you might like to look at my breasts, because you're vain and narcissistic, but cannot love a fat woman?"

"No idea," he said defiantly.

"Not a bad answer," she said.

"Do you judge all your friends? Do you judge what they say and think and do?"

She cocked her head. "Ouch. And yes, I do. Quite often. So?"

"I really need to make that hockey game."

She turned on her heel and left him with the *Grevenhorster Anzeiger*.

Benno sighed and returned to March 22, 1965, and the triplets who had been born that day. He had to hurry.

On March 27, a Sunday, shots had been fired on two policemen. Benno's eyes were tired and dry, and he rubbed them and could feel how red they had to be. But his pulse quickened—Gruber had been one of the cops. He and his former supervisor, Sergeant Reuter, had been on their way to Strathleven. The perpetrator or perpetrators hadn't been caught, but had fired on the police car from a hiding spot near the psychiatric hospital Huginwalde. The shooter or shooters had apparently fled on foot. The police officers had not seen anybody.

Gruber. He must have been a young man at that time, thought Benno. He had suffered a flesh wound. His colleague, who had been behind the wheel, had escaped unharmed, but had lost control of the car and hit a tree.

The motive of the perpetrator remained unclear. Benno was looking for other entries, but could not find anything further. Lübeck had apparently lost interest in the story.

He closed the folder, made a few notes and was about to open the *Grevenhorster Anzeiger*, when the speaker system was turned on, and a woman's voice announced that the library would close in half an hour. A short time later Hanne came into the reading room.

"How's it going in here?"

Benno groaned. "I need more time."

"But you have to be at your hockey game."

"It's not a joke."

"Not even funny."

"They expect a report tomorrow."

"I can help you."

"We only have twenty minutes."

She looked at him with pity. "I'm the librarian here."

"And you can just stay?"

She shrugged. "You have to catch a game."

"And if I cancel?"

"Are you not going to be missed?"

He shook his head.

She looked at him for a long time. Her voice was very quiet, without any expression, when she said, "That won't be cheap."

Benno exhaled, looked from her face to the microfiche folder.

"Let's stay then."

"Not that way," she replied.

He looked at her in confusion.

"You have to ask me. I'm not making you do anything. You have to want it."

He nodded and closed his eyes for a second and realized he was holding his breath. He nodded again, and his voice croaked. "Please stay."

When the lights in the building were turned off, Benno already regretted his decision. Muted voices reached him from the staircase, shuffling shoes, echoing steps, and then silence. He stood at the information desk on the third floor. His heart pounded and he felt like an intruder. Five minutes later, Hanne joined him. "Ready?" she asked.

Benno kissed her. Her neck smelled of cheap perfume, of crumpled pillows. She grabbed his hair and pulled him closer. He thought of Strathleven, saw the courtyard of the car dealer, his Christmas tree, and was afraid one of Hanne's colleagues might surprise them. They stood for several minutes, completely silent. The noise in Benno's ears made him deaf, he could not even hear his own breath.

Then, on cue, they slowly let go of each other, and Hanne smiled at him almost shyly. Together they went into the still-lit reading room. He switched on a second reader, happy to do something so simple and mechanical. Maybe he should call Carolin, maybe he should just storm out of the library. There was still time, there had been only a kiss, he could still retreat, he could still appease his conscience. He was married, he had a son, a dog, a house, a car, a job and . . . a silver chain around his neck.

"What I'm seeking is a report on Egon Friedrich's death. It was probably a suicide, but that may not have been mentioned in the newspaper. It must have happened sometime in March. I think, anyway. And maybe there are other things." He sat down in front of the screen.

"Other things," she said.

He laughed with her, relaxed somewhat. "The police officers who were shot—no idea what they wanted in Strathleven. My neighbor has only made hints, but there must have been a reason. Maybe it had to do with Friedrich, maybe not." He sighed. "And maybe it wasn't even in March. Anything that has to do with Strathleven."

"Anything?"

He nodded and went searching through the local section. "Something," he muttered to himself, like an incantation.

"No corpses," Hanne said. "If you were hoping for those. Shooting festival."

"Shooting festival?" He looked up. "In Strathleven?"

She nodded. "On March 26th. That appeared in the newspaper on the 28th. Brief report."

"Isn't that too early? In our village that was always in June. June or July."

She shrugged her shoulders. "Robert Wennersten was crowned. There's also a photo."

He rolled on his chair toward her. The man was wearing one of the big necklaces that Benno had observed during the autumn ball, a hat with a feather, and together with his wife he was laughing into the camera.

"Wennersten," repeated Benno. He had heard the name, but he hadn't met the family.

He wanted to kiss her neck, but she turned her head and offered him her lips.

"Am I working off my debt?"

"Is it hard work?" she asked.

He shook his head, rolled back to his reader. Ten minutes later, he finally found what he was looking for—Egon Friedrich's obituary. Beloved husband, father, member of the community . . . Friedrich had left behind three children, two sons, and a daughter. Otto was the eldest, the other children Benno couldn't remember meeting at all.

When he showed his find to Hanne, her first question was, "Nothing else?"

"There is another one," he said, pointing to the obituary paid for by the shooting club. "Seems to have been popular. Was only fifty-nine."

"This is much larger than that of the family," said Hanne.

"Quarter-page."

"Couldn't celebrate with the other shooters."

"No great loss," Benno said with a grin. "I was at the autumn ball and I . . ." He paused, leaned forward and read the obituary again. "But he was not the king."

Hanne looked at him blankly.

"The king must die," he said, and told her about New Year's Eve, the attack on the pastor and the wooden figurine in Heintz' workshop.

"When your son receives a crown, it doesn't mean that it has to involve the shooting club, right?"

"But I had hoped it would. So it's just a silly game. Like a scavenger hunt. Or this guy they burn every year. In England."

"Guy Fawkes?"

Benno nodded. "The pastor doesn't seem to like the shooters much."

"Really?" asked Hanne. "In the article about the shooting festival they say that the church congregation and the shooters held a common church service."

"When?"

"On Sunday. After the festival."

Benno scratched his head. That Friedrich had died on the day of the shooting competition could have been a coincidence, but why was somebody shooting at the police the day after? Also a coincidence? Friedrich had been found in the old hospital. That's what Wehrke had told him anyway, and Gruber and Reuter had been in an accident. Huginwalde. He had never heard the name of the clinic before. Were the three events connected? And what did they have to do with Tim and Pastor Cornelius?

It was almost eight o'clock. The hockey game had started half an hour earlier without him. Tomorrow he would have to plagiarize the report from the *Lübecker Nachrichten* and he felt already guilty.

"How much time do you have?" she asked.

He shrugged and looked at his fingernails, which were not very well cut. What did he want from Hanne? Did he really want to put his marriage in jeopardy?

"Let's go."

———————

In light, snowy rain they ran through the streets of Lübeck's old town. Hanne gave him occasional kisses, like breadcrumbs. He followed their trail. The cold couldn't sober him up.

Her apartment was on the third floor. His shoes left dirty, wet tracks, and she took them off in the hallway. He felt oddly reassured. He carefully removed the little silver cross and put it in a pocket. He did not want to leave it lying around. He almost believed Carolin could watch him otherwise.

"Magic," he said.

"Did you expect unicorn posters?"

"A cauldron," he said softly. Then he unbuttoned her shirt. She kissed him, but otherwise remained completely motionless.

The tattoos started just below the deep neckline. How strange it was that she was wearing a white bra on top of the images and symbols. He took his time playing with his panic, his guilt, but still didn't want to miss a single moment. A wild joy rose up in him, a joy which he couldn't explain and that stung his hands like so many needles.

Benno pulled Hanne away from the lit hallway to a room whose door stood half- open. It was probably her living room—the sofa, the small stereo system and the bookshelves said so. It smelled cold, somewhat flowery, and Benno led her to the surprisingly large windows through which light from the street lamps below reached them. The sound of footsteps on the pavement was audible.

He pulled down her shirt and took off her bra. Her breasts stretched, the nipples were pierced with rings.

He followed the lines of the tattoos on her back, drew them with his finger. In the middle was a leopard in black. Pale green, gray and red leaves and plants stretched out at his sides, but they were soon replaced by geometrical figures and symbols. Hanne's forearms were designed more playfully—Buddha and sun were paired with a geisha and a galloping horse, with flowers and leaves—it seemed as though she had only been practicing. But her upper arms and shoulders were covered with jagged rectangles, through which green and red snakes slithered. These appeared to be the armor of a medieval knight, who was preparing for battle.

He unbuttoned her pants and let them fall to the ground. Knelt down and slipped off her black socks. Her nails were too long, her feet wide but well-formed and completely naked, the tattoos only reached to just below the calves. He took three steps back and let the hazy light fall on Hanne's body. He tried to memorize it.

There were steps on the stairs, then they heard the slamming of a door. He almost wanted to tear open the window and—and what? Raise his arms skyward and scream and howl or sing? Her apartment was full of noises.

The leopard also stretched out on her stomach, his legs reached down to her thighs. She had turned to him and looked pitiable, grotesque, frightening, and silly. And a lump in his throat told him that he cared, that this body excited him, shook him. He felt very tender toward her, and the next moment he wanted to slap her. She was a few years older than Benno, her skin wasn't as tight as that of a young girl. Her legs weren't muscular. He himself had a sprawling varicose vein in his left leg and flat feet. His forehead had to shine even in the room's darkness. All this he was aware of, and yet it did nothing to cool him off.

—18—

The new edition of the *Kurier* had come out, and Benno looked sullenly at his stolen piece. It wasn't bad, read quite well, but somehow it didn't sound as though he had been there.

"And you weren't," Holger said cheerfully. "Welcome to the club. You didn't think that I'm the only one here who is lazy?" Benno sighed.

"I have a long article on page five. Scrupulously researched. Should interest you."

Benno flipped to page five. Since Christmas he had thought little about the dead waitress. But this Thursday she was worth three columns—Holger had obviously been unable to think of anything better. The too-ornate turns of phrase left little doubt that Holger had copied them from several newspapers. But when Benno glanced at the photo of the victim, the one that had been in every paper three weeks prior, he paused. His irritation with Carolin, even the night with Hanne disappeared from his head.

"You're trembling," Holger observed soberly. "Has Bad Segeberg won again?"

"The photo," Benno said, holding out the article, "where do you have it?"

He had seen it a dozen times. A laughing Irina, somewhere in a park or a wooded area. It was the photo that had been issued by the police. But all the papers had cropped it to include only Irina's face and upper body. Benno had never seen the entire photo. Holger had certainly been too lazy to edit it for publication. Now he rummaged through his drawers and finally found a copy, which the police had made in the hope of receiving leads.

Irina Sobieski stood smiling in the grass, the trees behind her sharper now. She wore a striped blouse, her hands were folded in front of her body, and in her fingers she held a leash. At her feet sat a large dog with a short, dense coat, and it seemed almost as if he was laughing at the camera. Around his neck the coat was thick and bulky. His right eye was still intact. It was Rasmus.

Around midnight Benno was awakened by Carolin's scream. He jumped off the couch and ran to the second floor. Tim was not in his room, his bed was rumpled, but neither the boy nor Rasmus were anywhere in the house.

He grabbed one of the magazines that lay on Tim's desk. *Tattoo* was the simple title, and the paper was cheap. But the pages were printed in color and women and men showed off their half-naked bodies. Tattoo artists gave interviews about their work. But there were other articles, reports about people who scarred themselves deliberately and buried small objects under their skin. There were dozens of pictures of scars arranged in patterns, forming intricate drawings. Most of them covered arms and legs, where others could see them well. Benno couldn't help thinking of Hanne's Leopard.

"How long has he had these?" asked Benno. He was wearing only his pajama pants and felt naked all of a sudden.

"What does that mean?" Carolin stared at the magazine and then yanked open the drawers. Other issues came to light, the whole drawer was full of them. All of a sudden she held something in her hands and gasped.

Benno came up to her and grabbed what Carolin had found. Slowly he pulled the knife from the leather sheath. He recognized it: it was the same knife Manfred had shown him in summer. A hunting scene was engraved on the blade. And while he still stared at the knife, looking for possible answers, Carolin emptied the trash on the ground, tore open Tim's closet and threw clothes and toys in a big pile. "Shit, shit, shit," she swore.

Benno turned and ran out of the bedroom, rushed down the stairs into the hall. He slipped into his sandals, took his coat out and yelled, "Call the police!"

But when he pulled open the entrance door, there stood Tim with dirty feet and dirty pajamas. Beside him sat a wet and disheveled Rasmus.

"Tim." Carolin came down the stairs and pushed past Benno. Benno felt nauseous, as if someone had kicked him in the stomach. Something was wrong with Tim's face.

Carolin held her son in her embrace. But Benno gently took her shoulders and pulled her away.

"Tim," he said, hoping that saying the name might work a miracle. He grabbed him by the shoulders and turned him into the light to get a better look at his face.

Carolin's scream made the boy wince, then both began to cry.

"Why did you do that?" Carolin was struggling with tears. "This is not going to smooth out again. People who mutilate themselves are not like you."

Tim wept. "You're not like me. No one is like me."

His left eye was half closed, a scar ran from one corner of his mouth to his ear. His new injuries gave his face a sinister expression.

"I didn't do it on purpose," he said tearfully. "I didn't see the branch."

Benno pulled Tim closer and stroked his head. "It's all right," he said. "You're back, you're back," he whispered, and the boy relaxed. "You're back." Following a sudden impulse, he asked, "You went to the Miracle Oak?" Even before Tim had time to reply, Benno knew the answer.

The boy nodded. "But it was so tight, I barely fit through the hole."

———

At three o'clock in the morning, Benno was still awake, and he got up quietly and went over to Tim's room. He switched on the lamp on the bedside table, one of those rotating apparatuses, which threw its light through transparent paper and made animal shapes run in a circle along the walls. It was a gentle light, but it woke Tim within a second.

"What's up?" His face was puffy, his eyes squeezed shut.

"Come on." Benno led the boy down the stairs into the dining room.

Tim wore clean yellow pajamas, with ships and lighthouses printed on the material. It wasn't one of his favorite pajamas. Rasmus trotted after them, shook himself, and sat down in front of Benno, as if he expected his food. He still smelled damp.

"Do you want a glass of water? Or a hot chocolate?"

"With marshmallows?" Tim asked.

"Sure."

"Is Mom coming too?"

"No."

Benno heated the milk, fished in the overcrowded closet for cocoa powder, and found a half-empty pack of marshmallows. Tim's eyes followed him closely, though his face was still creased from the pillows.

"Are you mad?" he asked.

"No," Benno said. "I'm worried about you."

"Can I tell Mom about this?"

"What the hell," Benno blurted out. "What is it? Are you afraid of me?"

"Can I?"

"Sure thing." Benno exhaled. He suddenly felt guilty. "I just don't want to wake her." Why wouldn't Tim trust him? Why was he nervous when Carolin was not around?

"Thank you," Tim said when Benno handed him the steaming cup of hot chocolate. The sugar foam on the surface died a slow death.

"So," Benno began, and poured himself a cup. "I just wanted to have a little talk with you." He pulled out Manfred's knife and put it on the table. "Did you steal it?"

The boy shook his head. "He gave it to me." He stared in front of him and blew on the sinking marshmallow. Rasmus was lying down at his feet, looking up from time to time in hopes he might snatch a treat.

"I just want to tell you that we won't give up."

"What?"

"We will continue to fight. You shouldn't feel as though you are alone."

"Okay." It was obvious that Tim had no idea what Benno wanted to tell him.

"I don't think that you cut yourself just out of curiosity." All of a sudden he realized that Tim had done it more often than they had assumed. Already in Berlin, that was for certain. How could he and Carolin not have noticed? Even the bicycle accident might have been intentional. Tim swallowed, held on to his hot chocolate.

"You're mad at me," he said.

"No," said Benno, "but to cut yourself is dangerous. You're not one of those . . ." He could only come up with a vague gesture. "These people with their injuries. You cannot help it. They have been disfigured, they would do everything to be normal again. And the others, those who pierce themselves or get tattooed . . . for them it's only pictures, jewelry." Benno's mouth was dry. "With you it's different. This is not like a fad or a haircut. You can't remove your scars, ever."

"They can't remove their tattoos either," Tim said. His hands were still clutching the cup.

Benno was suddenly aware of the absurdity of the situation. He had a tattooed lover in Lübeck. Two days ago, he had traced the legs of a leopard with his mouth. He could no longer speak with Tim, as though he were an adult. He was only a seven-year-old boy.

"But they do it voluntarily and without harming themselves." Benno knew that anger would not help him with Tim. "I'm afraid for you. You have nothing to prove to the people in the village. You're not a king, and whatever they see in you is just their imagination. You are Tim, you're our son. That's it."

Tears fell on Tim's lighthouse pajamas. He tried not to let it show, tried to suppress every sound coming from his throat. His face suddenly became red, his lips trembled. "They didn't come."

Benno looked at him puzzled. "Who didn't?"

"You said that the king must die, and then they appeared on New Year's Eve at the church. But no one took me away."

Benno walked around Rasmus and picked up the boy.

"Damn it," he said softly, squeezing the warm body. "Damn you." Tim wasn't disappointed that the doctors hadn't found a cure, but because no one had tried to kill him.

"Don't do that again. Do you hear? Can you promise me?" The boy sank into Benno's arms, suddenly became heavy. He sobbed, and it was an ugly sound. Benno felt his shirt getting wet, but he only held Tim tighter. The boy wrapped his arms around Benno's neck. Then he whispered, "But it feels good."

— 19 —

The restaurant where Irina had been working was not hard to find, but the colleague who had contacted the police no longer worked there. When Benno remarked that he was from the newspaper, the bartender went into the kitchen and returned a little later with the name and phone number. Benno thanked him, and called Ania Walczak from the phone in the foyer. No one answered.

When he later tried again, a man answered and mumbled something unintelligible.

"Is Ms. Walczak home?" he asked, and a second later it clacked, and he could hear someone walk off and softly call to Ania.

Finally, the receiver was picked up again, and a timid voice said, "Yes, hello?"

Benno pretended he was writing an article about the murder case.

"I've already told you everything," the woman's voice said. "I've already had enough problems."

"Problems?"

"With the authorities. My documents. I don't want to talk to anyone."

Before she could hang up, Benno said quickly, "I have Rasmus."

"Who?"

"Irina's dog. I found him. In my village. I'm worried."

"Voytek? What do you mean, you worry? Irina is dead."

Benno tried to explain, got tangled up in the web of scars, kings, his gruesome discovery two days after he'd moved to Strathleven. Finally he said, "I believe that the killer is from my village. And I'm afraid for my boy. Could we maybe meet somewhere? In a coffee shop? I won't make any trouble for you." For a moment there was only silence.

"Hello?"

"Yes, yes," said the woman on the other end. "But it will cost you something."

Benno inhaled deeply, tried to stay calm. "How much?"

"Three hundred."

"Do you have time today?"

"No, not today. I can meet you tomorrow afternoon. At four o'clock."

"Tomorrow afternoon," repeated Benno and wrote down the address Walczak gave him.

"The sergeant is on patrol."

"Can I find him anywhere?" Benno asked the woman at the front desk. "Does he have a prescribed route?"

The woman had a bad perm, and her face was small and looked stony, but as soon as he had asked, she smiled, revealing small, yellow teeth. She looked at her wrist where she wore a huge diver's watch. "Right now he is probably in the Café Horst, eating his almond croissant," she said. "If you hurry, you can catch him there."

Just as she had said, Gruber sat with a colleague inside the pastry shop. In front of him stood a cup of coffee and an empty plate.

"Good morning, Sergeant," greeted Benno. "Almond croissant?"

Gruber looked at him with wide eyes, apparently not recognizing his visitor. Then he grinned. "Did Frieda tell on me again?"

"May I sit down?"

Gruber glanced at his colleague, pressed his lips together and said, "It's a free world. Sit down. How can we help you?" He pointed to the second officer. "This is Sergeant Herrmann. And you are?"

"I was at your office in early December, because of the murder case. Benno Diedrich."

Gruber nodded. "Yes, quite right," he said eagerly, but it still didn't seem to register. "Do you want anything?" He turned to the waitress and waved, then pointed a finger at Benno.

"Well, who's dead now?"

"I'm not here because someone died," Benno said.

"You're not?"

"You were shot at twenty-four years ago."

Gruber's brow furrowed, then he shook his head in resignation. "You're rummaging around in old stuff?"

"Have you ever found out who it was?"

"Torsten, that was before your time," Gruber told the second officer. "When this was still the Wild North." Then he turned back to Benno. "Didn't have much time to look around that day. Reuter was in a hurry to pick out the biggest tree. There were a lot of tracks and footprints at the site—it has always attracted lovers and other idiots—but we didn't find anything, not even the cartridges."

"You had just found Egon Friedrich's corpse."

Gruber took off his cap and scratched his small curly hair. "You're right. I had forgotten about the incident."

"Suicide," Benno said. "But in the village it is rumored that Friedrich was stabbed to death."

Gruber turned around to get the waitress' attention. "Barbara, I could still . . ." He didn't have to finish his sentence, the waitress was already nodding eagerly. "Who told you that?"

"Someone who was at the funeral."

Gruber nodded. "I didn't take old Mr. Friedrich down, but he was hanging from the balcony of Huginwald clinic."

"Huginwald?" asked the younger officer.

"Insane asylum," Gruber said.

"I thought maybe you knew something, and that was why they shot at you. As a kind of warning?"

Gruber laughed uproariously. When the waitress put the almond croissant before him, and he wanted to thank her, he choked instead and began to cough. "Listen," he brought out with difficulty. "You're a strange clan, you Strathleven people." He took a deep breath, and his flushed face slowly relaxed. "That happened so long ago, it's not even true anymore. And if Friedrich had been murdered, I'm sure the doctor would have noticed it."

"So you weren't in the village to investigate Egon Friedrich's death? To ask questions?"

"Good heavens, no. We were probably just driving around in the area.

Reuter loved his liquor, always kept a flask in the glove compartment. After the accident, he never touched another drink."

"Were you perhaps at the shooting festival?"

Gruber was taken aback. "The what?"

"Strathleven celebrated its shooting festival the day before. Were you there? Perhaps because of a fight? An accident?"

The police officer nodded at his young colleague. "Torsten, go ahead to the car. I'll be right there."

Sergeant Herrmann blushed before he rose, pulled his cap down over his forehead and left the table.

"So what's really on your mind?"

Benno sighed and told the policeman about the slogans, Tim and the crown, from the upcoming shooting festival and the attack on the pastor. Gruber listened attentively. He just nodded from time to time, stirring his coffee.

"The pastor hasn't contacted us," he said, when Benno had ended. "As far as I know."

"He hasn't. Says it was just child's play. Doesn't want to make enemies in town, not for himself and not for his church."

"He's a smart man."

"Why?"

"Are you always asking this many questions?"

"Why? I'm a journalist."

"Oh, is that what it's called now? Last time I talked to you you were at the *Strandkurier*." Gruber laughed and didn't take notice of Benno's irritated gaze. "You won't make many friends running around asking questions."

"Have you ever wondered who shot at you and why?"

"Sure I did. We're the police. We can't just let everyone shoot at us."

"And have you found out who did it?"

Gruber took a final sip of coffee. A crumb from the almond croissant hung in one corner of his mouth.

"We have Ingo Schmoeh," he said ambiguously.

"He comes from Strathleven. Meets the local businessmen every Sunday at the inn."

"Does he? Is there a law against it? Ingo understands his work. Before him, we had a Hubert, and before that a Gottfried. People know Ingo. He knows who he can talk to and who he should leave alone."

"And who are the people he leaves alone?"

"You have to ask him. I don't need or want to know. I don't give a damn. Strathleven is Strathleven, and I don't show my face there if I don't have to."

"Is that why you sent Officer Herrmann away?"

Gruber spread his arms theatrically. "Who did I send away? I haven't sent anyone away. But you, Mr. . . .'"

"Diedrich."

"I have no idea why we were at the hospital that day, and I don't know what happened back then at the shooting festival. Maybe not everything was the way it should have been, but then again, the police don't tell people how they should live their lives. If we get a call, we'll go check it out. Period. Just because someone smears slogans on the walls, doesn't mean we're going to start a murder investigation. If the pastor doesn't come to us, we won't come to him. And anyway—what do you really want?"

"What do I want?" Benno was puzzled.

"Move away, if Strathleven frightens you. I guess the village will get along without you. It's a free country, anybody can move to all sorts of places. Today you see slogans, and twenty years ago, someone hanged himself. So what? Is someone going to hang himself again? Because it happened in your village twenty years ago? Is that your theory?"

"I don't have a theory. Not really," Benno admitted.

"There you go! That's the smartest thing you've said so far." Gruber stood up abruptly, grabbed his hat and walked to the checkout.

"Wait!" Benno ran after the officer. "Do you have any suspects in the rape of Sybille Antler?" The girl might have remembered the offender, or his car. Benno still believed that she had to have known him. Or the attacker had known her. "Have the parents filed a report?"

Gruber turned crimson, paid, and then walked out to the parking lot without another word.

"Because it happened in your village twenty years ago," muttered

Benno. He sat back down at the table. The sun shone through the windows on the white tablecloth.

"Twenty years ago," he repeated, and rolled a crumb between his fingers. Something took shape in his mind, but for the life of him, he couldn't tell what it was.

———

He called Martin Wehrke from the Café Horst, but there was no answer. Nevertheless, he went back to Strathleven and stopped at Wehrke's house on Rensfelder Kirchenweg. His car was parked outside, and Wehrke opened the door before Benno had the opportunity to ring the bell.

"I tried to call," Benno apologized. "Didn't want to barge in on you again."

"You're always welcome," Wehrke said. "I just came back from Hamburg. Would you like some coffee?"

Benno eagerly accepted. He felt that Wehrke was the only one in the village who didn't belong here. Although he had been born in Strathleven and had returned after retiring from the university, the village didn't seem to have claimed him.

"It's a Kona blend. Hawaii. You'll like it."

While Wehrke was busy in the kitchen, Benno went to one of the large living room windows. A few weeks ago the strange Christmas tree had stood here and blocked the view. Now over the brown fields hung white, wispy clouds. The blue of the sky seemed not quite clean and deathly pale, and the sun was as bright as a torch. He closed his eyes for a moment, felt a pain behind his right ear.

He turned to Wehrke and asked, "What does your nephew actually study?"

"Law. Last semester it was still law, I think. But that could change quickly."

"He's young."

"And stupid. He has no business sense. If it were up to him, he would sell the store. It's about to go bankrupt anyway. But don't spread the news." He sighed. "Probably everyone in the village knows it anyway."

"Nobody is buying tractors?"

"They want to, but the farmers have no money. The harvests have been poor, the farmers lack funds and credit. Also, they can buy everything cheaper in Lübeck. It's a miracle my brother has hung on for this long.

"And the concrete plant?"

Wehrke shrugged. "It hangs in the balance. Andreas has an offer from a competitor, but he would shut down the plant immediately. And then people here would lose their jobs."

Benno shook his head. "I just came back from Grevenhorst. Spoke with Sergeant Gruber."

"He didn't talk."

Benno was taken aback. "You know him?"

"That would be an exaggeration. He's not retired yet?" He shook his head. "Not a bad man, but not very imaginative."

"Somebody here tried to shoot him once."

"In Strathleven?"

"In 1965. Just a day after a shooting festival. Do you know Ingo Schmoeh?"

Wehrke shook his head, and poured coffee into two large cups. He handed one to Benno and then sat down in a chair in the living room. Benno took a seat opposite him.

"There has to be a king," he exclaimed. "My son received a crown for Christmas, by whom we don't know. But he cannot be the king." Then he told Wehrke what had happened in the meantime.

"You're worried about your boy," said his host. "The King. What did Gruber say?"

"He doesn't want to get involved in Strathleven's business."

Wehrke nodded, took a sip of coffee and then adjusted his glasses. "Wotan's hunting party is an old tradition. This explains the two ravens that you found during the first of the Twelve Nights. The birds were Wotan's companions, Hugin and Munin. At daybreak, they left to explore the world and later told Wotan the news."

"The old hospital."

"Yes, its name was inspired by the legend. Hugin means 'thought.' Although Munin, 'memory,' would have been a better fit for a psychiatric hospital, don't you think? Hundreds of years ago, it was the custom to appoint a member of the community to be a kind of representative of the gods. In this area he served Wotan."

"A representative of the gods? Like the pastor?"

Wehrke nodded. "Cornelius has a tough time here. The people are superstitious, and before he moved to the village, his predecessor never interfered with the affairs of the village. Cornelius has made it clear that he wants nothing to do with the Twelve Nights." He thought for a while. "Have the people been hostile toward your son?"

"On the contrary. They seem . . . to consider him something special."

"Because of his skin?"

Benno nodded. "But why should they give him a crown, only to kill him later? He's only just arrived, nobody knew about his condition." Then he said quietly, "Can I confide in you? I hardly know you, but . . ."

"I'm gay, and the pastor does not like me."

Benno's laughter died quickly. "No, but . . ."

"I have good whiskey. Want one? And before you tell me any secrets— are you sure you can trust me? After all, I could be the king. If there is one."

"No. So, yes. But . . ." For a moment, Benno closed his eyes, then opened them again and said, "The murderer must come from the village."

"What?"

"The woman the pastor and I found last summer. Most people assume that someone from Lübeck or elsewhere just used Strathleven to get rid of the body. But our dog, Rasmus, he belonged to the dead woman."

Wehrke looked at him with wide eyes. "Your dog?"

Benno told him how they had found Rasmus, and that he had recognized him in the police shot.

"But the killer could have released him at the same time he dumped the corpse."

"But Bauer Reincke said that Rasmus had been in the village since the previous winter. He called him the ghost dog because he was so thin. Rasmus must have been nearly a year in Strathleven."

For a few moments it was completely silent in Wehrke's living room. The sunlight on the floor suddenly disappeared, and when Benno turned his head, he saw that dark clouds had moved in. The pain behind his ear had increased, and his stomach growled uncomfortably.

"That could mean," Wehrke said, putting his coffee on a small table, "that the woman knew someone from the village."

"But wouldn't she have come looking for her dog?"

There was no answer, and after a few moments of silence Benno stood up to say goodbye. "Thank you," he said, shaking Wehrke's hand.

"Maybe you should talk to Gruber again." Wehrke sighed. "Or go directly to the Lübeck police."

"Yeah, maybe," Benno agreed. "You have a nice place here," he said. "You could almost forget that you are in the country."

Wehrke followed Benno to the door.

"Sometimes I forget myself."

Benno was too nervous to go to the office, and he had almost two hours left until his meeting with Ania Walczak. After he had bought Boxazin at a pharmacy, he sat down at a cafe, ordered some water and dissolved two tablets in it.

For a few minutes he read the sports section of the *Lübecker Nachrichten* and skimmed the reports he would later rewrite. It was cheating, but the alternative didn't look better. His head was filled with metallic echoes. He had told Wehrke about Rasmus, and he almost regretted it. He trusted the former professor, but what if he told his brother anything about Benno's suspicions? Benno didn't even know if the two were still on friendly terms, but it seemed likely. What if the village started talking about his investigation? He should have kept his mouth shut. He had to protect Tim, even though he had no idea from whom or what.

Whom could Irina have known in the village? Who might have seen her? Who had attacked Sybille Antler to find out what she knew about the dead woman?

At half past three, he made his way to Fleischhauerstraße. He found the Café Affenbrot, which was known for its brightly painted walls and an exclusively vegetarian menu. Benno ordered a tea and a piece of cake that was as colorful as the walls. His stomach could hardly stand it.

Ten minutes after the appointed time, a small, slender woman with a narrow face and long, bleached hair entered the premises. When her searching gaze met Benno's, she came over to his table.

"Nice here, yes?" Ania Walczak put her purse on the table and smiled at him. "Have you remembered to bring the money?" she asked without lowering her voice.

"Yes, yes," Benno said. "Right now?"

"Right now. Then I'll talk to you."

"But I don't know if you can tell me anything at all."

"Risk." Her teeth were as white as china and gleamed slightly bluish.

Benno reached for his wallet and took out three one-hundred mark bills, which he had withdrawn in the morning. Walczak put them in her purse.

"Good," she said, sitting down opposite him. "What do you want?"

"When did you see Irina for the last time?"

"We weren't friends."

"But you knew her."

"We worked together. And then she stopped coming one day. She wasn't here legally."

"And you never asked yourself what became of her?"

Walczak shook her head. "It was September. Or maybe October. In 1987."

"Did she ever mention that she met a man here?"

"Maybe."

"Maybe? Who was he?"

A smile crossed Walczak's face, and Benno could now see the freckles under her makeup. "He was married."

"Do you know where he came from?"

She shook her head, and a faint smell of hairspray reached Benno. His stomach started to turn. "What did he look like? Did he ever come to the restaurant?"

Walczak nodded. "He was tall, maybe as old as you. Or a little older."

"Did he come from Lübeck?"

She shrugged her shoulders. "I don't think so."

Benno swallowed. "As I said, my son found Rasmus—Voytek. And . . . I cannot explain everything, but it could be that your friend got into trouble in our village."

"You live where Irina was found? Do you want to pin anything on me?"

"No, no," Benno assured her. "I'm just trying to figure out what happened."

"For your newspaper?"

"No, not anymore. Just to make sure that nothing is going to happen to my son."

Ania Walczak seemed to think about this. "No story?"

He shook his head.

She leaned forward, her bangles scraping across the table.

"I think Irina's friend was a . . . man of the church."

"A pastor?" Benno sank back in his chair. "Was he tall? A bit bulky? Thin hair?"

She nodded. "Yes, that could have been him. I only saw him once, I think. But he was tall and not thin. Irina liked him."

"Do you know what kind of car he drove? Maybe his name?"

She shook her head. "He was married. Irina was very discreet."

Benno sighed. His hands were sweaty, and he wanted nothing more than to lie down, to darken the windows and hide from the world around him.

"Are we done?" Ania Walczak asked.

"Yes, I think so. Thank you," Benno stammered. "But why didn't you tell the police? About the affair?"

Walczak grinned. "I'm not here legally. Just like Irina. I don't want any trouble. It could be that he is coming back. That he might try to kill me."

"And why did you tell me?"

She shrugged. "You're not the police."

Benno nodded. "Can I call you maybe, if I have more questions?"

She nodded, stood up, and smiled.

"Good luck." Then she added with a straight face, "No story. I read the newspapers."

"No story," Benno assured her again. He could hardly look at the bright walls and lights anymore, but he forced himself to watch Irina's colleague until she had left the cafe. But the only thing he saw in his mind was Pastor Cornelius' head bandage and his crooked smile.

=== 20 ===

Hanne led him to a worn, green sofa, which stood in the break room of the library.

"Just lie down," she said. "You look pale. Goes nicely with the couch."

Benno tried to smile.

"I'll come back later."

To keep out the harsh light, he took off his coat and pulled it over his face. Within minutes he was asleep.

On waking, the room was completely dark. He sat up quickly and listened. He could not see the face of his clock. His head was free of pain, but it felt as though all its interior walls had collapsed like aging concrete and been removed by an excavator.

"Finally awake?"

He spun around and saw Hanne sitting in an armchair behind him. At least, he saw her silhouette there. "What time is it?" he asked. "I have to go home."

"After eight. Do you want to call first?"

"Yes, yes. No, or maybe yes." He sank back on the sofa. The conversations of the morning and afternoon returned in small shreds, mixed and mingled in his ears until he could hear nothing else. "The pastor . . . he was Irina's friend. Her lover."

"Your pastor? The Baptist?"

"Yes," Benno said in the darkness. He could make out a table and several chairs now, and Hanne's face and hands seemed slightly brighter than her clothes. "Is everyone gone?"

"Yes," she said.

"And they think it's normal that you stay behind with some strange guy?"

"I told them you were my half brother. Terminal disease. Only a few months to live."

"You did not."

"Sure did."

There was a rustling, and a few seconds later, she knelt on the floor beside him. Benno did not resist, lay very still and let Hanne have her way.

A deer jumped out onto the road and froze, getting larger and larger, almost filling the whole windscreen, but before the car came to a stop, it galloped back in the direction from which it had come.

It all felt very new and wrong, as if someone had taken apart the parts of his life and glued them back together at will. The car did not feel like his family's anymore, but like the car in which he drove to meet his lover. Lübeck no longer meant afternoons in the office, but a jumble of excuses, lies, and bad conscience. Whatever he believed to be reality in Lübeck—that Cornelius had been Irina's lover, and that Rasmus had belonged to the now dead waitress—appeared laughable in Strathleven. An obscene fantasy.

And Tim? He was a stranger who lived in a village full of strangers, and Carolin had become someone he could barely recognize. Nothing around him seemed recognizable anymore, and when he looked in the rearview mirror, he no longer recognized himself.

What should he do with Walczak's information? Ask the pastor to confess? In front of his wife and children? Should he go to Gruber, and tell on Cornelius?

First the pastor killed his lover—maybe she had wanted to be more than a lover, maybe she had come to Strathleven to confront him—and then he dragged her into a field and let the children find the body and ask him for help. That he hadn't wanted to mention the children in the police report seemed obvious now. Not because he wanted to protect them, but because he didn't want them to testify against him. Even if the children had seen or found something strange, no one would ask.

The dog. Rasmus made no sense. Why had he been in the village for so long? Irina had died last summer, the body had not been decomposed. Yet Rasmus had appeared already the previous winter in Strathleven.

Irina was murdered in the summer. If no one had seen her in Lübeck during the months prior, and Rasmus had been in Strathleven since at least December, there could be a simple explanation.

But what had she done for nine or ten months in Strathleven?

———

Tim was already in bed, but Carolin was still sitting with a magazine and a glass of wine in the living room. Already in the hall, where it smelled of wet dog, he could feel that their conversation would not be peaceful.

He deserved it. But that made it even harder. Benno put his bag down in the hallway, and hung up his coat. Then he went into the kitchen, took a glass from the cupboard and poured himself some of the cheap red wine. The bottle was half empty.

"Hey," he said when he finally stepped into the living room.

Carolin sat down her glass on the table and turned her head in his direction. It seemed to take her a big effort.

"Where were you?"

Benno looked at his clock. It was half past ten. No party in Berlin had begun before ten o'clock. He sat down opposite Carolin and tried a partial truth. He could not even remember which handball or hockey club had played tonight.

"I made some inquiries."

He could see that she had expected something different, and that she had already devised a strategy for that 'something different.' Her answer was delayed.

"And why didn't you call? I called the newsroom, and they had no idea where you were. Margit told me that you hadn't even shown up in the office."

Benno sighed. He should have called the newsroom to establish an alibi.

"They haven't fired you, right?"

"Margit probably would have told you."

"And what kind of research did you do?"

"You weren't at a peace rally. Cornelius' kids blabbed. You were protesting against abortion. Together with Pastor Thomas."

Carolin looked at him in silence, seemed to want to say something. Her lips were stained with wine. But eventually she took her half-empty glass, stood up and walked out of the room.

Benno remained in his armchair. What would he tell Carolin? That he had paid a waitress three hundred marks to talk about her dead colleague? That the pastor had maybe killed a woman and stabbed her with knives and forks? That there was a king in the village, but no one wanted to talk about him?

Suddenly he felt a hand on his head and the next moment Carolin said, "I should have told you."

His initial alarm gave way to tenderness, and he grabbed her hand and pulled Carolin down to him. "It was because of the murder," he said. "And because people constantly stare at Tim. I was worried."

"Because of the murder? What in the world does that have to do with us?" She sat down on his lap, pressed herself against him.

"I don't know yet," he said, "but . . ." He broke off. Could he tell Carolin about Rasmus? Of his suspicions against the pastor? "But I wasn't even mentioned in the police report. They messed up everything."

"Who cares if you're in the police report?" It was not an accusation, but astonishment. "Her killer is long gone. Does it still upset you?"

"Yes," he said. "I didn't want to tell you anything, because, because . . ."

"Don't you trust me?"

"I don't trust the police. And I don't want to drag Tim into this."

Carolin stared at him. "Then simply stop it. You can't undo the murder."

He closed his eyes for a moment and then said incoherently, "Manfred jerked off on our car. The old one, the Beetle."

"What?" She punched his shoulder. "Why didn't you tell me?"

He shrugged, and warmed himself in her sudden attention. How long this moment would last, he didn't know, but he felt so guilty that he completely devoted himself to it.

"Did he do it on Heintz' car too?"

"I think he doesn't like Fords."

His affair with Hanne made this moment even sweeter, because he had not earned it, would never be able to earn it again. And the affair wasn't over yet; two hours ago, Hanne had opened his zipper. He was guilty, and that guilt made him suspicious of Carolin, yet it also made him fall in love with her again. What had happened in Lauenburg? His own escapade made Carolin's lies and omissions look more serious, made her unfaithfulness seem likely. What if she had fallen back into old patterns? If she was looking for love and encouragement in men's restrooms and in the rear seats of cars? The more this uncertainty plagued him, the more he loved Carolin, the tighter he held her. "Maybe we should move away from Strathleven," he whispered. "We can go anywhere."

"Where to?" She nibbled gently on his ear.

"No idea. To Lake Constance, Munich or Wiesbaden."

"Not a city."

"Hinteruppermeadowharborarbor."

"I'd love to go to Hinteruppermeadowharborarbor," she purred. "But we already live there. I like it here."

"Me too," he said. "But the people here are so strange."

"I think it's beautiful here. Tim likes it too."

"That's what worries me."

She pulled away from him, looked at him with slightly narrowed eyes. "It worries you that my son has settled in here?"

"No, no." He tried to laugh and could feel Carolin's body stiffen.

"But the crown. They bring him gifts, stare at him strangely."

"That scared me too, but they probably just think that he's something special. And it's nice for him not to be viewed as sick."

Benno sighed. She was right, Tim enjoyed the attention. But he also ran through the streets with a dead woman's dog, and the pastor had known and killed Rasmus' owner.

He didn't want to destroy the peace, but he could no longer hold back. He grabbed his bag and pulled out the photo of Irina and Rasmus. "Look," he said, and handed it to Carolin.

She looked at it closely. "Who is that?"

"The woman I found last summer. Look at the dog. I only discovered the photo this week."

Carolin held it close to her face. "Looks like Rasmus. Is that what you mean?"

"I'm certain it's Rasmus."

Carolin looked very serious for a moment, then she laughed uproariously. "Is that why you're so strange? Because Rasmus looks like this dog? He is a mutt, thousands of dogs look like him. And his eye doesn't even look black."

"But Rasmus was here in the village. He was probably shot here." Benno could not longer hide his agitation. "I found the dead woman. We have her dog. He was called Voytek."

"How do you know that?"

Benno noticed that he had made a mistake, but it was too late to keep his meeting with Ania Walczak secret. "I spoke with her former colleague."

"Why? You're not the police."

"This," he held up the photo, "scared me."

"But that's just coincidence. And didn't the farmer say that Rasmus roamed the village for a long time? This may not have been her dog. The woman died in the summer." Her cheeks were flushed, her back completely straight. Now she stood up and walked back to the couch. "Is that why you come home so late? Because you're spying on the dead? Was her colleague at least pretty?"

Benno decided to ignore the question. "She hadn't seen Irina Sobieski since last winter. Irina just stopped coming to work."

"And? Did she abandon her dog here and then get killed half a year later? That's nonsense." Her voice was suddenly very loud. "What were you really doing in Lübeck?"

"What?" Benno did his best to sound completely unconcerned. But he was sure that he only achieved the opposite effect.

"You stink of perfume. Is that colleague your girlfriend?"

"That's absurd."

"What is it? Magie Noir? Opium?"

"No idea. Probably whatever Margit always wears." He couldn't tell her about Hanne, not even mention her as a friend. "I'm worried about what's happening here."

"You smell like Margit, even though you weren't even in the office? And you care about a dog who resembles Rasmus? Just go to the police. Show them the photo. Explain that you smell like perfume, that you come home late for no good reason, that you don't see your son before he's going to sleep, because you care about him so much."

You're right, he wanted to say. I have a mistress in Lübeck, I have deceived you, and will probably do it again, and yes, it has to do with you, but that's no excuse, and I'm really worried, and the pastor is not who he to pretends to be, and it would be better if you no longer went to church and stayed away from him. But please, please, just move away with me. We still have some money in the bank, and we can still move away. I can drive a cab until I find something better, and you can teach sports again, and we will move into a small backwater village where there is no death, and I love you, I really love you, even if I just saw another woman and still smell of her perfume. Let us move away together.

Instead he said, "Rasmus belonged to the dead woman. And whoever killed her, certainly knows that Tim has her dog."

"That's totally insane." Her mouth was open, she wasn't finished with him yet, but she stopped suddenly.

Benno had heard it too, and together they jumped up and ran into the hallway. There was Tim sitting on the stairs, with shaggy hair and bare feet. He looked heartbroken. "Do I have to give back Rasmus?"

21

It was twenty-five kilometers to Wengsten. At eight o'clock in the morning Benno stood at the entrance of the branch office of the Traveland county archives and asked for the death registers.

"Who are you looking for?" the attendant asked.

"I don't know exactly." Then he told the woman which years he was interested in.

"Before 1878, we don't have anything," she said.

"Then only the others," Benno said.

"It will take two days. We don't store them here."

He nodded. "But I can search them?"

She looked at him sharply. "But you mustn't copy anything. You will need to fill out an application to get permission."

Last night Benno had pushed the sofa into his study, and set up his sleeping quarters there. Carolin had not protested. The couch wasn't comfortable, but at least he had some peace there. Still, he was tired and didn't want to think about his marriage or the future.

In the newsroom, advertising customers had to be called in the afternoon before the next issue went to print. No one seemed to have noticed his absence yesterday. Although he had gone to Wengsten to confirm his suspicions, they now appeared absurd. It was so much easier to attribute all events to an unfortunate coincidence. So much easier to ignore Walczak's story, and to laugh at the strange behavior of Strathleven's citizens.

At four o'clock he was done with his work. Music sounded from a portable radio. Someone had bought cake and left it on the kitchen table.

Benno had had neither breakfast nor lunch. Cognac made the rounds. Rarely had he felt so happy in recent weeks. Holger announced that he would defend his dissertation in June, and then spend a year in Florence. He had applied for a scholarship in the fall and received his acceptance that morning.

Heidrun Michalski, who worked in the archives, looked sheepish as Holger announced his imminent departure. "Then you've got only a couple of months left," she said. She gulped silently, but Holger didn't seem to notice. Her eyes were very watery.

It was fine with Benno that everybody was focusing on Holger and wanted to drink to him. He sat on his desk, feet on the swivel chair, and looked from time to time out the window, where an orange afternoon sky slowly sank into blackness.

Shortly after six o'clock he left with Holger and stood with him on Hüxstraße. The last buyers rushed home, and the air smelled of fried food. "Hungry?" Holger asked. "I could eat an elephant."

Benno shook his head. "Heidrun has a crush on you."

Holger took off his glasses and wiped them with a shirtsleeve. "Are you sure?"

"Very. Maybe you should invite her for dinner."

"Maybe," Holger replied thoughtfully. "But that has to do with feelings."

Benno laughed. "And you don't have any?"

"No, I have them alright."

"But?"

He put his glasses back on and looked around. "Why are you standing with me in the street?"

Benno looked at him questioningly.

"We've had nothing to do for hours. I have no girlfriend. Nobody is waiting for me. But you have a family, and where are you? Are you going to see your mistress?"

"My what?"

"You guys held hands at the Indian place. And she visited you in the newsroom." His tone was without reproach, but his smug grin grew wider.

Benno smiled a little too rigidly. "Until tomorrow then," he said, turned abruptly and walked away. His car was in the opposite direction, but he didn't care.

On Hundestraße he stood in front of the entrance to the library. A visitor bumped him with his bag full of books. He didn't know if he really wanted to see Hanne, but she was the only other person he knew in Lübeck and would be happy to see him. Currently, she was perhaps the only person who would welcome a visit from him.

How many people might have seen him with Hanne? If Holger knew of his affair, his other colleagues might too. If Holger hadn't kept quiet, perhaps the whole newsroom knew.

He waited several minutes, but he neither saw Hanne through the glass front door, nor could he come to a decision.

After a long detour to his car, he made his way to the Burgfeld Hall, to see the first games of the city handball championships. Normally he would have shirked such an evening and invented a thousand excuses, but today he didn't want to go home. Today he welcomed the smell of floor wax and the sweat of men from the 2nd and 3rd tier leagues.

He joined a colleague from the *Nachrichten*, Hendrick Führholz, who sat on a wooden bench near the roof.

The game was well attended, and most of the audience seemed to play themselves or root for family members.

"You haven't missed much," said Führholz with a straight face. "But the goalkeeper is spectacular."

Benno nodded, looked at the tournament schedule, which he'd received at the entrance. "Who is playing now?" he asked, looking at the clock. It was shortly after seven, and the air was hot and without any oxygen.

"HSV Lübeck versus FLV Travemünde."

Who the spectacular goalkeeper was, he could see immediately. He was a thin, wiry man in his forties and of medium height, and seemed as agile as an octopus. Travemünde could barely get the ball past him, and the final score was 15:3.

"Fabulous," shouted Führholz, jumping up and clapping after the final whistle.

The next match was a sad spectacle, full of random hits and fouls. A player with a good-sized potbelly hit the ground, and strands of his hair, which had been glued to his bald head, peeled off.

In the ensuing break, Benno searched for the refreshment stand. The air was much cooler here, and he sucked it in greedily. He bought a Coke and looked at the men in their cheap, colorful jerseys, their old shoes. The faces were flushed, their eyes bright and radiant, as if this were the Olympic finals. They were all looking forward to the next match. With their gray hair, sweaty faces and thick glasses, they looked like school-boys with big dreams.

***

He had already turned onto Schulstraße when he braked and made a U-turn. He had a flashlight in the trunk and his camera in the glove compartment. He also had a pair of leather gloves in there—he didn't have to stop at home.

Benno was sure that Pastor Cornelius had not used his own basement to hide Irina Sobieski. With five children in the house, that seemed too risky. Someone would have discovered her there.

He could still remember the afternoon when the pastor had asked him to drive to the place where he had seen the corpse. He had paid little attention to Cornelius' words, but the pastor had been agitated. "How in the world did she get out?" he had said, and his words finally made sense. Irina had escaped him, and he had killed her in panic. That explained the many stab wounds.

Benno drove along the dark roads, only an occasional car passing him. At Huginwald clinic he turned off the highway and parked the car under some trees. The clinic was the ideal place to hide someone. Granted, sometimes teenagers came out to smoke pot, but they would probably not try to open locked basement doors. Who would search for a missing woman in the boiler room? In the storage rooms? There were a thousand opportunities to hide a woman.

Branches slapped him in the face as he fought his way to the wall. He trudged through brown, knee-high grass and walked farther and farther away from the road. Near the heating plant, he finally found a nearly crumbled pillar, which he climbed to pull himself over the wall.

But when he landed on the other side, his foot hit uneven ground. He twisted his ankle and screamed.

Cursing, he hobbled toward the heating plant. If anyone else was here tonight, he was warned now.

The gate to the heating plant was closed. Through a small side window, the beam of his flashlight revealed two huge boilers. Otherwise, he could see nothing. How should he get in there? He walked around the building, kept looking for another entrance, but the locked door was the only one. And it did not move a millimeter, no matter how hard he pulled. If Cornelius had a key, this was a safe hiding place.

Discouraged, he made his way to the main building. The pain in his ankle slowly subsided, and he was again able to put some weight on his foot. Although the night was cloudy and neither moon nor stars visible, he did not turn on his flashlight again—he wanted to attract as little attention as possible.

The smell that hit him was even worse than on his first visit. Or maybe it just seemed that way because he couldn't see much of anything.

Where would the pastor have kept a prisoner? Not on the upper floors—it seemed too difficult to push or drag a tied woman up the stairs. Plus, most of the upper rooms, as far as he could remember, had windows. And even if there was a windowless closet, the risk of being surprised by teenagers seemed too high.

That left the basement. Benno leaned heavily on the railing to relieve his sore ankle. He walked into the kitchen and tried to avoid the shards and utensils lying on the ground. He opened the refrigerator room, but it was completely empty. It just smelled damp and moldy. Of course, the pastor had had time enough to erase all evidence of his crime, and Benno felt his enthusiasm wane. His right shoe grew tighter and tighter, and the possibility of finding any trace of Irina Sobieski's captivity seemed ridiculously small.

He left the kitchen and stumbled through the hallways. Here was a small chamber, the door ajar. Benno switched on his dimming flashlight. Soon it might give up the ghost entirely, so he had to be economical. Two old washing machines stood here, and sheets and checkered duvet covers lay scattered on shelves and the floor. Two small windows did not let in enough light for him to discover anything more. He didn't see any shackles, no women's clothing, and the existence of the window spoke against the laundry room.

In the hallway, he heard a noise in front of him on the floor, and in the dying light of his lamp he saw two shadows scurrying away. Rats. They were the last thing he needed.

He found a broom closet and two washrooms and shower rooms. But the closet was too small, and the door could not be locked. The washrooms had no doors at all.

Disappointed, he went up to the reception. He had to stop his search for tonight. The batteries were now completely exhausted, and his right ankle was two or three times bigger than his left. If he wanted to make it home, he had to be on his way.

Slowly, he crossed what had once been the park. When he arrived back at the wall near the heating plant, he could see that the pillars on this side were largely intact and offered no opportunity to climb up.

Limping and cursing Benno walked along the wall, and after fifteen minutes he was at the main gate. On his last visit a new lock had kept the iron bars closed, but the lock lay on the ground tonight, the door was wide open.

Smiling, he walked out to the road and made his way back to his car. He was relieved and overjoyed when he put the key in the door and threw the flashlight on the passenger seat. Only when he straightened up to take off his filthy coat, he was blinded by someone's flashlight.

"Look here, it's Diedrich."

The back seat of the VW Passat was tight, and he had sprained his foot anew while getting in.

"Can't you just give me a warning? I didn't steal anything or set the place on fire. I just thought . . ." Benno fell silent. He couldn't tell the officers the real reason for his visit.

"Yes? We're all ears."

"I just wanted to look around. Simple curiosity."

"At eleven o'clock at night? You do that often?" Ingo Schmoeh, the officer who had kept his name out of the police report, held Benno's identity card and driver's license in his hand, and looked at a clipboard.

He picked up the pen, which was attached to the clipboard with string. His colleague, a slightly older, but equally large man, sat in the passenger seat and looked at the brightly lit dirt path ahead of them, and at Benno's car.

"You won't drag me to the police station, right?"

The colleague was silent, and Schmoeh grunted something unintelligible.

"If you write me a ticket, that's enough, right?" He hated how high his voice was. He had never overcome this strange fear of the police.

"What were you really doing here?" Schmoeh put the clipboard on top of the dashboard. He nodded to the second officer, who got out, walked around the car and opened Benno's door.

"Get out," he said. "We haven't searched you yet."

"I don't have anything," Benno said.

"Get out."

Slowly Benno followed the command. Once he stood upright in front of the car, the officer hit his left kidney. Benno screamed, and while he was still gasping, he felt the second blow, this time in the stomach. He tried to hold on to the doorframe, but the policeman pulled him off and placed a fist below his chest. Benno's scream died, he had no air left to scream. In the dim light from the car's interior, he could see the officer's face for the first time. It was a kindly face, used to smiling. A face that inspired confidence. A kick hit him in the stomach.

Benno fell to the ground and wrapped his arms around his head. But a toe hit his neck under the chin.

Then Schmoeh's door opened. Seconds later, the arms of the officer grabbed him and pulled him to his feet. "You have sprained your foot, eh?" he said quietly. "Well, come on, get up."

Benno stood trembling, leaning against the back of the car. He looked at the policemen with narrowed eyes.

Schmoeh cocked his head. "You've talked to Gruber. Snooped around. But Irina Sobieski is none of your business."

"What did you do with her? Did you keep her hidden here? Made sure she wouldn't escape? Have you been spying on me all this time?"

"You really take yourself way too seriously. And again, for the record, the dead woman is none of your business."

Benno's knees buckled. He knew what to say, but wasn't fast enough. His ribs made a peculiar sound. His stomach was swimming with acid. Schmoeh stepped with all his might on Benno's right ankle.

"Now you've made a mess," the colleague said half a minute later, when Benno caught his breath. His voice sounded like that of an advertising spokesperson.

"I've never seen that woman," Benno squeezed out. "Never."

When Carolin arrived at the Grevenhorst precinct, Schmoeh and his colleague had long since left. Her face was gray, full of fear, and he was so happy to see her, tears welled up in his eyes.

"You look terrible," she said. Benno wanted to get up and greet her, but his foot didn't want to support him. His clothes smelled of vomit, his pants were wet and dirty.

The police officer on duty asked Carolin for her ID, and a few moments later he dismissed Benno. He would get charged for trespassing and resisting arrest. "Schmoeh was very lenient," the old officer told Carolin. He gave Benno a look of disgust and pity.

Carolin had to support Benno; he couldn't walk down the few stairs on his own.

"What were you doing there?" Carolin said in an icy voice.

Benno was sweating, the pain in his leg spreading through his whole body.

"Later," he said, gritting his teeth. His tongue felt swollen.

"Did you fall?" she asked.

He didn't answer, focused on his feet instead.

In the parking lot behind the precinct stood Heintz' old Taunus. "He wanted to drive himself. I had to beg," said Carolin. "I told Tim only that I was going to pick you up. You can think of a good story." She closed her door. "Where is our car?"

"At the clinic," Benno said quietly.

"Can you drive with your bum foot?"

He wasn't so sure, but what could he do? Somehow he would manage. All he wanted now was a bathroom and some ice for his foot. He hoped that he hadn't broken anything, because his body felt like a bag full of broken glass.

He sank into the passenger seat. The car smelled of tobacco and paint thinner, but that was alright with him.

"Try not to get anything dirty," said Carolin. "You smell like a skunk." Then she laughed tonelessly. "When the police called, I was happy at first. I thought, finally. Finally."

"What?" asked Benno. "What do you mean?"

"Finally, someone stands up to you and your antics. Why did you have to crawl around there in the dark? Without even calling me? I had no idea where you were or what you were doing."

"I didn't think you were interested."

"We are still married," said Carolin.

"I discovered something terrible," Benno blurted out. "I didn't want to tell you at first, it's so . . . so outrageous. But that's why I went there. We need Tim to get out of here."

"There you go again."

"I'm serious. The pastor held Irina Sobieski captive for nearly a year. And then he killed her. And now he's after Tim. Cornelius is probably in cahoots with the police. The officers who arrested me tonight, they knew exactly why I was at the clinic . . ."

Her shrill laughter interrupted him, tore his words to shreds. "Are you in your right mind? The pastor a killer?"

"It's true," Benno insisted. "Irina's colleague said that she saw him in Lübeck. He was Irina's lover."

"You are making these things up."

"No," parried Benno. They weren't far from the clinic, and Benno looked out for a police car. He was afraid that the two cops would be lying in wait for him a second time.

"Just because you have a mistress."

"I don't have a lover." It was a lie, but in this moment it felt like the truth to Benno.

"You know what? You get in your car, and then you can drive to Lübeck. I don't want you in my house."

"But Cornelius . . ."

"Stop it," she snapped. "Don't we have everything we ever dreamed of? A house in a small village, a job, a family? And you, you've ruined everything. Didn't take you long. Half a year. That's all. Half a year, and now you're coming up with crazy stories about murder and kidnapping." She paused. "Who was with you at the old hospital? Do you have a sweetheart around here?" She slapped her forehead. "I'm so stupid. Lübeck. Your lover lives here. Who is she? I probably even know her."

Benno shook his head. "No, I've been searching for the hideout. Where Cornelius held Irina."

Carolin's laughter rang in his ears. "You know what? I'm letting you out here, and when you get home, there'll be a suitcase with your things in the yard. You take it and get out of Strathleven. Everything else, your precious records and books you can pick up next week. Call me, we'll make an appointment. So that I'm not alone in the house when you arrive. So you're not getting any ideas."

Benno nodded. "If that's what you want."

"Yes," said Carolin. "That's what I want." Seconds later, they stopped in front of the main gate of the hospital. Benno didn't feel like arguing, didn't want to explain that his car was parked a few hundred yards away. He got out with difficulty, looked back at her and said, "I . . ."

But Carolin sang at the top of her lungs, "Lord, your love is like grass and shore," and all he could do was slam the door shut. "Like wind and vastness and like home and hearth," came from the inside, before the car sped away.

Even with a thick branch as a prop, it took him nearly fifteen minutes before he reached his car. The Ford was still where he had parked it, and Schmoeh was nowhere to be seen. Almost happily he dropped into the seat.

After a few seconds he started the engine and drove cautiously back to the highway. Here, too, no police car was in sight. Everything around him was silent.

Braking proved to be a bit problematic, but driving was easier than he had thought. Once in Strathleven, he turned off the main road and onto Schulstraße. When he pulled up at the old school, he was greeted by an unexpected sight. The light above the entrance was on, but there was no suitcase in the yard. Instead, the door stood wide open, and Rasmus was chained to the banister jumping around furiously, trying to pull his head out of the collar. He growled and barked incessantly. Mrs. Schmied's and Mr. Heintz' doors were open too, and as Benno got out of the car, the old man came running from the house.

"Where the hell were you?" he shouted at Benno.

"I was . . ."

"I don't give a shit. Have you seen him?"

"Who?"

"The boy, of course."

Benno hobbled past Heintz to his front door. Carolin came running down the stairs, and behind her appeared a red-faced Manfred.

"What took you so long?" Her voice cracked, her lips trembled. "You got him?"

Benno shook his head. Carolin burst into tears. "All this is because of you, just because you had to let yourself get arrested at the old hospital." She sobbed and ran toward the street. Lights came on in the pastor's home, and a window opened on the second floor. Rasmus wouldn't stop barking. He yanked at the leash, and his feet scratched over the floor.

"What happened?" Benno asked, but no one paid him any attention. Only Manfred came up to him. "You stink," he said and turned to his mother, who was stepping out of her house with a robe slung over her nightgown.

"Tim is gone," he said softly, as if afraid to be overheard by someone. "They came and took him away."

22

He awoke in a muted gray. It smelled unfamiliar, and somewhat sweet and insubstantial, as though he might have been awakened to a more shallow life. He turned his head to the left, but there was only one chair, a silk coat hanging over the back.

Benno pulled back the blanket and looked at his ankle. It was bandaged, his foot still swollen.

His chest was dotted in blue and yellow, as if he were growing moldy from the inside. The pain hit him the moment he tried to sit up. He was naked.

Getting out of bed was a difficult balancing act, and even tying the robe caused him pain. Hanne was no longer in her apartment. The living room was empty, flooded with gray daylight; he could hardly keep his eyes open. He found a second, smaller room. A study, it seemed, with books on the influence of names, the healing powers of indigenous herbs, about tarot and astrology. On her desk was a small plate full of colorful semi-precious stones. He felt safe in this strange room.

She wasn't in the kitchen either, but the clock on the wall showed that it was almost ten. After he had waited five more minutes, he called Carolin. He hadn't expected her to be home, but she picked up after the second ring.

"Hello," she said breathlessly.

"It's me. Did you find Tim?"

"No," she said and hung up.

Benno exhaled. He was to blame for everything. He had put her son in danger, she didn't want to see him.

At four in the morning, Benno had rung Hanne's doorbell. He was still in the same filthy clothes, and she took them off in the hallway, but this time slower, gentler. She almost cried when she saw his ribs and ankle. He felt embarrassed. While sitting in the bathtub, she wrapped his foot in ice.

She had silently listened to his story, dried him off and helped him into the bedroom. He had fallen asleep in her arms.

He called the *Strandkurier*, was put through to Jochen Hecht, and then told the publisher of Tim's disappearance.

"Take your time, Diedrich." Hecht's voice was calm and soothing. "But once your boy has turned up again, we need to talk."

Benno closed his eyes and nodded into the phone. "Yes," he said.

"Your work. Maybe it's my fault, maybe I've given you too much freedom." Hecht sighed and continued. "Find your boy, Diedrich." Then he hung up.

Benno kept the receiver in his hand for a long time, unable to hang up. Carolin was right: he had screwed up.

Half an hour later, Hanne came home, her hands full of shopping bags.

"You can exchange everything." She put the bags onto the couch in the living room and showed him her purchases. "How are you?" she suddenly asked, while still holding a gray sweater to her chest. "Did you call your wife?"

"Peek and Cloppenburg?" He came up to Hanne and hugged her and the sweater. Her coat smelled cold, and of coffee and croissants and spring rain.

"Tim didn't come home?"

His nose pressed against her neck, he gently shook his head.

"Now what?"

"No idea." Benno dropped his arms at his side.

"She kicked you out. What if she wants you back? Do you want to go back to her? Where will you stay in the meantime?"

He stared blankly ahead. Without thinking, he had assumed that she would want him to stay with her. What a fool he was, he thought. A conceited, arrogant fool. "I'll have to find something."

Hanne folded the sweater, put it on the coffee table. "Take your time," she said, without looking at him.

"Thank you."

"As long as you're sexually available to me, of course."

He opened his silk robe. "Right now?"

"You should find your son."

The police car in front of the house almost made him turn back. The sun, which was all too easily escaping the clouds and finding open skies yet again, didn't fit this occasion. Nothing seemed to fit. Church and village looked too ordinary, and the air was relatively mild, with a slight hint of cow dung. As he walked toward the house, he wasn't sure what the confusing mix of police, church, wife and disappearance meant to him. Different laws seemed to be at work in Strathleven, and the meaning of events could be changed depending on the wishes of the residents. He would never find his assumptions confirmed, never find his way.

Ingo Schmoeh was without his partner this time and slowly and carefully took down Carolin's description of Tim. He nodded at Benno, without moving a muscle in his face. Last night he had stepped on Benno's ankle, today he was searching for his son.

"And you don't believe he ran away?" asked Schmoeh. "Has he been fighting with you, does he have problems at school?"

Carolin shook her head. "He has an illness and the people here have reacted very strangely to him, but no, I think he felt comfortable." She paused. "Rasmus was chained to the railing. Tim would never have done that."

"Your dog?" Schmoeh looked away from Carolin and nodded toward the large window overlooking the yard. Rasmus sat in front of it, with his paws on the windowsill, and looked out onto the yard. Not even on Benno's coming home had he left his post. "You suspect that he left with someone else?"

Carolin kneaded her hands, didn't look at the policeman. "I know. This sounds stupid. Who is going to kidnap a little boy?"

"Kidnap?" Schmoeh's voice was businesslike, but his question made Carolin shrink.

"Maybe it was just his friends, maybe they wanted to play a prank on him."

Twenty minutes later Schmoeh left the house, after he had asked Benno for clues about Tim's whereabouts and not received any. When he closed the door behind him, the silence in the house glued their ears shut. Carolin hugged her knees, hair covering her face. From the kitchen sounded the ticking of the wall clock.

Rasmus whimpered softly and slowly trotted toward the entrance. When Benno let him out, he sniffed the ground, ran towards the sandbox, then back. He looked at Benno and cocked his head. He barked twice, whined again, then looked around as if searching. His limp had become more pronounced, his movements were stiff and angular. His eyes seemed dead. Within one night he had turned into the ghost dog again.

Benno waited until the dog had finished his business, then he went back into the house. Carolin was making coffee. She stood by the window, her face like that of a young girl. She had taken off her glasses, her eyes stared out toward the garden, and yet they couldn't see anything.

As the coffee maker began to wheeze, she poured two cups and handed one to Benno.

"What are you wearing?" She reached for her glasses, pushed them back on her nose.

"Had to buy something," Benno said. The clothes still smelled brand new.

She nodded. "I have put two suitcases in your room."

"You still don't believe me?"

"You smell like her."

"Because of Tim?"

She looked up from her coffee, too tired or too controlled to lash out at him. "That Cornelius is a killer and that there is a conspiracy against Tim?" She waited a few seconds and when Benno didn't reply, she continued, "No, I don't believe that." She seemed to listen to the echo of her voice, tried the word again. "No."

"Tim is gone."

"But he will come back."

"You said yourself that people look at him strangely. The gifts, the crown, all that doesn't frighten you?"

She seemed to think, sipped hot coffee, then looked for Rasmus, who had resumed his observation post by the front window.

"That's nothing compared to what Tim would have experienced in Berlin. What I experienced in Berlin. Daniel and Jens—I acted like a crazy woman in front of Mrs. Stroth, but it was harmless." She suddenly shook his head. "He will come back today. I'm sure of it."

The suitcases lay open on the ground, as if they had landed there just a few minutes ago. Large spots of light played on the carpet. Benno put his coffee on the desk, trying to concentrate—what was he to pack, what could stay behind for now? For a few minutes he stood around, before he randomly threw writing pads and pens in the first suitcase. Carolin came up behind him in the doorway.

"Are you staying with her?"

"She's a friend." He wasn't sure why he was still lying. Perhaps for Tim's sake, so Carolin could not invalidate his suspicion against Cornelius. For Tim's sake? No, he couldn't claim to be so unselfish. He didn't want to be treated like a cheater, he didn't want to look the way he really was.

"You haven't even asked if I would like to have you here."

"You've thrown me out." He tried to filter all his anger from his voice.

"That was last night."

"Do you want me to stay?"

She looked directly at him, adjusted her glasses. "Do you want to stay?"

He looked at the books in his suitcase. He wanted to leave, he wanted to go back to Lübeck, back to Hanne, to colorful semi-precious stones and silk robes. When he thought of unpacking his bags again, something in his stomach clenched. But Carolin was his wife, Tim was his son. He could not just leave and abandon them now.

"I didn't expect you to," she said softly, turned around and walked back into the living room.

After he had put the luggage in the car, Benno went over to the rectory. Mrs. Cornelius came to the door.

"Have you found Tim?" She blinked in the sunlight.

What did she know about her husband? Had she been helping him all along? Maybe she had carried food to their prisoner?

Benno shook his head. "Is your husband home?"

"He is in the church. If you hurry, you can still catch him, he has to be in Grevenhorst later."

Benno thanked her and walked over to the church. The red VW bus stood in front of the side entrance, and the door was open.

"Hello?" Benno called. For a moment he imagined the pastor waiting with an axe behind the door, but no, Cornelius couldn't possibly know that he had spoken with Ania Walczak. Unless Carolin had told him everything.

"Hello?" It smelled of cheap wood, closed windows, and sweat. Benno walked through the small, narrow room and a moment later entered the church, where the pastor was standing on a ladder changing light bulbs in the chandeliers. Sunlight flooded through the windows and framed him as though he might be a heavenly apparition.

"Is it time?" he asked, without turning around.

"It's me," Benno said.

Cornelius stopped. "Oh, Mr. Diedrich. Have you found Tim?"

Benno took a few steps closer. "You know where he is, right? Maybe he's even here somewhere?"

"What?" The pastor turned so quickly that the ladder started to sway. Benno lunged forward and held on to it. His ankle protested on the spot.

"Thank you." Cornelius descended slowly, his face was sweaty. "What did you say?"

Benno let go of the ladder, kept his distance from Cornelius. "I know that you were Irina's lover."

"Irina?" The pastor seemed surprised, then his face reddened. "What do you want, Diedrich?"

"You imprisoned her somewhere in the village. But something went wrong, she tried to escape, and you killed her." Benno expected an explosion, but Cornelius' face only darkened. "And you've seen Irina's dog every day. Right next door, in our house. Every day you saw Tim walking him. And you've kept your mouth shut, hoping that no one would find out about your affair. Is that why you've kidnapped Tim? Where is he?"

The pastor seemed to inflate and suck in all the air around him, but suddenly he stopped to let out a huff. "You've got it all wrong."

"Where is Tim? Is he here? Do you have a basement?"

"This is a tragedy." Cornelius voice was thick with feeling. "You have no idea what you're talking about."

"You were Irina's lover."

"Who gave you that idea?" He seemed truly offended.

"I know it."

"And when should I have had time for that?"

"You were seen in the restaurant."

"What?" The pastor gasped. "In what restaurant?"

"You picked up Irina."

"I did not," Cornelius cried indignantly. "What a cunning lie. I understand that . . ."

"And you told my wife to throw away her medication. Where is Tim?"

Cornelius' mouth snapped shut, he swallowed his protest. Instead he threw his arms in the air and shook his head. "What do you want?"

"My marriage is broken. Tim, where is he?"

"I don't have the slightest idea," the pastor said gloomily. "And your wife does not need medication. She needs her God and her faith, not pills."

"And you're the expert?" Benno said. "Who's the king?"

"My good man . . ."

"At the time I didn't really think about it," Benno interrupted the pastor. "But when you and I were driving out to that meadow, you said, 'How in the world did she get out?' I didn't suspect you, of course, but you had kept her hidden all that time. Where? Where did you keep her? Where is Tim? Who is the king of the village? Why does he have to die?"

Cornelius took the ladder, folded it and let it slide to the ground. "Just look around. Look at everything. And then you are welcome to call the police."

"And they'll beat me up again?"

The pastor went past Benno without looking at him. "You have brought this on yourself."

Wehrke wasn't home, his car was nowhere to be seen. Nevertheless, Benno got out and looked around on the property. The house stood back from the road and was protected from prying eyes by trees and hedges. No one would be able to watch him.

To his left was the garage, but through the window he could see that it was empty except for a bicycle and garden equipment. He followed the gravel path past the garage and along the left side of the house to the garden, while trying to protect his ankle as much as possible. The sun disappeared behind the clouds more often now, but it was still mild enough that Benno almost wanted to take off his new coat.

He had only ever seen the garden from the living room window. It seemed old, right out of another century, with thick hedges and a low stone wall. Except for a few fruit trees, there was nothing that blocked the view onto the fields beyond.

A light was burning in the living room; maybe Wehrke had forgotten to switch it off. Benno was looking through a window at a wooden door with tigers painted on its panels when the glass broke into a thousand pieces. The crack of a rifle made him jump, but the pain in his foot forced him to his knees. Benno looked around. A second blast followed, and behind him a brick shattered.

Benno threw himself flat on the ground. He didn't know where the shooter was hiding, didn't know if he was already running towards the house. He didn't dare move. After a minute he crawled to the right, trying to put weight mostly on his arms to protect his ankle. He could hear nothing but the blood rushing in his ears, and hoped that he wasn't making any noise, hoped that he could no longer be seen.

Cautiously, he peeked around the corner. He could see the rear of his car. Behind him lay the garden, and nothing moved around in it. As fast as he could, he crawled on hands and knees toward his car. He stopped once more when he finally had to give up the protection of the house, but he still couldn't detect anything. Slowly he straightened up, took a deep breath and ran. His foot was raging, his teeth gnashing so loudly that it echoed in his ears, but he ran, and heard the cracking sound only when it was already over. Before him, pebbles went flying and a second shot went straight into the radiator of the car. But Benno didn't stop. I am a huge target, I'm tall, I'm too slow, I have to run back, I have to protect myself . . . but he managed to tear open the passenger door and throw himself on the seat. He twisted his body to get his feet on the pedals, lost the key, fished it out of the gap between the seat and handbrake. He writhed, the fifth shot had to come at any moment . . .

But the fifth shot didn't come. The engine howled, because he hadn't selected a gear. The gearbox crunched while Benno struggled with the shifter. Half blind with fear, he drove off, almost rammed one of the large, white boulders that stood at the entrance of the yard, and then raced toward the entrance to the highway. A truck came from the left and was able to dodge him at the last moment. The horn made Benno jump. When he stepped on the accelerator, he could no longer feel his ankle.

On Friedrich's lot, he remained in the car for long minutes. The engine was running, warm air flowed over his face and his feet, and yet he was freezing. The pastor. He must have followed him. Or one of his accomplices, whoever they might be. Why did he have to confront Cornelius with the truth? Without witnesses, without being able to share his suspicions with anyone. Except for Carolin, of course, but she didn't believe a single word he said.

No, he had to confide in someone, had to seek help. But who in the village could he trust? Who did he really know? Martin Wehrke was himself an outsider, and neither the postman nor the shopkeeper Johannsen he deemed trustworthy. But Otto Friedrich? Through the window of the showroom he saw salespeople behind their desks, two families looking at the shiny, clean cars inside. The children squeezed behind the wheel and were pulled out immediately by their parents.

Benno looked at the clothes Hanne had bought him just this morning. His knees were dirty, his coat stained. He wished himself at his desk in the office, wished for nothing more than to stop at a Chinese restaurant and walk with a bag of spring rolls and noodles to Hanne's apartment. Carolin would be able to cope, might even be happier without him. But Tim. He couldn't simply disappear and let down the boy. He had to find him.

"Can I speak to you for a moment?"

Friedrich wasn't alone, but Benno didn't want to be deterred by indecisive customers. The dealer looked at him, nodded and said, "You can sit in my office. I'll be with you in just a minute."

Benno sat down on one of the stained chairs and waited. A digital clock flickered on the desk. He leaned forward and grabbed the photo of Friedrich's daughters. Corinna stood in the middle and smiled a little too persistently into the camera. The background was a dark brown color, probably taken in a photo studio in Grevenhorst. The photo looked too stiff and carefully lit not to be the product of a professional photographer. The girls had daffodils in their hands, and their faces looked completely lifeless.

"What's going on? You look awful." Friedrich walked around the desk and sank into his leather chair.

"Tim has been kidnapped."

"Kidnapped?" The car dealer raised his eyebrows. "I heard something else."

"Have you?"

"Yes, that he ran away. We are a small town, news get around real fast."

"He didn't run away."

"Excuse my bluntness, but your marriage is . . . you're having problems, right?"

"Did that also get around?" Benno couldn't decide whether to be angry or ashamed, but his face felt hot anyway.

"Maybe he wants to teach you a lesson?" Friedrich seemed genuinely concerned, his forehead was creased, his voice soft, his smile kind. It was the same expression that he'd worn when they had refused to buy the bigger Scorpio.

"He would never leave his dog behind."

"Oh," Friedrich said ambiguously. "But who could have kidnapped Tim? And why? Have you notified the police in Grevenhorst?"

"We have. But . . ."

"You don't trust them?"

Benno shook his head.

"May I ask why?"

Could he really trust Friedrich? The question still banged around in his head. He was respected in the village, he had business dealings with everyone—he must have little interest in the concerns of a newcomer. But Friedrich didn't like the pastor, and Cornelius seemed to hate the car dealer. Benno had little choice.

"The pastor," he started, but all of a sudden his suspicions against Cornelius seemed outrageous even to himself. A village pastor who killed waitresses and kidnapped little boys—who would believe this? Then he thought of Tim and of Carolin, who was waiting for him at home. He thought of Irina Sobieski's body, how it had looked when he'd found her in the summer, and with a jerk, he sat up and told Friedrich everything he knew. He even mentioned his arrest the night before. He needed help, and Friedrich knew the village. They had to find Tim.

Afterward it was very quiet in Friedrich's office. Across the car dealer's face ran different expressions, like clouds in fast motion, but none stuck. He asked, "Can you prove any of this?"

"I have a witness remembering that the pastor visited Irina Sobieski in Lübeck. And a bullet is still stuck in my car."

"The pastor." Friedrich laughed sadly. "I never thought that someone from the village could have anything to do with the murder. Never in my life."

"And now he's got Tim." Benno watched the car dealer for a long time, but he seemed to be lost in thought.

"Who's the king?" Benno asked into the silence.

"Yes," Friedrich sat up. "Who? And what does that have to do with your boy?"

"I had hoped . . ."

"That I could tell you."

"The Wild Hunt, the crown, someone has to know what is actually going on here. The way people stare at Tim—they must know something."

"But you don't belong here. Why should they trust you?" Friedrich emphasized his words with a nod. "And I have no idea what to make of the king. Sounds mysterious."

"Did you see your father back then? Before the funeral?"

Friedrich frowned. "Why do you ask?"

"I've heard . . . maybe just a rumor. That your father was killed. I thought maybe he was . . . involved in something. Every twenty-four years . . . some terrible thing seems to happen here."

An ugly laugh gurgled up Friedrich's throat. His face contorted as if someone had hit him. "You know," he said. "If you weren't worried about your son, I would throw you out right now." His right hand clenched into a fist, slowly opened and then closed again quickly. "That would have been almost a relief," he said. "If someone would have killed him. But no, he had to kill himself, and let his family down. It just brought grief to everyone involved. Grief and shame. I've done my best to get over it, but every time I look in the mirror, I see my father tying a noose around his neck. I look exactly like him, and I am almost his age now. Not a day passes that I don't think of him. I've even taken over his business. I'm his spitting image, both inside and out."

"I'm sorry," Benno said.

"There's tons of rumors in the village. It's more interesting than what we see on television about the big, wide world."

"Sure," Benno admitted. "I just thought . . ."

"Of course. How would you know whom to believe? I'm not taking offense. But what are we going to do? My father is dead and buried, and he cannot help us find your son."

For the 'we' and 'us,' Benno could have hugged Friedrich. It was the first offer of help he had received.

"I'll keep my eyes open, ask some people," promised the dealer and grinned. "We don't have any caves or secret bunkers, as far as I know. If someone in the village kidnapped your boy, we'll find him."

"Thank you." Benno struggled to suppress tears. "Thank you. I was afraid you'd think I'm crazy."

The car dealer smiled. "Granted, your story is strong stuff. The pastor in cahoots with the police. But Tim is gone. Everything else is secondary at the moment."

Benno shook Friedrich's hand far too long and then limped out of the office into the disappearing day. It was past four o'clock, the sky was clear and sinking into a strange high-pitched red.

With a sigh of relief Benno got in the car. He had done the right thing. It almost felt as though he had already found Tim, and with renewed energy he drove to Schulstraße and parked in front of his house. Carolin ran to meet him, but when she saw that he was alone, her face turned pale.

"You don't have him," she said.

He shook his head. "We'll find him, definitely." The shots and his talk with the pastor he didn't mention, nor did he tell Carolin that he had just confided in Otto Friedrich.

"I have to go again," he said, "but I'll be back in two hours."

Carolin said nothing, just nodded.

I won't let you down, he wanted to add, but she had already turned away and was walking back inside with her head down.

23

He arrived just in time to be still admitted into the archives, but the attendant looked at him reproachfully as she handed him the two registers. "You have twenty-five minutes," she said, after checking her little gold watch.

Benno took the books and sat at a small table. When he opened the first, he felt almost dizzy—he could barely read the tall, sharply curved font. In 1941, the so-called Sütterlin longhand had still been taught in schools.

The entries were sparse, not many people had died in Strathleven. When had the shooting festival been celebrated? He hoped that the March date had been the same, and he copied all the names, without knowing what they said.

The speaker system crackled, and a tinny voice let him know that the archive would close in fifteen minutes. Benno closed the first register, and then devoted himself to the year 1917. As before, he simply copied all the names as best he could. Even though they looked like Osnfom, Ohngruft, and Viutnu, he hoped that maybe Hanne could decipher them.

For 1893, there were only three entries in March, and these he could read with some effort. Only two were men.

At three minutes to five, he gave back the registers and received an icy look from the archivist. Then he limped back to his car. At the town's exit, he stopped at a phone booth and called Hanne, but no one answered, and no answering machine came on. He didn't have the number of the library with him, and the Lübeck phone book had only ten or fifteen pages left—the rest had been torn out.

His breath steamed up the windows. The cheerful yellow paint had never looked so gleeful. He hated the countryside, the loneliness, the darkness. He hated the flickering light of TV sets behind the curtains, the brick façades, and timid neon signs. Most of all he hated himself. He couldn't even remain faithful to Carolin, couldn't feel guilty when he called Hanne. He couldn't find his son, and that made his infidelity only worse. As though Tim had to suffer for his father's faithlessness. With his right foot Benno kicked the phone booth's window. The sharp, red-hot pain stopped his tears and made his loneliness nearly bearable.

When he stopped in front of the sandbox, the headlights struck the pastor and seemed to pin him against the house wall. He was hugging Carolin and then turned into the light, his eyes small slits, his face fleshy, naked and radiant.

Furiously, Benno pushed open his car door. "Go away," he shouted. "Where is my son? Where are you hiding him? Yes, I'm still alive. Where do you have your gun? Where do you hide it? Where?"

The pastor turned and walked over to his house. Carolin waited patiently at the front door.

"What did he want?" Benno's voice cracked. "Caro, he's got Tim. He is behind everything. You mustn't let him into the house. He shot at me."

"Benno." Her voice was very quiet, completely even. "You should really talk to Cornelius. He told me everything, and he is not angry with you. He knows that you're worried."

"He's not angry?" Benno forced himself not to scream, but his voice fluttered nervously. "He's not angry? He almost killed me."

"He understands that you suspect him."

"Caro, he killed the woman. He's behind everything."

Carolin laughed. "Nonsense. How should he have done that? Where should he have been hiding her?" Before he could answer, she said, "come," and led the way into the kitchen, where she poured two glasses of wine. Her hands didn't even tremble. The bottle was almost empty.

"Has the police called?" Benno asked. "Because of Tim?"

"Have you called your lover?" Carolin asked quietly. Her face was as full and soft as that of a much younger woman.

He took the glass, but he didn't feel at home. He missed this house already, as if he were standing in a memory.

"I don't have a lover," he insisted.

"And you call the pastor a liar?" She drank the blue-red liquid, which immediately stained her bitten lips.

He was silent. She was right, he was a liar. For a while he stared in front of him, looked at a tiny piece of cork. Then he took a deep breath, and without looking at Carolin, he said: "Yes, I lied." Hastily he added, "But that doesn't exonerate the pastor."

"Do you still have a job?"

Benno nodded. "Yes. For now."

"Is she beautiful?"

He didn't know how to answer that question. Whatever he said, he would betray and destroy something he loved. "That's not it."

"What is it, then?"

"We have to get out of here."

"We?"

"For Tim's sake."

"You're sweet," she said, and smiled timidly. "You really think that Cornelius is hiding him?"

Benno nodded.

"You're really sweet. I know that you care about him." She put down her glass of wine and walked into the living room. He followed her silently, sat down beside her on the sofa. Rasmus was sleeping in his bed under the window, from time to time making small noises, as though he were hunting squirrels or rabbits in his sleep.

"How are you?" Her voice was too serious, too gentle, to laugh at her question. She grabbed his knees, looked at the dark stains on his pants.

"They shot at me today." The sound of his words was all wrong; he wasn't someone people shot at. It sounded like a stupid lie.

"They?"

"I know that you trust the pastor. And the police. And the people in the village."

"But you love it, right?"

"What do you mean?"

She ran a finger over his shoulder and down his arm. "I haven't seen you so happy in a long time. Your face glows like a little boy's."

"How are *you*?" he asked, instead of answering her.

"The uncertainty is eating at me." She wiped her face, it glistened wet. "And what's worse . . ." A strange sound came from her mouth, almost like a burp. "Sometimes I catch myself wishing he wouldn't come back."

Benno remained at her side, took one of her hands in his. A moment later, she leaned her head on his shoulder.

"The doctor visits, the tissue and blood tests, the scrapes and scars. I wouldn't have to worry anymore."

His shirtsleeve was wet, and still he said nothing.

"It was so nice to think that he would be normal. A real boy."

For several minutes they sat in the darkness, listening to the snoring of the dog. Only their hands moved in and around each other, sweaty and as if they'd taken on a life of their own.

"I don't want you in the house," she said softly.

He nodded and still didn't let go of her hand. His throat felt impossibly narrow, a ball of fire seemed to rage in his stomach, but he held her hand, and she held his. They didn't let go of the other. He realized that this moment with Carolin was only possible because they had already given up on each other. Not yet completely, not yet without pain, but the break was irrevocable.

What would she do? Would she stay here? Would he stay in Lübeck or return to Berlin? What would Tim say to that?

"That doesn't matter," she said into the silence. She had to know what was going on inside him. "Tomorrow, Cornelius will ask the congregation to help look for Tim."

"But . . ."

"Yeah, as if he were already dead." Carolin sobbed. "I know you don't trust Cornelius, but that's none of your concern. You can do whatever you want, but I won't refuse his help because of you."

He nodded. "Well." After a while he added, "Call me when you have found him."

"Where?"

"At the *Strandkurier*. I have to look for an apartment first."

"Yes," she said softly.

"If you need anything . . ."

"Yes," she said again, and as if on cue, they huddled together. Entangled into each other they sat silently on the couch, and Rasmus opened his eyes and whimpered. Only when her breathing had calmed and her head suddenly grew very heavy and rolled to one side, did Benno pull away, grab his coat and step outside. The light above the entrance wasn't on. Carefully, he pulled the door shut.

What should he say? How should he begin? 'Can your daughter remember the rapist? What did he really want from your daughter? Had it something to do with the dead woman?'

For a long time he stood before the Antlers' house. It was one of those white-washed buildings that seemed to come from a kit. The color was not quite fresh, and the garden looked unkempt. Then he pulled himself together and rang the doorbell. A woman in her forties opened the door and looked at him questioningly.

"Excuse me," Benno began. "I am . . ."

"I know who you are. It's already late."

Benno nodded. He waited for a sudden inspiration, but it wouldn't come. "I'm not here as a journalist," he stammered."I just wanted to ask . . . because of my son . . . does Sybille remember anything? Who attacked her?"

The door was slammed shut so quickly that it almost hit him in the face. Benno rang again, then a third time, and finally a man's voice shouted from inside, "Go away! I'll call the police."

He had to talk to Sybille. Limping, he left the Antler's house.

It was only ten o'clock when he arrived in Lübeck and took a room in a guesthouse in Mariesgrube. He had no toothbrush or pajamas or anything clean to wear. Only his dirty clothes, car keys, and Wehrke's family history, which he had taken from the trunk. He lay down on the bed and stared at the white ceiling. The curtains were made of rough polyester and were a toxic shade of green. Through the window he could see the roof of the house on the opposite side of the street and a church tower in the distance, a red light flashing on top of its spire. He had eaten nothing since breakfast, his stomach growled, but his ankle felt so hot and bruised that he rejected the idea of walking to a restaurant.

After ten minutes he sat up, took off his right sock and unwrapped the bandage. It was an ugly sight. Red, blue, brown and green intermingled, and the swelling had hardly gone down, if at all.

Hanne picked up after the second ring. "Where are you?" she asked.

"I didn't want to get on your nerves," he said, after he had given her the address.

"Oh." She stretched the syllable until it sounded like a very long word. "Do you want company in your little room?"

He longed for attention, but he could still feel Carolin on his body.

"The silence probably means 'no'?"

Benno groaned, laughed, felt tears come and swallowed hard.

"Can you read Sütterlin, set feet straight, shrink swellings, buy toothbrushes and lend me a sweater and socks?"

"In 1893. Brunhild Schreier. Egon Busse. August Wehrke."

"He was 56."

"Children?"

"Five." Benno pointed to the family tree in Martin Wehrke's book. "Sophie, Margot, Hans-Rudolph, Ernst and Günther." He bit into a spring roll Hanne had brought, and burned his mouth. Hanne had been let into his room without difficulties.

"People think that there are no fat whores," she said with a mirthless grin. "They probably thought I was your mother." She pointed with a chopstick to an entry on his notepad. "You have a second Wehrke here. In 1917."

Benno stared at his scribbles, trying to see which name she was talking about. "This here means Wehrke?"

"Hans-Rudolph."

With his still clean pinkie, he searched for the correct entry on the family tree. "He had no children."

"Right. And in 1941, there are no Wehrkes among the dead."

"Who do we have?"

"Else Johannsen. Ingeborg Fries. Martin Witte. Bernhard Wohlfarth. Ernst-Otto Wegner."

"That really spells Bernhard?" asked Benno.

"Probably. Your handwriting is terrible."

"Witte is our mailman."

"And when did the shooting festivals take place?"

Benno shrugged, causing a piece of chicken to slip from his chopsticks onto his lap. He cursed as sauce spread on the fabric. "Every twenty-four years."

"Every year," Hanne said.

"Every year what?"

"People die. The twenty-four years could be a coincidence. You are looking for a connection. If you had looked at a different set of years, you would also have discovered names you know."

"Two Wehrkes?"

"There's a lot of them. Just look."

She was right. The family tree was huge, and family members were born or died almost every year. In Strathleven and in other cities in Schleswig-Holstein. Throughout Germany.

"Both in March?"

She raised her eyebrows, the corners of her mouth pointed downward. "That's strange, but no evidence. Your foot smells."

"Only one? But what does that have to do with Irina?"

"Maybe nothing. The pastor may have killed the woman, but he's not a member of the shooting club. No, not just the one, but the other one is too far away. You need a bath."

The bathtub of the hotel had barely enough room for both of them, and when Benno finally dropped into the water, it spilled over and drenched his dirty clothes on the floor.

"Now I have nothing to wear," he said. How coldhearted to sit in the tub with his mistress, while his wife waited at home for a call that her son was still alive. Who was this Benno, whose foot was now carefully soaped and tended to? Who was this guy who let everything happen to him, and who knew that he would eventually pay a price for his actions and omissions, and who still didn't care?

"I have to drive to the village tomorrow morning," he said.

"Did you recognize the shooter? Or have any idea who he was?"

He shook his head. "Perhaps Cornelius. I have no idea who else might be in on this."

She put his foot gently on her breast. "Actually, you know pretty much nothing at all, right?"

Benno looked at her for a long time. "In Wehrke's book it says nothing of a king."

"He wouldn't shout it from the rooftops."

"If you say that, it sounds almost obscene," he remarked with a smile.

Before going to sleep they lay in bed and flipped through Martin Wehrke's family history.

"No photo of August," Hanne said. "And here," she pointed with her finger to a paragraph, "only his death is mentioned, but not the cause."

"And Hans-Rudolph was his heir." Some pages later, they came across a family photo, Hans-Rudolph with his siblings and their children in front of the family home. "Martin never met him. He is the son of Hans-Rudolph's brother Eugen. Born in 1933. Eugen took his jolly good time before producing any offspring." Hans-Rudolph wore a thick white beard, a coarsely woven yet elegant-looking suit and a grim expression. All Wehrkes favored this same expression.

"He's not wearing a crown," Hanne said.

"No children. Maybe Hans-Rudolph was gay or infertile. Or a woman-hater."

"Maybe he just didn't want to."

Benno stared at the photo until it began to flicker before his eyes. Then finally everything seemed to add up. "The first Wehrke had children, then his son died twenty-four years after him. But he had no offspring, no son. So another family's turn."

"To do what?"

"Friedrich was the next, and Otto . . ." He trailed off. "Otto has three daughters."

"And Otto . . . ?"

"And I told him everything." Benno's face was hot, he had spoiled everything. Frantically he asked, "Why did Cornelius kill her? Because of Friedrich?"

"Maybe it was just jealousy, maybe she was blackmailing him."

Benno had the urge to immediately drive back to Strathleven. But how should he proceed? How would that help his son? He still had no idea who might have kidnapped Tim.

"Thank you for coming into my small room," he said softly.

She put a tattooed arm around his waist. The demon grinned at him.

"Can we leave the lights on?" He was afraid that without light he might disappear and get lost almost as if by accident. And as if she understood, Hanne also put one leg around him, holding him so tightly that he could feel himself. It hurt, but he didn't dare move.

— 24 —

In the morning, the world outside his guesthouse window was chilly, the window itself full of frost patterns. Snow was in the air.

Hanne was sitting naked on the bed, and he ran his hands over her drawings, the leopard on her belly lying in folds. He had inspected her, she was his mistress. This woman was the reason why he no longer slept at home. No, not the reason, just the occasion for his infidelity.

"And?" she finally asked.

He spread her like a map. "My hands are too small."

The van of a Lübeck glazier stood in front of the house when Benno drove into the yard. He rang the bell, and when no one came to the door, he walked around the house into the garden. Martin Wehrke and a man in overalls stood outside the newly inserted window. When he saw Benno, Wehrke's serious face brightened. "What happened to your foot?"

"Kicked someone," Benno grinned.

The glazier whistled and looked at the sky. Single snowflakes scouted out the garden. "I'm finished here in ten minutes," he said. "Just in time."

"Someone shot at the window," Wehrke said and shook his head.

"Shot at it?" Benno tried to sound surprised.

Wehrke shrugged. "When I was young, we shot at street signs."

"Do you have a minute?" Benno asked, glancing quickly in the direction of the glazier, who was wiping down the new window.

"Come," Wehrke invited him and walked to the front of the house. "Coffee?"

Benno followed Wehrke's example and took off his shoes, grateful for Hanne's thick black socks. They were a little too small and fit snugly around his foot. Gingerly, he walked behind Wehrke into the kitchen.

"Last night I read your book again."

"Oh yes? How are you getting on with your research?"

Benno leaned against the counter to relieve his right foot. From where he stood, he could see the glazier standing in the garden, in almost exactly the same spot where he had been shot. "You didn't write anything about the king."

"The king? The old legend still fascinates you?"

Benno watched his host, but nothing in his face changed. He inserted a filter, poured water into the container, and soon the machine started to gurgle.

"Two of your ancestors. And they had to die for it. Why?"

Wehrke sighed. "Does this have still to do with your article?"

"My son has been kidnapped," Benno said.

"Yes, the news has spread in the village."

"And has the news about who did it spread too?"

"The village isn't happy."

"Not happy?"

"Many people had placed great hope in him."

"Who?"

"The harvest was dismal, the last few years haven't been good here."

"But then why has he been kidnapped?"

Wehrke did not respond to Benno's question. Instead, he said, "Maybe you should call next time before you come to see me." When he saw Benno's questioning look, he added, "I'll have to be more careful. You'll also need to be more careful."

"And what or whom should I be careful of?"

"My brother. The pastor. Friedrich. The whole village. We don't have much time, and you should stop interfering. You currently live in Lübeck, right?"

Benno looked at him with growing unease. "Who is the king? Wotan's representative? You've known all along that there's still a king. Who is it?"

"That's the most important question, isn't it? And you know already. Why don't you confront him? What are you waiting for?"

"Why does he have to die? Why did your relatives have to die?"

"You still don't get it." Wehrke looked at him calmly, adjusted his glasses. "But until then we'll keep our guns ready."

"Our guns?"

"I grew up here, I shot my first deer at age six. Just because I'm gay, doesn't mean I can't handle a gun. When someone intrudes on my property and peeks through my windows, he should better be prepared for my response." He paused for a moment, looked at the steaming coffee, and said, "Maybe I should drink my coffee alone."

———

Sybille Antler arrived around two o'clock in the afternoon by bus. Benno had been patiently waiting on the street corner, letting the engine idle from time to time to warm up, but now his toes were numb. Snow fell on the windshield and melted.

She was a lanky girl and was wearing a black anorak, jeans, and a Walkman. When Benno got out of the car and approached her, she cocked her head. "What are you doing here?"

Benno looked at her in surprise. "Is it illegal?"

She took off the headphones. "No," she drawled, rolling her eyes as if he had said something terribly stupid. "But my parents don't want me to talk to you. You know that."

"What are you listening to?" he asked.

She shifted from one foot to the other, biting her lip, and remained silent.

"You found the dead woman, right?"

The girl placed a gloved hand on the fence, looked quickly toward her house, then nodded.

Sybille had been kidnapped about a month ago and abandoned in the woods. Benno was aware of this fact, could feel the many eyes of the neighborhood on him. They would probably suspect him now. Loudly, way too loudly, he asked, "And one of the boys stole something, right?"

"Who told you that?" Sybille asked. Her eyes narrowed to slits.

"Doesn't matter."

"Was it Volker?"

Benno knew no Volker, but said nothing, just looked sternly at the girl. She avoided his eyes, put the other hand on the fence as well and wobbled on the crooked heels of her boots. "Is that why you were kidnapped? Someone wanted to intimidate you? That was no coincidence, right? You knew the driver."

The girl swallowed. Her nearly black eyes had no shine.

"I'm sorry," Benno said quickly. "I didn't mean to stalk . . ."

"The miracle boy is gone." She gave him a quick look.

"Do you know where he is?"

She shook her head. Music came from the headphones around her neck.

"Who was that man?"

She shook her head vigorously. "I can't say. My . . ." She trailed off again.

"What did the boy find at the body? The man wanted to know, didn't he?"

"Why are you asking about that?"

"I want to find Tim." Benno exhaled, forced himself to unclench his fists. "Who was the boy? I won't drag him to the police. I won't hurt him."

"You will never see your son again. Completely impossible," Sybille said matter-of-factly.

The next moment, Benno could hear steps behind him and Sybille's mother, wearing a kitchen apron and high-heeled slippers, came up to them. "Sybille," she shouted angrily, and fixed her eyes on Benno. "What are you doing with my daughter? What are you thinking?"

"Nothing," said Benno and felt caught anyway, as though he had really stalked the girl.

"Then leave us alone. You only bring evil upon our village."

"My son is gone," Benno said pleadingly. "I'm just trying to find him."

"That means nothing to me," the woman said. "Don't drag my daughter into this. She has suffered enough. Sybille!"

The girl was still clutching the fence, looking down at the ground. Her mother was strongly built, and she tried to grab her daughter's hand. "Are you finally coming?"

"My fault," Benno said.

Sybille finally let go of the fence, put the headphones back on and began to nod to the beat. With shuffling steps, she followed her mother down the road. Mrs. Antler disappeared quickly in her house, as though Benno were giving pursuit. But Sybille took her time. At the garden gate she lifted her head again.

"Ralf Witte," she said, loud enough that he could hear it. "I didn't rat him out. But he's an asshole."

The postman lived in an old brick house with a crooked but neatly painted porch. When Benno rang the door, he was greeted by loud barking, and seconds later a small black terrier scratched on the frosted glass. Steps became audible, then the door was opened a crack by a teenage boy of about seventeen.

"Ralf?" asked Benno.

"My brother," said the boy. "You're the guy who lives in the old school."

"Yes," Benno said. "Is Ralf here?"

"Well yes, but . . ." He obviously didn't know what to do next. "One moment," he murmured and left the door ajar, without asking Benno inside. The terrier forced his nose through the narrow slit and growled softly.

Two or three minutes later, a freckled boy came to the door and pushed the dog aside. He might have been a little older than Sybille. His hair was cropped short and red, and his eyelids seemed almost translucent.

"What's up?" he asked. His voice broke.

"I wanted to talk to you."

"My parents aren't here."

"It won't take long."

"We can't let you in."

"We can talk out here."

Ralf furrowed his brow. "Okay." In socks he stepped out onto the porch. "What do you want?"

Benno explained that he was looking for Tim. "I've heard that you took something from the dead woman's body," he said.

Ralf fidgeted; his feet had to be freezing. The sleeves of his Norwegian sweater he had pulled over his hands. He couldn't stand still. "Who said that?" he asked.

"Do you still have it?"

"What?"

"The thing you took."

"Why?" Ralf grinned.

"I can also talk to your father," Benno said. "And tell him that you stole evidence."

"I'm cold," the boy said with hostility. "Why are you still sneaking around here? Your wife has thrown you out."

Benno had difficulty staying calm. "I'll talk to your father," he said and left the porch. When he was at the fence, he heard Ralf's voice. "Hey, wait."

Benno turned and paused for a moment.

Ralf was standing on the stairs, scratching his head. "Come back!"

Benno remained at the gate. "What did you steal?"

The boy looked around, put a finger to his mouth and on tiptoes came running towards Benno.

"Come, come!" He grabbed Benno's hand and pulled him back to the house. He opened the door and marched toward the kitchen. "We were just joking," he said.

"We?" asked Benno. It smelled like re-heated potatoes and vegetables. A light gray plastic clock ticked on one of the cabinets, and above the old corner bench hung a china plate with the inscription 'Dad is the best.' Benno fervently hoped that Witte would not show up now. He would probably react the same way Sybille's mother had and throw him out. He looked at his wet shoes and the footprints he left on the bright linoleum. "We?" he asked again.

Ralf sucked in his upper lip, which gave him a goofy expression. Then he let it go with a smacking sound. "Volker, Sybille, Silke, Torsten, Bernd and me. But she was already dead."

"And what did you take?"

The boy ran out of the kitchen, and Benno could hear his footsteps on the stairs. A door opened and slammed shut again, then it was quiet in the house. Benno went to the window. From here you could see the church steeple and the roof of the old school, and the sight cut into his heart. What was Carolin doing now? Maybe she was sitting at home and waiting for the phone to ring. Maybe she was in church and sought solace from Cornelius. Cornelius, who had killed his lover. Benno grabbed the roll of paper towels that hung next to the stove and began to wipe his footprints.

A door opened, and seconds later Ralf appeared on the landing. With one hand he held something hidden under his sweater, and when he arrived outside the kitchen, he stopped with a jerk.

"What are you giving me for this?"

"I won't tell on you."

Ralf grimaced. "Not good enough."

"I guess it's just a sock or an old shirt." Benno tried to sound disinterested. "I don't have time for games."

"But you've come to me, not I to you."

"What do you want?"

"What do you have?"

Benno stepped toward Ralf, but the boy stepped back and shook his head. "Not a good idea. My brother is upstairs, and he's stronger than you."

"Who's the king?" Benno asked.

The question seemed to confuse the boy. He raised his eyebrows and stared at Benno. "Everybody knows that."

"Who then?"

"Your son. If he comes back."

"But why should he die? If he's the king?"

Ralf stared at Benno with a mixture of pity and disgust. "Not Tim. Friedrich, his reign is over."

"His reign over what?"

"The village. Us." The boy shrugged.

"And that's why he has to die?"

"Sure thing."

"But why? He's not old. "

"That's just how it is."

"But why has Tim disappeared? Who has him?"

Ralf pursed his lips and shook his head. Benno thought he heard a car outside the house. He quickly reached into his pocket and pulled out a few crumpled bills. "Here, take that," he said.

The boy took the money, and as he began to count it, the object he had kept hidden under the sweater fell to the kitchen floor. Benno hastily grabbed it, but as soon as he held it in his hands, he let go again.

"Nasty, huh?" Ralf said with satisfaction and smoothed out the bills. "Thirty marks? Is that all you have?"

Benno bent down again, looked at the little doll that was lying on her back in front of him. It was covered with dried, almost black, blood.

"Stuck out of her abdomen. Nobody wanted to pull it out, so I did."

Benno grabbed a kitchen towel and lifted the doll by one leg. It was made of plastic. The thumb of her right hand was stuck in the blood-smeared mouth.

"There's something written on it," Benno said. "Did you write that?"

"Nonsense," the boy said.

"Who did you tell about this?"

"No one. The others ran away screaming. They didn't even look at the doll. They thought it was real."

Benno nodded, wrapped the doll in paper towels and went past Ralf to the entrance.

"It was Sybille, right?" the boy asked.

Benno turned his head, but didn't answer. Then he pulled the door open and stepped out onto the porch. He walked through the increasingly heavy snow to his car. He only remembered where he was when he stopped at the edge of town and with trembling hands opened the package. The little baby doll grinned at him. On her belly was written, "Another girl."

25

No one answered the door. After several minutes he pulled his keys from his pocket and unlocked it. Rasmus jumped up on him and pressed himself against his legs. He held very still as Benno knelt beside him and stroked his head.

Without a clear plan Benno sat down on the couch and stared out at the yard, the sandbox, Heintz' old yellow Taurus, snow collecting on its roof and windows. Rasmus jumped on the cushion beside him, looking threatening, perhaps, or simply confused. Maybe it was only the black eye that made him appear frightening.

Benno felt all of a sudden how tired he was, and only the prospect of Carolin coming home kept him from curling up and falling asleep. It was nearly five o'clock, and snow and gray clouds made off with the last light of the day.

The receiver seemed infinitely heavy, and he dialed a wrong number twice, three times, until he finally got through. Then he let it ring until a woman's voice said, "Hello?"

"Benno, the guy you met at the cafe."

"Yes?"

"You said I could call you if I had a question."

"And?" Ania Walczak's voice was calm, more whispered than spoken, as if she had just awakened from a nap.

"Describe the man you saw with Irina at the restaurant. Her lover."

"But I already did."

"Do it again, please."

Silence followed, then a slight cough. "It's been so long. I paid Irina little attention back then."

"I gave you three hundred marks."

Silence again, this time even longer. "Maybe as big as you, dark hair. He was a pastor."

"Without glasses."

"Yes, without glasses."

"And pretty thin. Almost lanky?"

A hesitant, stretched Yes was the answer.

Benno sighed, closed his eyes and pressed the phone hard against his ear. "You never saw him, right? Irina had no lover."

"She did, I remember him exactly."

"And he was not a pastor."

"But I tell you . . ."

"What kind of car was the man driving?"

"I . . . it was a large car."

Benno sank back deep into the couch, and as though he had sensed something, Rasmus came closer and put his head in his lap. For several seconds, only static could be heard on the line. Rasmus closed his eyes.

"I'm sorry. The money. I thought . . . every village has a pastor."

Benno hung up. Blackness surrounded him. Tim wasn't home. Carolin was not here, and he felt for the first time how cool it was in the apartment. Gratefully, he stroked the large, soft head in his lap. There was so much to do, but he could hardly move. Sybille Antler—who had kidnapped and raped her? Who had questioned her and tried to intimidate her? Who had known that the children had discovered the corpse?

Corinna, Friedrich's daughter, had told him about the painted doll. Who else had she confided in? Her boyfriend? Harald Wehrke, the son of the champion shooter? But why would he kill Irina? What had he to fear from Sybille?

Benno tried to calm his breathing. He knew that the whole village was watching his house. The entire village was awaiting his next step and preparing an answer for him. While he kept his eyes closed, others were making plans for his son and himself. But he didn't move, only felt his own breath and the fear that penetrated his body together with the cold. Rasmus sniffled loudly and curled up.

He wrote her a message. He took Rasmus into the garden where the dog eagerly took to the snow and finally stopped at a huge brown tuft of grass. He lifted his leg and looked reproachfully at Benno.

He hadn't meant to take him. But the dog didn't want to go back into the house, pulled away and instead ran to the car. There he sat down in the snow, in front of the right rear door.

Benno looked at him puzzled, looked at the sky and felt the snow on his face, the flakes so small and gentle, no moon in the sky.

"Okay, then come with me," he said and opened the car door. Rasmus jumped with a bark onto the backseat and lay down at once, as if he feared that he might be thrown out again.

Benno opened the trunk and lifted the lid of his toolbox. He fished around in it, but his fingers wouldn't obey him.

"What are you doing?"

Benno spun around, hitting his head against the trunk lid. Manfred stood wide-eyed behind him, his head half-hidden by the hood of his anorak.

"I liked you old car better," he said, almost wistfully.

"Do you know where my wife is?" Benno cut him off.

Manfred shook his head.

"Can you tell her that I have Rasmus?"

"You have to find Tim," he said. "He'll be afraid, all by himself. And he didn't take my knife with him. Otherwise he could stab his captors or dig a tunnel."

Benno nodded, closed the trunk and got in the car. Manfred was still standing near the trunk; for him the conversation wasn't finished yet. "I'll go inside now. Hopefully Tim has something to eat. It's time to eat." Then he trotted toward his front door.

Hopefully his son had something to eat. Where could he be? Where did they hide him? Or had they already buried him in a field or ditch? The engine howled furiously as Benno left the yard.

It was five minutes before closing time, and the brightly lit showroom was almost empty. Two salesmen rummaged through their papers, closed drawers and file folders. He nodded at them, figuring they recognized his face by now. Did they know what was going on here? Or did they hail from Wengsten or Kamitz or Grevenhorst? Would they pick up the phone and report his visit as soon as he turned his back on them?

"Is the boss around?" Benno asked.

One of the salespeople, a fifty-year-old man in a white shirt and a yellow tie, pointed behind him.

"He's in the spare parts warehouse."

Benno turned and walked back out onto the lot and over to the low-slung building. Stifling heat greeted him. Without a sound he closed the door and started looking for Friedrich. He found the dealer in a small office where he was flipping through a catalog and taking notes on a pad. When he saw Benno, he smiled and stood up.

"How can I help you?"

Benno didn't know if any mechanics were still present, or who else was still at work, but when Friedrich came toward him, he lost his nerve, and instead of waiting for an opportune moment, he pulled the metal flashlight from his sleeve and hit the smiling face.

But Friedrich had enough time to take a step back—the blow only struck his shoulder. The second also missed its target, but Benno lunged forward. The third blow struck Friedrich's skull, and the sound turned Benno's stomach. Once again he struck, and finally the dealer's legs gave out and he slumped to the ground. His raised hands could not protect him from the next blows. They hit the chair, the desk, the shelves, the floor, and again and again Otto Friedrich.

The Scotch tape and office chair squeaked when Friedrich began to stir again. Benno hadn't been prepared, and after Friedrich had collapsed, he panicked. He bent over the lifeless body and looked for signs of life. Then, when it was clear that he hadn't killed Friedrich, he had noticed that he hadn't brought any restraints. Wide scotch tape and a few cables were all he found.

"The scribbler," were Friedrich's first words. Then he closed his eyes and moaned softly.

Benno rolled the chair into a corner of the small office, to make sure that Friedrich couldn't fall over. "If you do something stupid, I'll kill you," he hissed.

"Go ahead," Friedrich whispered. "Better than what I'll suffer at the hands of my own people." A smile flickered on his lips.

Benno sat down on the desk opposite him. Naked neon lights hung from the ceiling and buzzed loudly. On the wall in front of him hung a Ford calendar and photocopied office jokes.

"How long do you have?" he asked. "End of March?"

Friedrich nodded almost imperceptibly.

"Where were you hiding Irina Sobieski? Here? In your home?"

Friedrich smiled at him weakly.

"You still don't know?"

Benno's face turned red. He had beaten Friedrich, he had tied him up in his own chair, and yet he still felt like a schoolboy who played a trick on the teacher and knew that in the end he would get punished.

"Where? In the clinic?"

"You Romantic," Friedrich said. "You've fallen in love with the old shed." He paused for a moment before he cleared his throat and said, "She lived right next door to you. Under the same roof."

Friedrich's words were so matter-of-fact that they left no doubt.

"Most of the time she lived in Heintz' basement. He hasn't given you a full tour of the house, has he? He was faithful to me for a long time, knew what would happen if I had no successor. But during visiting hours, Mrs. Schmied let us have her room."

"Visiting hours?"

The car dealer groaned. "With a son I could have bought time. With a son I could have convinced them."

"Who kidnaps a woman in the hope that she'll give birth to a son?"

"Someone who fears for his life. I knew Irina from Lübeck, I knew that she had no relatives or friends. A desperate plan. But with an heir they would have let me live, with an heir nobody would have stood a chance against me. I had no reason to kill a pregnant woman."

"But it was another girl."

"Did they tell you that?"

"Who?"

Friedrich was silent, letting his chin fall to his chest. "I have long tried to bring new life to Strathleven, but the problem is that new life doesn't necessarily bring more life into the village. It's blind to the old. New and old don't mix. They simply live side by side."

Something cracked behind Benno's back. He turned, but there was nothing. He grabbed the flashlight, turned it in his hand. "Where is Tim?" he asked.

Friedrich shook his head.

"You kidnapped him."

"I should have."

"Then who has him?"

"Andreas Wehrke. He hasn't forgotten the old magic, he brought the Twelve Nights back to the village. The slogans that the king must die? All Wehrke. The people in the village love their TVs and their fast cars and cruises, but horses and bells for New Year's Eve still frighten them to death."

"What's in it for him? He'll have to die himself."

"Not him. He is much smarter. He wants to avoid bankruptcy."

"He still has the concrete plant."

"Did he tell you that? The farmers here are impoverished, the harvests are bad. His store is almost broke, and have you ever counted the trucks that come from the factory through the village? They're working only one shift there. And when I'm dead, he will find a way to take over my business. Although I doubt he'll leave it to his son. He's a dud." Friedrich chuckled. "Harald. He's the new king. That's how Wehrke gets around dying."

"Don't people believe that Tim is the new king?"

Friedrich now looked at him with a serious face. "Sure. I've told anyone who would listen. His skin—that's something you don't see every day. I've been telling everyone that it was a sign. Didn't you get that pretty crown? I had it made. Here in my shop."

"You gave Tim the crown?" Benno asked.

"I was scared," Friedrich said. "When I was twenty-three, I was called back to the village. I was studying in Kiel at the time, had my own apartment. It was the beginning of the 60s—it was a great time to be young." He laughed. "Hell, it's always a great time to be young."

"Your father was murdered."

Friedrich looked up, directly at Benno. "He wasn't murdered," he said contemptuously. His mouth and eyes twitched. "He absconded from this town." His voice was trembling. "My father always knew what awaited him, and he preferred to die by his own hand rather than to be hacked to pieces by his friends and neighbors. Wehrke wanted to be king at that time, spread rumors that I was a coward and slept with men. Wanted to do away with his brother too and said we had a relationship." He paused for a moment. "My father was already dead when they descended on him. They put a knife in my hand, wanted to test my resolve. You found Irina. That wasn't a pretty sight, now was it?"

"And if you hadn't done it? If you had refused to become king?"

"That would have served Wehrke well. They would have killed me. You cannot reject the honor."

Benno looked at the car dealer, looked at his hands, looking for any sign that this man could really be a killer. A murderer, kidnapper, and rapist. But there was nothing. He had bruises on his face where Benno had hit him, but otherwise he didn't look particularly aggressive. The gray suit was now full of dust and stains.

"You didn't kill Irina?"

"Before she could give birth to my child?" Friedrich laughed bitterly. "You must think I'm a monster, but no. I had nothing to do with it. I had no reason to kill her."

"Wouldn't you have been able to bed any woman in the village?"

"We're not barbarians, I'm not a feudal lord. Don't think I haven't tried to produce an heir. But my only son . . ." He broke off.

"Your son?"

Friedrich nodded. "You know him. Manfred."

Benno stared at him. The widow had never mentioned her husband. "Mrs. Schmied is not a widow?"

"She is, but she wasn't always old. Thirty years ago, she was a beauty, even if you can no longer see it."

"And your wife?"

"She grew up here. She understands what's going on." Friedrich's face seemed to become narrower, older, tougher. "I'm the king," he said. "Of what? Of a few farms and people who don't know if they should listen to Abba, Nena, or some other silly nonsense, or if they should believe in Wotan, Miracle Oaks and wizardry. I have enjoyed the benefits of my so-called rule. Don't you think the people here could have bought their shitty cars cheaper in Lübeck or Hamburg? Fear and a sense of duty have saved me more than once. The old order says that the king rules for twenty-four years and guarantees the welfare of the village. Then he must die in order to make place for the new one. Twenty-four years, no more. He should never grow frail and weak. He is a representative of Wotan, a higher order. And he lives in the village."

"And people still believe in this nonsense?"

"Of course not. They haven't believed in any of it since before the war. In Wotan, I mean. My father, after he was chosen, wanted nothing to do with the old superstition. But he wanted a good life, and people believe in power and violence. And where else should they go? Move away to the city? Leave the farm? Abandon their business? The King is still important here, even if he can't perform any magic."

"And Cornelius?"

Friedrich laughed. "He represents the new God. Only that this God cannot be held accountable. They leave the pastor alone, they don't kill him. His God is already dead." He tried to sit up in his chair. "Without me, Cornelius would never have set foot in the village."

"What do you mean?"

Friedrich looked at him with a mixture of pride and scorn, but there was something else, something that Benno could not interpret.

"The old pastor was one of us. He was always there when we murdered the old king. Cornelius was my choice. He wanted souls. Damn Baptists. Wanted to sell us his God. That was fine with me. For twenty-four years I've been trying to undermine my own position."

Benno sat very straight, his fingers clenched around the torch. His hands were all wet.

"Nothing happens without my approval," Friedrich said. "The widow needed my permission to rent your apartment. And you looked quite harmless. Young guy with a wife and child. Quite what I needed. And you, you are really quite harmless, stumbling awkwardly about and asking your stupid and impertinent questions. And so vain. You wanted to play family, but you don't have what it takes. Am I wrong? But the boy . . ." He did not finish his thought.

Benno looked at his clock. Almost an hour had passed since he had attacked the dealer. He had to hurry if he didn't want to run the risk of being surprised by Friedrich's family.

"Where is Tim?"

Without answering the question, Friedrich said, "This year I must step down, but I don't want to die. I'm not old and weak. Look at me! Why do we have modern medicine and health insurance? We live to 80 years and longer. I am 47, I don't intend to be slaughtered. A lot of people don't like that." He paused for a moment. "Who is responsible if corn prices fall, or if cows don't give enough milk anymore? If the competition in Lübeck undercuts Johannsen's prices? God?"

"Where is Tim?" Benno asked again.

"The pastor had to endear himself to my successor. He knew everything."

"I believed he had killed Irina."

"The pastor?" Friedrich shook his head and smiled. "Never. But he knew where I kept her hidden. I told him myself." He sighed.

"And Cornelius told Wehrke?"

Friedrich shrugged. "Or his wife. Or my wife. It would have been better not to marry, not to have children. In the past, kings often preferred to remain childless. Without children, the curse would hit another family when their reign was over."

Benno stood up, weighed the flashlight in his hand. "Where is Tim?"

Friedrich laughed. "I don't have him. Wehrke and his Twelve Nights spectacle have put fear in people, and fear is stronger than faith in a miracle skin. I didn't wish the boy any harm, I just wanted to save my own skin. So Wehrke had to take him. It's that simple. It's my fault. Go on, hit me. Don't you stop!"

———

Music came from the speakers, and the driver's door was wide open and let the densely falling snow drift inside. A man in the passenger seat fed Rasmus something Benno couldn't make out.

From the interior of the car came Andreas Wehrke's voice, which sounded very gentle, despite its volume. "Good evening, Diedrich. Your dog here is such a sweetheart."

Benno slowly approached the car. Snow hit his neck. Had Wehrke passed the dealership by accident and discovered the car? Or did he know what had happened inside the warehouse?

"Good evening," he said.

"Don't look so mad. Your dog and I are already great friends. Do you want another piece?" The question was addressed to Rasmus, and Benno saw that Wehrke held a bar of chocolate in his hand.

"Stop," he yelled, "you're poisoning the dog."

"Is that right?" asked Wehrke. "But he seems to enjoy it."

Benno tore open the back door, but the next moment he was grabbed from behind and pressed against the fender. "Take it easy," said a voice that seemed strangely familiar to him. And a second added, "Search him." Benno felt how one of the men groped his legs and emptied his pockets onto the ground. Then he was released.

With difficulty, Benno stood up and turned around. Günther Dithmann, the tow truck driver, and Wehrke's son Harald stood before him and looked amused.

"What have you done to Friedrich?" Wehrke got out of the car, crumpled the purple paper, threw it to the ground, walked around the car and joined his son. "Have you done our dirty work for us?"

Benno shook his head. "What have you done with Tim?" From the car came a faint whimper.

"Did he tell you how ill he felt back then? How the new king almost fainted when his dead father lay before him? How he gagged when I pressed the knife into his hand? That was a bad sign. But this time we will crown a real king. You will have to hurry, though," said Wehrke. "Your boy will soon run out of breath."

Günther grimaced and quickly lowered his head. Wehrke seemed not to notice. He put his hands on his son's shoulders and said, "Time to claim your inheritance."

Bewildered, Harald turned to his father. "The shooting festival . . ."

"We won't wait any longer. Go and show yourself worthy of the honor."

"Right now? Alone?"

Wehrke took a step back and slapped Harald. "Yes, right now. Alone."

Harald held his cheek, looked from his father to Günther and finally addressed Benno. "Don't look at me like that!"

"You're the new king? Because of you that woman had to be murdered. Then you found out that I was searching for Irina's killer, and you got cold feet. You kidnapped Sybille and made sure that she would not reveal what she had found on the corpse. Corinna had told you about the corpse and about Sybille. And you took advantage of her trust. Sybille didn't tell on the boy. She didn't tell you who had the doll. And now you've kidnapped Tim." Benno's voice cracked. Then he forced himself to calm down. "Have you no fear of being killed?"

The young Wehrke had listened without blinking. He said, "It's not yet time to die." Then he clenched his fists, swung quickly and struck Benno in the face.

Benno could hear his nose break, and tears came to his eyes. Instinctively, he held his arms over his face, but nothing happened. Instead, he heard how Harald stepped away in the direction of the spare parts inventory.

"Well, come on, Diedrich," said Wehrke. He went to Benno, took his arms away from his face, looked at the injury. "Not too bad," he said with satisfaction. "My brother found the conversations with you very entertaining, but he knows who he depends on for his pension. Nothing personal. He really regrets that you are leaving the village."

"That I am leaving the village?" stammered Benno. Tears ran down his cheeks, he could hardly keep his eyes open.

"Yes, right now. Don't you want to save your dog? And see your lover again?"

"You're letting me go?" He could hear the greed in his question, the irrepressible desire to escape.

"Sure. We could make you disappear, but in such a tight-knit community such as ours, you have to be careful. You cannot trust anyone, can you, Günther? Take Günther, for example. Friedrich treated him almost like a son. An illegitimate, ill-bred son, but still. And how does this lad thank him?"

Günther's face hardened. All life disappeared from the surface, even his eyes seemed to go out. His cap was already covered in snow.

"I will prove myself grateful. He will be part of the family, my family. He will continue to run the business here. Without Friedrich." He turned back to Benno. "You will leave now, and never show your face here again. Your own life should be worth more to you than that of your stepson. Go away, forget about us. Your wife has already forgotten about you." He turned to leave, but stopped suddenly. "The doll," he said. "Where is it?"

Benno opened the trunk. Wehrke took it, whistling through his teeth. "Ralf confessed right after you left. Got cold feet. His father knew what to do." Then he stepped away from the trunk and walked back to his own car, a Mercedes Benno hadn't noticed before. For a brief moment Wehrke turned his face, but Benno couldn't make out his features. Seconds later, the car slipped from the lot.

"Well, get out of here already," Günther raised his fists.

Benno ducked, and got in the car. "Where is Tim?"

"Go," Guenther said, looking in the direction of the spare parts inventory.

"Where is he? Is he still alive?"

"Enough of that, fuck off!"

"Please?"

Günther's face twitched, his fists fell to his side. Once again he glanced at the warehouse, then said quietly, "Widow Schmied." And when Benno kept waiting for an explanation, he repeated, "Fuck off."

26

His house lay in darkness, and no lights were visible behind Mrs. Schmied's curtains, but from the half-open church door came a faint glow.

As fast as his ankle allowed, Benno ran into the house and into Tim's room. There on the desk was the brown bottle with hydrogen peroxide. The vet had advised him to keep it, and it sat next to the pictures of mutilated faces.

After a few seconds Rasmus puked on the car seat. To make sure, Benno gave him a second spoon. The dog choked until nothing more was coming. Then he stared at his vomit, but before he could lick it up, Benno pulled him from the car. He greedily drank the water Benno poured for him.

The church door was still open, and carefully Benno stepped inside. He shook the snow from his clothes, but he was completely soaked. When he entered from the vestibule, a single candelabrum was burning, and no one seemed to be present.

"Hello," he shouted, and got an uncertain echo in reply. Benno was grateful that no crucified Jesus stared at him while he was trudging past the pews. Rasmus followed him half-stunned, but unwilling to be left alone.

They found Cornelius in the sacristy. The pastor knelt at the baptismal font, and his glasses had slipped down his nose and fallen into the basin. His arms were spread out, almost tenderly he held the font in an embrace, and his head was bent over an old inscription, as though he wanted to study it yet again. The hole in his head was as big as a five-mark piece, the right side of his face hung in tatters.

Rasmus approached the dead man and sniffed at his clothes. Then he pricked his ears.

Benno could hear the voices too. He backed away from the baptismal font and looked around the corner into the church. Carolin stood in the open door, together with Pastor Thomas. She wore a light down jacket, kept her hand in the pocket of his black wool coat. Benno's heart couldn't keep up with his eyes, and it nearly forgot to beat. Rasmus trotted toward his mistress, bushy tail wagging.

"What are you doing here?" she said in high voice reserved for small children and pets. Only then she looked up and saw Benno, and the tender expression on her face faded. "What are you doing here?" she asked.

Her question sent a chill through Benno. He would have liked to hobble toward Thomas and break his thin nose. But wordlessly, he walked past the couple, stepped into the vestibule, where fliers announced the next church services, and from there into the open.

Only his own tracks, and those of Thomas and Carolin appeared in the snow. The VW Golf of the young pastor stood next to his own car. The silence around him was hard to bear.

The moment Gustav Heintz flung open the door and stepped outside, a rifle in his hands, Benno could hear Carolin cry out. He looked at the old man's face and could see that he knew that she had found the dead pastor.

"What are you doing here?" Heintz said angrily.

"Why have you betrayed Friedrich?" Without waiting for an answer, Benno stepped toward the old man until Heintz pushed the muzzle of the gun against his chest. "I'm going down to the basement and I will get my boy," he said softly.

"The hell you are," Heintz said. Despite the cold, he wore only a white undershirt. His muscles were hard and tough, his arms gnarled. "Piss off, Diedrich. Or I'll shoot you right here."

"Like the pastor?" asked Benno.

Heintz hesitated, his mouth open. "Yeah, like the pastor. He told Wehrke about Irina, told him that I had her. Wanted to be in the new king's good graces and save his church. But then he didn't want to get his hands dirty. First he tells on me, and then he calls me a murderer."

Snowflakes flew in Benno's eyes, he squinted against his will, pressing his chest against the gun muzzle. "When I was at the police station, you grabbed the boy. My wife borrowed your car and you went straight next door. Tim probably didn't even put up a fight. He trusted you. Did Wehrke put you up to this? What has he promised you? Or have you done it for free to save your own skin?" His voice was shrill. "But you won't shoot me from behind. You have to shoot me in the face." He broke off, fear constricted his throat. He didn't want to die, not now.

He hadn't noticed Manfred approach. All of a sudden he stood behind Heintz, his arm wrapped around the neck of the old man, the engraved blade held under his chin. Heintz' face turned red, blood ran into the white undershirt. "This is how it's done," Manfred said through clenched teeth as though he were giving instructions to an invisible student. "This is how it's done right." Benno grabbed the rifle, tore it from Heintz' hands. He had never owned a firearm. He didn't even know if the gun was loaded or how to release the safety.

"I got him," Manfred said, panting, and pulled Heintz inside the house.

Benno hurried past him and crossed the workshop. On the walls hung Snow White and Cinderella and the Pied Piper of Hamelin, curiously watching the commotion.

The basement door was locked. With the rifle butt, he hit the latch, even though he understood how futile that was.

"Let him go, you silly boy." Mrs. Schmied's voice came from the workshop. She looked like a ghostly apparition. Her customary bun was gone, long white hair flowed around her face, and she was wearing her nightgown beneath a robe. For the first time he could see what Friedrich had said about her beauty. It was still there, had not completely drained from her face. Anger and fear animated her face. With her bare hands she hit her son, who kept Heintz in a headlock. The old man barely struggled anymore, his face beet red.

"Leave him alone," cried Benno. "Where is the key to the basement?"

Startled, the widow looked at the gun, and let go of Manfred. She bent over Heintz' limp body, rummaged through his pockets. With trembling fingers she handed Benno a set of keys. She smelled of apple shampoo.

"Poor boy," she said. "The poor woman."

Benno backed away from her. Hadn't she known all along what was going on in her house? She had made her home available to Friedrich, she had followed his desperate plan. Had he offered her money? Had she done it for her son? Friedrich's son?

After the second attempt, the basement door opened. The steps were narrow and steep. In the dim light of a naked bulb, he descended the stairs. He kept the rifle at the ready.

The floor was covered with green carpet, and cocktail chairs from the Sixties stood around like lost sheep. A bar took up almost a third of the space. A strong odor entered his nostrils, his eyes kept searching for a light switch, and seconds later the room was bathed in greenish light coming from two overhead lamps.

Liquor and wine bottles stood on shelves behind the counter. In the back of the room, a short hallway with bare concrete walls branched off.

The steel door wasn't locked. It led into a small room, where a fabric-covered sun-lounger was the only furniture. A sink was mounted on a wall, and a toilet had been installed in the corner next to it. The room might have been nine or ten square meters, and was otherwise empty. Nothing indicated that Irina had ever lived here.

Nor was there any sign of Tim. Had Günther lied to him?

Benno laboriously climbed the stairs to Heintz' apartment. He didn't know how to handle the rifle, but it felt good in his hands. He carefully opened the door, thankful that it was still unlocked. Yet the sight that greeted him made his heart sink. Manfred sat on the floor, in his mother's arms. He was looking startled at his too-short gray pants, where a bloodstain spread. The handle of his knife protruded from his abdomen. Heintz was nowhere to be seen.

"Where is Tim?"

Benno spun around, almost pulled the trigger. In the door to Heintz' bedroom stood Carolin.

But he had no time for explanations. "Rasmus!" he shouted, and ran outside. Only his own car and Thomas' stood in the yard; the yellow Taunus was gone, its tracks visible in the snow. Rasmus crouched near the entrance to their own apartment. When he saw Benno, he came slowly toward him, but Benno had to grab him by the collar to drag him over the threshold into Heintz' house. At the basement door, the dog's demeanor changed. He growled, bared his teeth, then he barked and did a strange little dance on the landing. Finally he shot down the stairs.

Benno followed the dog, Carolin on his heels. They found Rasmus in front of the steel door, acting crazily. He had both paws on the doorknob and barked. Benno threw the door open, and the dog ran into the little room and jumped on the sun-lounger, sniffing wildly, lifting his head, howling, sniffing again. Then he sat down with a pitiful whimper. Confused, he looked around. He had found Irina, but where was she? He could smell her, but where had Benno hidden her?

"Rasmus." Reluctantly, the dog let himself be led from the room, but in the small hallway he became active again. He sniffed at the corners, smelled the stone walls, and then stood at the very end of the corridor. He turned his head to Benno and looked at him with his slightly cross-eyed stare.

Benno stepped closer and inspected the wall. The greenish light cast only a faint glow in the hall, but where the dog stood, the bricks were a little darker and wouldn't quite fit into the neat rows around them. Benno now recognized the odor that was so repugnant to him. It was fresh cement.

With his fists he hammered on the stone. "Tim," he shouted, and Carolin joined him. Then they listened, and Benno pressed his ear against the wall. They got no response.

The small table, with which he struck the wall, shattered. He found no tools behind the bar, nothing that would make the wall budge. Angry and with tears in his eyes, he made his way into Heintz' apartment. He had come too late, Tim was no longer alive. He himself would die here. Harald, Günther, Wehrke or Schmoeh would show up at any minute and make him disappear. They had allowed for Irina's body to be found only to taunt Friedrich and let the entire village know that the old king was weak. This time Wehrke wouldn't leave behind any evidence.

Mrs. Schmied knelt next to Manfred. They had locked the front door, and Thomas was on the phone, giving someone on the other end the address. He had taken off his coat, and sweat stains showed under his arms.

"Where does he keep his tools?" Benno asked.

The widow pointed in the direction of the garden. "In the shed."

Benno ran out into the snow, opened the squeaky doors of the old, wooden structure. There was no light, and his eyes could barely make out saws and screwdrivers attached to the walls. He tore rakes off the wall, hedge clippers, and finally his hands clasped the wooden handle of a hammer. Then he found a second, larger one, with a short handle and a heavy, broad head.

Carolin was still standing where he had left her. She had her hands pressed against the wall, sobbing and shaking.

He had never fought as a child, had been too inexperienced and too frightened. He remembered how it felt to lie helpless like a beetle on its back and to kick and scream and yet achieve nothing. After the first blow against the bare stone he felt his arms turn to mush. How foolish it was to fight against the truth. How foolish it was to hit with a hammer against this wall. But still he kept going. He brought the hammer down on the wall, over and over again. Carolin stood behind him, her eyes glued to what had once been a door.

And then they could smell it. They smelled it before Thomas came running into the basement. The old school was on fire, they had to flee. Benno barely listened to Thomas, he mustn't stop, mustn't stop for a single second, otherwise he would run away and try to save himself.

His arms roared in pain, and he knew that his strength was nearly exhausted. He needed air, he had to catch his breath, he no longer wanted to fight. And when he struck the wall once again, the stone gave. So he continued, continued to fight, and perhaps the cement was still fresh, maybe Heintz had finished his work only today, and the opening grew larger and chunks fell into the room behind it.

He paused. The smell of the fire was already very strong. Thomas stood in the middle of the basement room. He called for Carolin, demanded that she get to safety, but she didn't listen, squeezed her head and shoulders through the opening. The boy didn't answer to their shouting, Benno had to forcibly pull back his wife in order to keep going.

After two or three more minutes, he climbed into the space behind the wall. It smelled of earth, the cold hit him, and he could hardly breathe. It was just a dark hole, dug quickly, supported by slats and covered with plywood. Heintz had chosen this hole as Tim's grave.

In the far corner a bundle lay on the ground, and Benno picked it up.

The boy felt nearly weightless in his arms. He carried Tim to the opening and handed him to Carolin, then climbed back into Heintz' basement. He leaned over his son, put an ear to his mouth.

Tim's hands were bleeding and full of dirt. He must have tried to dig himself out, but had no longer been able to breathe. His face was grimy.

Thomas urged them to follow him. "The whole roof is already in flames."

Together they ran as fast as they could toward the stairs, Tim's lifeless body in Benno's arms. Heintz 'apartment was full of smoke, and Manfred and Mrs. Schmied were gone. Thomas raced frantically to the front door and threw it open. But there he stopped so abruptly that Carolin ran into him.

The front yard was brightly lit by the flames. The light flickered on the faces of the men who stared fixedly at the small group at the entrance. Witte was there, Johannsen, Bruno Maier, whom Benno had not seen since the autumn ball. Heintz stood in his stained undershirt among them.

"Get back inside!" Two of the men raised their rifles. There were ten or fifteen of them. Rasmus growled, his fur stood on end. Thomas raised his arms as though he were standing in the pulpit and blessing the congregation. Maybe he just wanted to show that he was unarmed.

The first shot stopped him, the second made him wince. After the next he went down on his knees.

"I have the king," Benno screamed like a madman. He hoisted Tim onto his shoulders.

"He's dead," cried one of the men, and a few laughed. Their cars stood parked behind them, almost like a corral.

Behind Benno and Carolin something burst and clattered to the floor. Rasmus jumped, ran to the left and off into the dark. Two shots rang out. Carolin stood motionless beside Benno. They had left Heintz's rifle in Irina's prison. They couldn't remain here forever; behind them, the wooden figurines had caught fire and hung like torches on the walls. Benno's back was boiling hot.

A white van appeared on the road and pulled into the yard of the old school. The men barely noticed it. Only when the driver did not slow and steered directly into the small group did they scatter. With a jerk, the van came to a stop in front of the house. In the light of the flames, Benno could only dimly see the driver's face, but he believed he recognized Günther's cap. The passenger door was pushed open, and a man fell out and then lay lifeless on the ground. The engine howled again, the van turned, broke through the sandbox and made for the road.

The armed attackers approached the lifeless body, turned the man on his back. Benno couldn't see who he was, but the sight of him made the group scatter once again. They hurried to their cars as if the burning school suddenly frightened them.

Benno ran out into the garden, stared after the disappearing rear lights. Carolin bent over the slumped Thomas.

"Get the car," she said.

He stopped at the dark shape that had so scared the men. Not much of the face remained recognizable. It was swollen and full of blood. Harald would never be king.

After they had exited the village, Benno looked for the first time in the rearview mirror. The old school was still burning, turning the night sky red. Before him, beyond the reach of his headlights, blackness spread. Only the snow brightened trees and fields around them.

The fan ran at the highest level. Carolin sat in the back seat, Tim's head in her lap, the down jacket wrapped around his body. Rasmus was crouched on the floor in front of her. Thomas sat next to Benno. Two of the bullets had hit him in the stomach. His breath rattled.

Benno tried not to think of Tim. He was still alive, Carolin claimed. He had survived, but he had to be half frozen. How long since he had last received food and water? When had Heintz walled him in?

What had become of Manfred, he didn't know. Maybe he had escaped with his mother. Maybe the village would take pity on them. Had Harald killed Friedrich before getting killed himself? Or was the car dealer still alive? Had he and Günther paid him back? But he mustn't think about that either. He had to drive, he mustn't lose his way in the snowstorm. He stared at the road ahead, at the flakes, which shone like thousands of little stars before him.

In the emergency room, they waited in silence. A doctor tended to Benno's face, bandaged his hands, gave him an injection.

In the early morning hours they were taken to Tim's room. His fingers looked crooked and deformed, and under the skin of his bare arms crept new beetles, new snakes. But it was their boy who had been hooked up to an IV, who raised his eyelids and couldn't keep them open. They remained in his room until a nurse asked them to leave.

"I'll check on Thomas," Carolin said in the hallway. Gray daylight filtered through snow-covered windows.

Benno nodded. For the first time he felt how heavily the weariness weighed on him. He could barely lift his shoulders, could barely stand straight. He had to get to the car and feed Rasmus. He had to call Hanne immediately, had to go to the Lübeck police.

"Should I wait for you?" he asked.

He couldn't read the expression of her face. Her chapped lips parted. "And then what?"